STOCKPORT
METROPOLITAN BOROUGH COUNCIL

*Libraries,
Advice and
Information*

cu s/22

WITHDRAWN
FROM
CIRCULATION

Please return/renew this item by the last date
shown.
Books may also be renewed by phone or the
Internet

TEL: 0161 217 6009
www.stockport.gov.uk/libraries

D0549169

BY THE SAME AUTHOR

Break Point

Battle Ready

Scar Tissue

ALL OR NOTHING

REVENGE IS A GAME YOU CAN'T AFFORD TO LOSE

OLLIE OLLERTON

BLINK
bringing you closer

First published in the UK by Blink Publishing
an imprint of Bonnier Books UK
4th Floor, Victoria House
Bloomsbury Square,
London, WC1B 4DA
England

Owned by Bonnier Books
Sveavägen 56, Stockholm, Sweden

facebook.com/blinkpublishing
twitter.com/blinkpublishing

Hardback – 978-1-788704-93-9
Trade Paperback – 978-1-788704-94-6
Paperback - 978-1-788704-97-7
Ebook – 978-1-788704-95-3
Audio Digital Download – 978-1-788704-96-0
CD – 978-1-788706-81-0

A CIP catalogue of this book is available from the British Library.

Designed and set by Envy Design Ltd
Printed and bound by Clays Ltd, Elcograf S.p.A

1 3 5 7 9 10 8 6 4 2

First published in hardback by Blink Publishing in 2021.
First published in paperback by Blink Publishing in 2022.

Blink Publishing is an imprint of Bonnier Books UK
www.bonnierbooks.co.uk

This book is dedicated to Laura who became my wife on my 50th birthday in December 2020. Our adventure is just beginning and having you by my side is fundamental to the strength and positivity I feel each day. I love you!

ACKNOWLEDGEMENTS

Writing *All Or Nothing* has been a labour of love. I'd like to thank everyone who has helped bring this book to life: Andrew Holmes, David Riding, Matt Phillips, Sophie Nevrkla, as well as everyone else at Bonnier Books UK. And, of course, my amazing family, especially my brilliant wife, Laura, without whom this would not have been possible. Thank you one and all.

PROLOGUE

On the carpet lay a dead man, and who knows what had gone on inside his head, but most of it now dripped down the walls. Blood and brain matter, incongruous in the suburban front room.

Sprawled on the sofa was another man. He had fought a brave battle marked by its brutality and longevity. He wore a bloodstained T-shirt bearing the words 'Finchley Sportsman', and though he had lost the battle, he was not dead. Not yet.

As for the victor, he stood in the middle of the devastated lounge. At his feet was a Heckler & Koch MP7 fitted with a suppressor and a sight, still warm. In his hand was a Glock, also suppressed. He watched the unconscious figure on the sofa carefully, ready to deliver the *coup de grâce* should the man awake, reflecting on the fact that he had been a fine and worthy opponent. When the skills of the combatants are matched, the outcome of a battle often comes down to chance. Luck, in other words. And one of them had been lucky.

The doorbell rang, and he went to it, used the chain and opened the door a crack. Outside lay a newbuild estate of nondescript boxes that right now, a Wednesday afternoon, was quiet. The kids at school, the adults either inside or at work.

Standing on the doorstep was the visitor, who seemed about to say something until he looked down and saw the suppressed barrel of the Glock, trained on his groin.

The gunman spoke. 'Sasquatch?' he said.

'We called him Bigfoot in our house,' came the reply.

'Then you would be Mr McGregor?'

'Aye, I am,' growled the visitor in broad Glaswegian. 'And that would make you Owen Flyte.'

'You don't look as if you've come to do the cleaning,' said Flyte warily. His Glock was still trained on McGregor.

'I'm what they call a right-hand man in this operation. I don't do the fuckin' cleaning, pal. I assess *ahead* of the cleaning. Now how about you lower the persuader and we continue this inside, eh?'

Flyte led McGregor through to the lounge, where a large TV was flecked with blood and the cream walls were splattered with it, too. A coffee table listed, two of its legs broken from some kind of impact. A box set of *Fast & Furious* movies lay on the floor, a tin of lager.

And the bodies.

'Christ,' grunted McGregor, employing commendable understatement as his gaze travelled the devastation. He indicated Flyte's Glock. 'And I guess from the lack of police sirens we can assume that your silencer works.'

'We call it a suppressor.'

McGregor pulled a face. 'Potato. Poh-tar-toe. If you're trying to convince me that you're a pro, then . . .' he indicated the carnage around them. 'Job fuckin' done, pal.' He approached the sofa and pointed to the guy in the Finchley Sportsman T-shirt. 'This guy?'

'Out cold.'

'I can see that, Doctor Zhivago. This is Alex Abbott, is it?'

'Yes.'

'And how do you know that?'

'It's him. He matches the description.'

'Well, you better finish the job.' McGregor indicated the state of Flyte's face. 'Better do it quick, too. Looks like he almost killed you.'

'Sure. He was tough.'

Flyte raised the weapon.

He pulled the trigger.

PART ONE

CHAPTER 1

As an elite member of the special forces and then in private security, Alex Abbott had fought all over the world. He'd gone up against the IRA in Northern Ireland, against drug dealers in the Indo-Pacific, child traffickers in Thailand and the usual suspects in the Middle East. He'd fought in bomb-scarred streets, in jungles, in deserts, and on storm-lashed seas.

But right now, he was fighting at the back of The Sportsman pub in North Finchley, in that shitty bit of the pub where they kept the empty barrels and the sticky wheelie bins; where the landlord sent customers who required physical resolution to disputes that had started indoors. As a regular, Abbott had seen it a dozen times. *Right, you two. Out!* Now he found himself with a starring role.

And the funny thing was that he couldn't even remember exactly how the argument had begun.

Something to do with . . .

No, it was gone.

Standing opposite him, two men brandished knives, both shouting something at him.

No. Wait.

Abbott slapped a hand over his left eye. One of the knifemen disappeared. That was better.

'Now come on, mate,' he heard himself say, without much conviction.

'You ain't the only one who's got it bad,' the knifeman wailed, slurring the words.

Now it came back to him. Abbott could remember being at the bar. That's right – he and the other bloke had been swapping sob stories and talking about football. At least that's what Abbott had thought at the time. But somehow, and for reasons that remained a mystery, the conversation had taken a nasty turn. The kind of voices-raised, kicking-back-of-stools turn that had Nigel the world-weary landlord pointing in the direction of the fire door. 'Right, you two. Out!'

And now here they were, gone from being best new buddies to mortal enemies in the space of a heartbeat.

'Leave it, will you?' repeated Abbott. 'Put down the blade. Let's go back in, have another drink.'

But the other man was red-faced, eyes streaming, still in his angry-drunk phase, attacking not Abbott but an idea of him – Abbott as an avatar of a world that had clearly abandoned him – and he raced forward, the knife held like a bayonet.

At the last second, Abbott saw what it was. A butter knife. And whether it was that sudden revelation, the complete ineptness of the whole thing, or more likely, because he was also very drunk and had been drunk for weeks, his reaction was slow, and the knife, yes, just a bit of cutlery, but still a knife, nicked his cheek and sent him off balance.

He tried to find his centre of gravity, attempting to summon whatever vestiges of SF training were left in his drink-sodden, pain-ridden head, but found his combat instinct AWOL, staggering to one knee and finding there was no fight left in him.

Instead, what he felt was . . .

Exhaustion. A fatigue that was as much mental as it was physical. As much driven by demons within as it was by the alcohol he used to try and silence them. He looked up to see his opponent, who instead of returning to finish his job had dropped the knife, braced himself against the wall and was throwing up, a copious, lager-rich spew.

Abbott, on one knee like an ardent suitor, and knowing he deserved no better, felt the vomit rain down around him.

'Do you know what? You're a right couple of fackin' twats,' barked Nigel the landlord, glowering at them from the back door. 'And you're both barred.'

CHAPTER 2

Two boys playing in a field. Abbott and his brother Chris. The river, not deep, but still, they'd been warned to stay away by their worried parents.

Abbott calling for his brother. 'Chris! Chris!'

This image intertwining with another. This one of a young man dying in a desert, Abbott kneeling over him, watching his son slip away, the light leaving his eyes.

Nathan. Son. Don't go.

And then, like a man escaping the clutches of hellspawn, Abbott wrenched himself from the dream and into the waking world.

And decided that frankly the nightmare was preferable.

There was the distinct smell of vomit in the room. No, not just in the room, in the bed, in his hair and in his nostrils. Fragments of the evening returned to him. Being outside. A guy wielding a butter knife. A guy who seemed especially irate about something, but for the life of him, Abbott could not remember what.

The pressing on his bladder sent him downstairs, steeling himself to join the queue for the communal bathroom. Sure enough, when he got there, the door was closed and locked but at least he was next.

The door opened. The face of a little Somalian boy appeared, his eyes widening in fear at the sight of Abbott, who as he shuffled shamefully past the kid and into the bathroom caught sight of himself in the mirror and saw the left side of his face crusted with dried blood from last night's wound. Beware men wielding butter knives, as Shakespeare never said.

He took a piss, grabbed a quick shower, and made it back to his room dripping wet but without being seen. He crawled back into bed, and although it still stank of sick, at least he was clean within his kingdom of puke, and for now that would have to do. He reached for the half-empty bottle of vodka that lay on the threadbare carpet beside his bed, thinking, *This is it. This is your life now.*

Time? The year of our Lord, 2004. Just a few months after . . . well . . . *after*.

Place? A B&B in Finchley used primarily for asylum seekers. Families who spoke in languages Abbott didn't understand and regarded him with outright suspicion and fear.

He drank. A quick swig. One or two gallops of the Adam's apple, needing just that one hit to straighten him out. An experienced all-day drinker, he knew better than to seek oblivion at such an early stage. The days were long, each was an endurance test for the soul. Oblivion? That would come later, ushering him into another nightmare-crowded sleep.

His room was mostly bare, just a few treasured possessions and a television that was quietly playing breakfast TV. He watched as the latest headlines scrolled across the bottom of the screen, one of which was the fact that the billionaire Sir

Charles Norton had died after a short illness. A short report about Norton, detailing how he'd begun by opening a small chain of bookies in his hometown of Derby, and how his company, Norton Gaming, had grown exponentially until it was a multi-billion-pound international concern with major casinos in Vegas and Atlantic City and dozens of other smaller ones dotted around. They owned three theme parks worldwide. One in Dubai, another close to Paris, one in New York state. Again, other smaller parks dotted around, with plans to expand further into Eastern Europe.

The picture of Norton showed a guy who was older than Abbott, but still not exactly ready for retirement. 'And now you're dead,' said Abbott, toasting him with the bottle. 'All that money and you can't cheat your fate.'

He switched off the TV, reaching instead for his iPod, inserting the earbuds and allowing the music to work its magic. LTJ Bukem, his go-to tunes for soothing himself.

Allowing, also, the booze to do its job.

As he settled back, the words of Tess came to him. 'Alex, I think that your parents lied to you.'

He and Tess had been in the London restaurant Kettner's at the time. A meal that he had hoped would be of great emotional significance considering that their last meeting had ended in bed. In fairness, it had indeed been of emotional significance, just not the kind he expected.

It went back to her, to Tess, he realised, as he lay, listening to Bukem and wondering how he found himself here, at this particular juncture in his life. It went back to her, but first, it went back to Chris.

Two boys playing in a field . . .

CHAPTER 3

They were just kids at the time, living in Matlock. Chris was eleven, Abbott nine. They had been playing near the river under strict instructions never to go past what the Abbott family knew as 'the second bridge'. Past the second bridge the water was deep and fast running. The banks on either side rose vertiginously. No place for children to be playing.

They had removed their shoes and were paddling. Chris had his plimsolls in his hand, but he'd lost his footing and one of his shoes slipped out of his grasp and went into the water. The next second they had watched helplessly as it bobbed along, caught up in the current and racing distressingly fast towards that feared 'second bridge'.

Chris had called out. '*Alex.*' And Abbott had gone racing along the river, aware that the water was getting deeper, coming up to his thighs. Aware, also, of being pummelled by the current. He reached the mouth of the tunnel where inside it was dark and dank and there was no sign of Chris, who must have been pulled through and out the other side.

'Chris,' Abbott had called at the top of his voice.

So deep was his fear of the tunnel that instead of risking it, he turned and ran to the safety of the shallow water, scrambled up the bank, and then went racing along the field.

'Chris,' he called some more, again in vain, unable to see Chris in the river.

But he never saw his brother again.

Abbott was later told that Chris had most likely been swept out to sea. For his family it was the beginning of a slow, unspoken slide into domestic dysfunctionality marked by his parents' gradual withdrawal from everyday life, both coping-but-not-really-coping with the death of their eldest. They had moved from Matlock to Burton-on-Trent, hoping that a change of scene might help. Maybe it did, but if so, the effect was microscopic, a case of delaying the inevitable, which was the break-up of the Abbott marriage. As for Alex, he started life at a new school where he met the girl who was to become the love of his life: Tess – Tess Lacey to give her her full name.

Looking back, he knew it was weird that they'd ever wound up together. He and Tess were such different animals. The young Alex Abbott . . . Well, you wouldn't exactly say that he had turned to crime, but he didn't go the other way either. He became the kind of tearaway who was known to the police but not the magistrates, and more than once he was delivered home in a squad car, long-suffering coppers knocking on his door, delivering him back to parents who were only semi-interested in his whereabouts, being too preoccupied with arguing, drinking, grieving – skills that Abbott, in later life, would acquire in full.

His time in a remand home had done a lot to repair the damage. Inside the home he was told, 'We've seen your sort before, mate, and we'll see you again,' to which his dad had said, 'Well, son, you prove them wrong, then.'

A rare moment of coherent parenting from his old man. And it worked. Because Abbott *had* proven them wrong. He had. Getting out of remand school, he pledged never to darken the police station door again, and one thing about Abbott, when he put his mind to something . . .

Tess had always stood by him. And if she was a little bit titillated by her jailbird boyfriend, and secretly loved the fact that it scandalised her parents, that didn't matter, because she loved him properly. He knew she did.

Just not quite enough to marry him. His was a proposal borne more out of hope than expectation and, sure enough, she turned him down. Tess, after all, was bound for Oxford University. She loved Abbott. And who knows, perhaps she did see some future in the relationship beyond uni. Just that she never let on, being Tess. If the world is split into dog people and cat people – dog people needing love and affection, giving it in return, getting kicked and coming back for more; cat people, inscrutable and unreadable, much more selective with their affection – then he was a dog person, Tess was a cat person. Perhaps they were destined never to be together.

Either way, the choice was not his to make, because on one of their famous breaks, Abbott had a one-night stand with a girl called Fiona. There had been an unfortunate contraception malfunction and from that moment on, fate was in the driving seat.

He did the decent thing. He stuck by Fiona, married her, fathered Nathan and loved that boy with all his heart. But although Fiona was a good woman – as canny with money as he was crap with it, a great mother, funny, witty, great-looking, and a tiger in bed – she had one drawback. She was not Tess.

Abbott had joined the military. Being in the Marines changed him more profoundly than any other event in his life, excluding, perhaps, the birth of Nathan. The military taught him to both read and control his instincts. It instilled in him discipline and organisation.

At home, however, things were not so good. The word 'divorce' was mentioned. Who had said it first? He couldn't remember. The point being that it was out there, and once it's out there, as soon as the concept takes breath, it's difficult to go back. Talk of separation and divorce, once taboo and either whispered or spoken of only in anger, now became commonplace, something they discussed as easily as who did the washing-up.

Until, by a slow process of osmosis, it became a reality.

There was no rancour, at first. They had agreed between themselves to keep things civil for the sake of the young Nathan. He was just ten years old when they finally went their separate ways. Abbott had been away for so long that although he absolutely doted on Nathan, he hardly knew him. But it was as though the separation wrenched something loose in Abbott, or maybe tightened it up, for suddenly he became a much more present father, taking every opportunity he could to see his son. This, though undoubtedly a good thing, came at the expense of his previous good relations with Fi, who was aghast at the change, unstinting in her contempt for Abbott's 'sudden change of heart', as she put it. He, meanwhile, felt the same when Fiona had so quickly moved on to another bloke, a guy who held an administrative role attached to the British Army's Intelligence Corps.

And in the background – something that was like a low hum

in his head whatever the drama and tragedy of his life – were thoughts of Tess.

Years passed, until the advent of the internet allowed him to look her up and he'd discovered that Tess was now married with two kids and worked as a lawyer at Fitzpatrick & Sims. They'd got in touch, met up, and during the subsequent meal he'd told her the story of how Chris had died.

Why did he feel the need to reveal something that he'd kept hidden from her all those years? He wasn't sure. Maybe because he'd wanted to explain what made him the way he was back then. Why he'd been such a mixed-up kid. After all, everything about Tess seemed so content and settled.

Later that night they ended up in bed together. To him it was seismic, but Tess had behaved like it was nothing, no more important than a goodnight kiss, and Abbott had been left feeling discarded somehow. Hating the sensation, hating how it made him feel weak, unmanly and vulnerable.

A short while afterwards, Nathan had gone missing.

And not long after that, Abbott had cradled Nathan as he lay dying in Iraq.

The next thing to happen was that Tess had got back in touch, telling him that she needed to see him right away.

Then, as now, he had been in the clutches of grief. Even so, he couldn't help but think about their night together, hoping that her reasons for seeing him were romantic. For if anybody could save him – if anybody could stop the downward trajectory he knew his life was taking, it was Tess.

Once again, they had met in Kettner's in London. 'I'm so glad you got in touch,' he'd said, 'I was worried you might not want to. You know, after . . .'

'After what?'

She'd looked confused for a moment before it dawned on her. 'Oh, that. Yes, of course. I think that was what they call a blast from the past.'

The joke didn't quite reach her eyes. Her fingers were restless on a small sheaf of papers that she had placed on the table.

He swallowed. 'Sure. But I mean, well, to me it wasn't *just* a shag.' She was looking uncomfortable so he tried thinking of something else to say, something lighter and more conversational, but all he could come out with instead was the one pathetic word 'sorry', leaning back in his chair, giving her space.

'No, look, I'm sorry, Alex. It *did* mean something, of course it did. And maybe one day we can organise a return visit,' but again the smile didn't quite get there, 'it's just that that's not why I'm here. Why I'm here is not about *us* at all. It's about you.'

'What about me?'

She held up a hand. *Wait.* 'I know that you told me that your mum has passed away,' she said. 'What about your dad? Where is he right now?'

'He's in a home.'

Abbott thought guiltily of his father. When was the last time he'd bothered to pay the old man a visit? 'Why? Why do you want to know?'

'I have something I need to tell you.'

'About my dad?'

'Sort of.'

'Go on.'

'It's to do with Chris,' she told him. 'About how he died.'

And if the line of questioning about his father was

unexpected, then that took him completely by surprise. What could she possibly have to say about Chris? About the *death* of Chris? A tragedy that had taken place so many years ago.

'It's something you said,' she told him. 'How your parents told you that Chris must have been swept out to sea. It didn't ring true somehow. Either way, I looked into it.' She had picked up some of the papers that she consulted now. 'I found something,' she said.

'What is it?'

'I think . . .'

'Yes.'

'Alex, I think that your parents lied to you.'

CHAPTER 4

'What do you mean they lied to me?'

'OK, I mean that if they really told you that Chris had been swept out to sea then they *definitely* lied to you. Look, I'm trying to choose my words carefully here. I don't want to appear insensitive. But it just sounds, I don't know, *unlikely* that a kid in a river in the East Midlands ends up in the sea, don't you think? Tell me, did you ever look into that?'

He shook his head. 'No, I never checked it out. I took what I was told at face value and . . .'

'Even with the passing of time? Something nagging at you? Some sense that things weren't quite right?'

He shook his head.

'Or had you simply accepted this notion of guilt, this sense that you should have done something more?'

He looked at her. 'Don't psychoanalyse me, Tess,' he said, perhaps more sharply than he had intended.

Her eyes flicked down to the glass of beer in front of him. Not far away was a second glass, this one of white wine. Neither were his first. 'I know this is painful territory for you, Alex,' she said, 'I know you're dealing with new stuff now.

Believe me, I thought long and hard about bringing this to your door.'

'No, no, you did the right thing. I'm sorry. Just, please, bear with me.'

'Sure, sure.'

'What else is there? I mean, there's more, right?' His gaze went to the papers.

She placed her hand on them palm down. 'Yes, there's more. But are you sure you want to hear it?'

He shrugged like, *Tell me and then we'll see . . .*

'This is going to be hard to hear, Alex.'

'It's getting even harder not to.'

'OK. So like I say, your brother wasn't swept out to sea. In fact, he was pulled from the river. It was Chris's misfortune that the man who rescued him from the river should be a known sex offender. He put Chris into his car. They must have driven for some distance. Perhaps Chris became suspicious, something about the way the guy was behaving, perhaps. Or possibly Chris knew that he wasn't being driven home. Either way, at some point Chris escaped from the guy's car.'

'He escaped . . .'

Tess held up a hand. Again: *wait*. Her eyes dropped. 'Not quite. He got out of the guy's car and ran into the path of another vehicle. I'm sorry, Alex, but he was killed instantly.' She paused, looking at Abbott as if to assess his reaction. 'There was no fault on the part of the other driver,' she told him. 'He wasn't speeding or drunk or anything. Chris literally ran out in front of him.'

Abbott absorbed the information, feeling what, he couldn't say for certain. Only that it was cushioned by a great numbness.

He reached for his drink, grateful of the excuse to take a good long swallow. 'What happened to him, the kidnapper?'

Tess continued. 'When the police got round to his house, they found him in the process of smashing computers and discovered that there was already a fire in the back garden. They did manage to retrieve some images of child sex abuse from a laptop that had not yet been thrown onto the fire, and that, plus the charge of attempted kidnapping, was enough to put him away.'

'So he went away?'

'Yes. For a long time.'

He nodded as though satisfied but the thought in his head was, *That's not enough.* 'How did you get this information?' he asked her.

'Well, I could have made a subject access request through the official channels, but instead I called in a favour. A favour with a warrant card, the necessary security clearance and access to a computer.'

Abbott nodded. 'Which prison?'

'He died inside,' she said. But Abbott watched her eyes slip away. A tell if ever he'd seen one. He filed the moment away for the time being.

'What was his name?' he asked.

'His name?'

'Yes. The name of the paedophile. The one who died in prison. What was his name?'

She looked at him.

'Go on,' prompted Abbott.

'I need you to tell me . . .'

'Tell you what? That I won't go after him? He's dead, remember?'

'Of course. But reassure me that you won't, I don't know, go after members of his family or something. That you'll leave it there.'

'I wouldn't take it out on his family,' said Abbott, surprised she'd even think so. 'I'd never do something like that.'

'OK. His name was Jason Scutter,' she told him.

'Jason Scutter *RIP*,' he said, watching her carefully.

'Yes,' she said.

No doubt about it. She was lying to him.

CHAPTER 5

Abbott took a train back to the place of his youth. Arriving, he realised that he'd been steeling himself for a memory rush – some good, some bad, all of it hard to handle in his weakened mental state – but instead was relieved to find that the station had been modernised and looked nothing like it had when he'd last seen it. Exiting the station, same again. It used to be that cars were parked outside. Now the area had been pedestrianised. Only taxis were allowed near the station front. It felt like the only thing unchanged was its name. Burton-on-Trent.

He gave the taxi driver an address – out of town, thankfully, also unlikely to evoke memories – settled in the back, had a surreptitious chug of vodka and caught sight of the guy watching him in the rear-view. He checked himself to see whether he cared about being judged and found that, no, he didn't, his thoughts going back to his old AA group in Singapore. Guys who talked about motoring past that point where you stopped worrying what other people thought. Where you stopped caring about yourself. About your family. You stopped caring about anything apart from the booze.

At the time he'd thought to himself, *That's what makes me different from these other guys. It's because I care.*

But you're getting there, aren't you? You're getting ready to join that group.

The driver was visibly relieved when Abbott came up with the cash at their destination. Abbott waited until he was gone, took another quick chug of the bottle and then turned to look at the care home.

Clearview was the name. This was where Abbott's father, Ted, lived now. He was only in his mid-seventies, but first alcoholism, and then a stroke had put him in a wheelchair needing around-the-clock care.

The last time Abbott saw him was Nathan's funeral when his dad had been accompanied by a male nurse from the home. Abbott had leaned in to embrace him after the service, but the moment had been awkward and weird. Had they spoken further? Abbott couldn't remember, although what he did recall was that as a Brucie bonus, the funeral had also included a moment when Fiona physically attacked him, accusing him of being responsible for Nathan's death. There wasn't much answer for that. She was right.

So to the Clearview complex where the only view, clear or not, was of more buildings associated with the care home. During the journey Abbott had been asking himself the purpose of his visit; after all, he knew the truth of Chris's death now. Why take time out of his busy schedule to spend precious money on trains and taxis to ask his father what he already knew?

Answer: because he wanted to confront his father with it. He wanted his father to know that his lies had been exposed.

A woman on reception directed him to another building

across the quad. There, he asked where he might find Ted Abbott, and was told to wait.

Inside was warm with a smell like school dining halls, not especially pleasant but at the same time almost nostalgic, making him feel like a kid again.

'Mr Abbott?'

Abbott looked up, startled, coming right back down to earth with a bump, his hand slapping his thigh before he realised that no sidearm was there.

'Yes?' he said. 'Sorry. I was miles away. Years away, actually.'

'That's quite all right,' she said, and to his surprise took a seat beside him. 'I was wondering if I could have a quick word before you go in to see your father?'

'Of course.' He leaned away slightly, worried she might smell the booze on him.

'As far as I know you haven't seen your father in a while, so you may not be aware of this – there's something I need to tell you before you go in.'

'Go on.'

'He was recently diagnosed with Parkinson's disease.'

'I see.'

'I'm sorry,' she said, and Abbott sat, nodding but shell-shocked as she went on to say that with any luck his father, being in his late-seventies, was likely to die *with* Parkinson's rather than of it, and how the onset of the condition was gradual, and that Abbott might not even be aware of its presence because sufferers could be quite lucid one moment, confused and incoherent the next. That their long-term memory was often much better than their short-term memory.

'You might find that you need to be very patient with him,'

she continued. 'I'm sure I don't need to tell you that whatever you do, you cannot lose your patience with him. Don't show irritation or anger.'

With that, she stood, indicating that he should follow, and led him along the hallway to his father's room. She knocked, ushered him in, announced him. 'Mr Abbott? Ted? It's your son Alex to see you.' She promised to organise some tea and then left them to it, closing the door gently behind her.

And there they were. Father and son. The older Abbott in his wheelchair, positioned in front of the TV, which was on, some antiques programme. The younger one hovering by the door, thinking, *My dad has Parkinson's. He's been given a death sentence.*

'Hi, Dad,' said Abbott, at last.

'Hi, Alex,' said his father.

Abbott, about to take a seat, stopped, excused himself to the en-suite bathroom and took a nip. He returned to find that his father had switched off the TV and positioned his wheelchair by the window, which although the radiator blazed away, was open a crack, letting in a welcome breath of fresh air.

'It's good of you to come,' said his father. He wore a pair of baggy faded jeans, shirt open at the neck and a brown cardigan. 'I can't think. When was the last time I saw you?'

Abbott was about to remind him when his father added, 'And how is that lovely wife of yours? And my grandson?'

The question was like a dagger. He swallowed. 'They're fine, Dad.' The words were croaked. 'They send their love.'

'Good to hear. Good to hear. He must be walking now, isn't he?'

Abbott thought of the last time he'd seen Nathan. Nathan

dying. He thought of a tiny little boy, pictures that appeared on his laptop screensaver: Nathan sitting up in his cot. Nathan crawling. Nathan sitting cross-legged on his bedroom carpet grinning up at the camera, no older than three. A perfect little boy. A wonder of possibility that had been snuffed out by greed and revenge.

'Bet he runs you a merry little dance,' chortled his father, happy and jowly, eyes bright with pleasure.

'Yes, he does, Dad. He does that.'

For a second, Abbott wondered whether it was worth pursuing any line of enquiry with his father let alone the one he had planned. Remembering what the nurse had said, how his dad's long-term memory was likely to be better than short-term, he thought, *Here goes nothing.*

'Dad, I need to talk to you about Chris.'

His father gave a small start. His brow clouded. For a moment, Abbott wondered if he would even remember Chris.

'We don't talk about that,' said his father, all that grand-fatherly happiness erased.

'No, we never talked about it when I was growing up,' said Abbott. 'But I want to talk about him now, please. I need to ask you something.'

Ted Abbott's fingers fretted at the denim of his jeans. His eyes went to the window, looking out into the car park. Abbott pressed him. 'I need you to tell me what happened that day.'

His dad looked at him, clear-eyed. 'Sounds to me like you already know. Sounds to me like you're trying to catch me out, make me feel bad for what happened years ago. Would that be right?'

All Abbott said in reply was, 'I need to hear it from you.'

CHAPTER 6

For a moment Abbott thought his father might simply clam up. But then he spoke. 'Your mother wanted to tell you the truth,' he said, 'but I wouldn't allow it. I couldn't see the use in it meself.' He threw up his hands as though considering the dilemma afresh. 'What could we say to you? When could we say it? What good would it have done you? Anyway.'

Abbott exhaled, rubbing his hands over his stubble. '"What good would it have done?" How about the fact that I would have known the truth?'

'Sounds like you know the truth now.'

'Yeah, Dad. Yeah, I know the truth now.'

'You feel better for it, do you?'

'No, you're right, I don't. But that's not the point.'

'What is the point, then?'

'That I grew up thinking the river killed him.'

'Does it make any difference now you know otherwise?'

'No. I mean, yes. Yes, it does.' Abbott stood abruptly, angrily. He saw fear flare in his father's eyes, which was enough to settle him a little, reminding him to take things gently. 'It means that I grew up thinking things were different to the way they really were. It means that I thought the river took him when a man took him. I always thought that if I'd tried harder, I could have saved him, but it turns out that had nothing to do with how he died.'

'But we knew that, son,' insisted his father. 'We knew you was riddled with guilt over it all. Why make it worse by telling you that Chris had been delivered into the hands of a nonce?'

'But I grew up thinking that we never knew for sure what had happened to him, when we did. Or everyone else did. Everyone else but me. I grew up with a lie, Dad.'

His dad was shaking his head. 'We never saw it like that. We didn't see it like lying. We saw it as keeping you safe. We wanted to prevent you from a lifelong feeling of hatred for a man you've never met and never will. I can see now that you reckon we did the wrong thing, but you'll know when that boy of yours gets older. You'll know that as a parent you don't always make the right decisions. You just make the decisions you think are right at the time. You make the decisions you think'll cause the least hurt.'

With a sigh, Abbott plonked himself back down, and they sat for a while, Abbott wondering if another nip would help him make sense of his father's excuses. Help him to accept them. It wasn't that, though. What he needed was to find forgiveness in his heart; he needed to remember that although the guy opposite had not been the best father, he in turn had not been the best son, and he thought of all those times that his father had made excuses for him, turned up at the police station when he was in trouble, tried his best to reassure him that Chris's death was not his fault, and how he, the young and youthful Abbott, had reacted, which was to give his father years and years of trouble, ending in that remand-home spell. The death of Chris had sent them all off the rails one way or another. There was no wondering who'd got it worst. From four Abbott family members there were only two left, and as they sat in this overheated room in a care home in Burton-upon-Trent the last thing they needed to do was despise one another.

It was as though his father had read his thoughts. 'I'm sorry, son,' he said.

'I'm sorry, too, Dad.'

They remained in silence for a while. A silence you might even have said was companionable, until Abbott almost regret-fully broke it. 'I'm going to have to go, Dad,' he said.

'You'll be coming back next week, will you?'

He looked at the old man, the reality of it all coming crashing back in on him. 'Yes. Next week, as usual,' and he stood. His emotions roiled. He turned to go, just as his dad said, 'He came to see me, you know.'

'Who came to see you? The kidnapper?' Abbott tried to recall the guy's name. 'Jason Scutter? Him?'

'No, not him. They sent him to jail. I'm talking about the bloke who ran into Chris. Mr Smith was his name. Driving a Rover. Devastated he was. He sat in our front room in front of your mother and me, and he cried his heart out for what he'd done. He said that even though it weren't his fault he could never forgive himself for what he'd done. I don't think I've ever felt more sorry for someone in me life than I did at that moment.'

Abbott knew. He knew that it didn't matter whether or not you were responsible, where the fault lay; that even when it wasn't your fault you still felt like it was, you still played it out in your head and made it end differently, wondered what you could have done.

'He said something else an' all.'

'What's that then, Dad?'

'He said he saw the bloke in his car, the nonce, the one you just said.'

Abbott found himself leaning forward. 'Jason Scutter?'

'Yeah, him.'

His dad was drifting a little. 'Yeah, go on,' pressed Abbott. 'He saw Scutter in his car?'

'Yeah, that's what he said. He said he saw him in his car . . .'

'Yeah. And?'

'He said there was another bloke with him.'

CHAPTER 7

It was rather – no, more than that – it was *really* childish. But when Fiona had got together with the guy from the Ministry of Defence, and when that guy had moved into the home that Fiona had previously shared with Abbott, Abbott had come up with a rather childish nickname for him.

He had called him Cuckoo.

He and Cuckoo had not exactly hit it off. Abbott was rough-hewn special forces. A soldier trained to kill and good at it. Cuckoo was, as far as Abbott was concerned, a pen pusher, a paper shuffler. The two men could hardly have been more different.

But then, when Nathan had disappeared, Cuckoo made the trip to Singapore to alert Abbott. The search to find Nathan could scarcely have ended more badly, but throughout it all, Cuckoo had been a huge help and support. To say that Abbott had gained a new understanding and respect for him was putting things mildly.

Still, when it was all over, Cuckoo had to go back to Fiona. The two were by now married and whatever she was told, Fiona could not let go of the notion that Abbott was primarily responsible for Nathan's death. That, more than anything, put a stop to any burgeoning friendship between the two men.

Well, that and the fact that Abbott's only true friend came in cans and bottles.

Fiona was right, of course, despite what Cuckoo told her. Abbott *was* responsible. Of course he was. Not directly. He had not literally lit the fire that ended up causing Nathan's death. But metaphorically? Yes, in many ways, he had. Fiona was right. The issue being that she could not possibly, not in a million years, have hated Abbott as much as he hated himself.

Now, Abbott found himself at RAF Chicksands, where he paid his way into the museum and had a wander around the Ministry of Defence exhibits, passing among other visitors, staring in at glass-fronted cabinets displaying weapons of the past, uniforms, as well as a reconstruction of an air-raid shelter where kids had their pictures taken wearing gas masks. Piped into the exhibits were sounds of battle, explosions and gunshots that made Abbott's palms sweat.

He located a quiet corner of the museum, unhooked his backpack and reached inside for the trusty bottle, took a quick hit and put it back, waited for the booze to do its job.

'Abbott.'

The voice came from behind and he wheeled quickly to see that Cuckoo stood behind him, wearing a suit.

'You look well, Cuckoo,' said Abbott, stuffing the bottle back in his bag under Cuckoo's disapproving gaze. 'Have you lost weight?'

'Fiona's got me on a diet,' nodded Cuckoo, patting a hand to what was indeed an admirably flat stomach.

'Talking of which, did you tell her we were meeting?'

'No, because I like my balls where they are, thank you very much.' A family arrived, little boy scampering forward. Cuckoo indicated for he and Abbott to leave. 'Outside?'

On a bench in the late-March sun they watched visitors come and go.

'So how is Fiona?' asked Abbott when they were settled.

Cuckoo sighed. 'To all intents and purposes she's coping. She's redecorating the house. She's got us on this diet. She's keeping herself occupied.'

'But . . .?'

'But she's hurting. During the days, she keeps herself busy. But she's crying herself to sleep most nights.'

'She still blames me?'

'No, she doesn't blame you, Abbott. She knows it's not your fault. That you did your best.'

Abbott closed eyes that were suddenly pricked by tears, taking a moment or so to compose himself. 'It didn't come across that way at the funeral.'

'I don't know, mate. All I can say is that she's mellowed in that regard.'

'But not enough that you could tell her about this meeting?'

Cuckoo chuckled. He stretched his legs out in front of him and pushed his hands into his pockets. 'No, Abbott, she hasn't mellowed that much. I don't think she will *ever* mellow that much.' A pause. 'What about you? No need to ask about your coping mechanism.'

It was Abbott's turn to chuckle. 'It's not decorating and diets, that much I can tell you.'

'You can't go on like it, you know.'

'I know.' Abbott had spent enough tortured, hungover

mornings telling himself exactly the same thing. Knowing that he needed something – anything – in his life. Something to help take the pain away.

'So anyway, to what do I owe the pleasure?' asked Cuckoo.

'It's about something that happened a long time ago.'

'Go on.'

'OK, do you know about my brother, Chris? Did Fiona ever tell you about that?'

Cuckoo nodded. 'She did. And I was very sorry to hear it.'

'Right. Park that for a second. I've got this ex called Tess . . .'

'I've heard of Tess.'

'Oh yeah? From Fi?'

'Well, who else? She was your girlfriend before her. Apparently, you've always carried a torch for her.'

'That's what she said, was it?'

'Yeah.'

'Not that it would bother her.'

'Well, I think it probably bothered her at the time.'

'Fair point.'

'Are you romantically attached now?'

'Me and Tess? No.'

'Would you like to be?'

'More than anything, mate. But she's married with kids, and anyway, that's not the point. The point is this.'

He told Cuckoo everything. All about Tess and their meetings at Kettner's and especially what she'd discovered regarding his brother. He missed out the bit where he and Tess slept together, because a gentleman never tells, and besides, how could he possibly explain that they'd slept together and yet there was still no romantic attachment? That they'd slept together and that while it had meant everything to him, it had apparently meant nothing to her?

Otherwise, everything else came out.

'OK,' said Cuckoo, when Abbott had finished, choosing his words carefully, still unsure where he fitted into all this. 'So that must have come as a shock.'

'That my entire childhood was a lie? You might say that. I went to see my dad afterwards.'

'Oh yeah? And how did that go?'

'Ups and downs. The main thing was that years ago he was visited by the guy who ran Chris down, and that guy said there was a second perp in Scutter's car.'

'OK . . .'

'A big fat bloke, according to the driver.'

'And this fat bloke – he was never found?'

Abbott shook his head. 'Never mentioned, never looked for, never found, never punished. Scutter goes to jail. This other bloke's a ghost.'

'What about your dad? Did he report it to the police?'

'He said that he did, but that the police never did anything about it.'

'OK, but did he follow it up? I mean, this was his son. Your brother.'

'I asked him about that. He said that the police got narky with them. Said they must be mistaken. Told them to leave well alone. All that kind of stuff. I tried pressing him on it, but he started to get a bit anxious. The nurse turned up, saw that he was a bit distressed and wasn't best pleased. She said I was upsetting him.' He looked away with a heavy heart. 'Which, I guess, I was.'

'I don't suppose it's ever a good look to be seen upsetting your wheelchair-bound father?'

'You suppose right. I was given my marching orders.'

'She didn't happen to get a whiff of your breath, did she?'

'Well, if she did, she didn't say anything.'

Cuckoo gave a slightly derisive snort. 'You're not pulling the wool over anybody's eyes, you know. You might think you are, with your secret little drinks. Vodka doesn't make your breath smell, is that it? But you're not fooling anybody. They all know.'

Abbott shrugged. Not sure if he cared.

'And so, on top of grieving for Nathan, you've now got this?' said Cuckoo.

'*This* being what? The boozing.'

'Well, yes, that. Also, *this* being the stuff about your brother.'

'I guess I have.'

Cuckoo made a noise – a disgusted noise. Shook his head.

'You think she shouldn't have told me?' Abbott asked him.

'I *know* she shouldn't have told you. She's a lawyer, you say. Skirting the truth should come as second nature.'

'Well, as a matter of fact I think that she has been a bit economical where that's concerned. She told me that Scutter was dead.'

'Yeah? And?'

'I reckon she was lying.'

'Why?'

'Call it an instinct.'

'OK, so she wanted you to know, but she also wanted you to consider the matter closed. So do that. Pack it up with the rest of your worries and concentrate on getting well.'

'What do you mean *getting well*?'

'I mean drying out, sorting your head. Dealing with your grief. Mate, have you considered therapy?'

'Therapy for me would be to find Scutter, if he really is alive. Find him and then find this second man. That would help me, Cuckoo. That for me is coping.'

'What about this?' Cuckoo reached to tap the rucksack that lay between them and there was the unmistakable sound of knuckle hitting bottle. 'Before you do anything you need to get off the booze.'

'Look, in SF, we'd drink like witches between operations. But as soon as the call came you put the bottle down. You went dry. It's the same in this situation.'

Cuckoo sighed. 'Well, OK, then. If I can help you do that, then I'm all ears.'

Not for the first time, Abbott wondered why he had ever felt any animosity towards Cuckoo, who had long since proved beyond doubt that he was one of the good guys, to the extent that Abbott felt eternally grateful that Cuckoo had made his way into Fiona's life. Small mercies and all that.

'So, what you want me to do?' asked Cuckoo.

'I'm hoping you can look into it for me. Find out if I'm right and that this Scutter guy is still alive, where he is now, and who he associates with.'

'Tess wants you to leave it.'

'She should have known better than to tell me, then.'

'Maybe I should tell you to leave it, too.'

'But you won't do that. Because you know that this is what I need.'

CHAPTER 8

Sitting in the lounge area of his palatial Swiss home, the playboy Ross Norton yawned. He wore a large robe and the relaxed air of a man who looked as though he was never happier than when slightly drunk or slightly hungover.

In the lounge, huge windows offered stunning views of blue skies and mountaintops, while a sunken area played host to white leather couches. Along one wall were bookcases. On another wall a large television.

'Are we ready, Kennedy?' said Ross Norton.

Kennedy, his assistant, wore a pair of neatly pressed jeans and a navy Lacoste polo shirt tucked in and fastened at the collar. His hair was short and neat, bald on top, monkish. 'I shall need the television controller, sir,' he said implacably.

Ross snatched up the controller and tossed it towards Kennedy.

'Perhaps you should change, sir,' suggested Kennedy, 'while I establish the connection and double-check the encryption.'

Ross Norton plucked at the robe that barely covered his nether regions. 'Change?' he said, as though he didn't understand the meaning.

'You are, after all, a bereaved grandson in mourning, sir.'

'And will my attire make any difference to the will reading?'

'I'm sure we wouldn't want your family to gain the wrong impression, sir.'

At the same time, Kennedy produced a framed photograph of Ross's grandfather, the late Sir Charles Norton, and placed it on a shelf in order that it should be prominently displayed during the meeting. 'Sir, I know that you're nervous . . .'

'Nervous? I'm not in the slightest bit nervous,' spluttered Ross, darkening.

'You have lost your grandfather.'

Ross shrugged.

'He was an important figure in your life.'

'I don't care. I'm not nervous, and if you carry on like this you'll find yourself cleaning chalets.'

Kennedy approached the sofa, his hands clasped behind his back. He leaned forward – leaning even as Ross pushed himself back into the sofa cushions, wanting to cringe away. 'Just you try it,' said Kennedy evenly, 'sir.'

Kennedy straightened. Ross recovered – or at least tried to recover – some composure. 'You should watch your tone, Kennedy. I'm about to become a very rich man,' he said, mustering a little defiance.

Kennedy made a small, sharp motion with his hand and allowed himself a smile as Ross Norton flinched. 'A very rich man who can't even tie his own shoelaces,' said Kennedy. 'Now get dressed in a manner appropriate for somebody who, first, has just lost his grandfather and, second, is about to speak to his beloved and grieving grandmother.'

Ross trooped off. Kennedy switched on the television,

established a link with the laptop. A screen appeared confirming that end-to-end encryption was successful and that the host would shortly be beginning the meeting.

Ross returned to the spacious lounge, looking smarter. He sat down until the television, which up until that moment had shown a black screen and the simple message 'waiting for host', suddenly changed, and a thirty-second countdown began.

Twenty-eight

Twenty-seven

The host had begun the meeting. They were live. And suddenly the screen was split, tiled into faces that Ross knew well.

First, there was the lawyer, Jeffrey Coombs. Coombs sat at his desk in London. Late-fifties but looking good on it, weathered, tanned skin merged with the wood panelling of his office behind.

He wore glasses that he removed, and he made a play of doing something with his mobile, as though to reassure the assembled surviving members of the Norton clan that they had his full attention and, for a handsome fee, would continue to command it for as long as needs be.

Then there was his mother, Montana Norton, who would have been horrified to discover that a word such as 'milf' even existed but flattered to find that she easily qualified. She was based in Malibu and if Ross's experience was anything to go by, would mention the fact that she had watched dolphins from the balcony of her beachfront home at least once over the course of the conversation.

For the moment she sat at what looked like her breakfast bar, exuding exactly the right amount of age-appropriate glamour, Liz Hurley's only real competition in this world.

'Ross, how are you?' she asked, and showed the usual lack of interest in his response.

'And how are you, Mother?' he asked in return.

'Lovely thank you, darling,' she glowed. 'This morning I had breakfast on the balcony and watched the dolphins.'

She stopped, interrupting a train of thought that would have probably gone on for quite some time were it not for the fact that something had just occurred to her. 'And where is Simon?' she said. 'Is this going to be another one of his no-shows?'

'No, Mother,' sighed Ross, 'I think *even* Simon is going to make the effort for this one.'

As if in response, his younger brother, Simon, flicked into view.

There were some whose money prevented their drug use from taking its toll on their looks. Ross should know, having been to school with a number of them. Some had quit, some had been to rehab, some were still what you might call 'functioning'. They all looked the picture of sun-dappled health.

Not Simon.

Simon looked as he always looked. Strung-out and needy. The sort of person from whom you averted your eyes in case their obvious addiction was catching.

Next to appear was Juliet Norton. Ross's grandmother and the wife of the deceased. Sir Charles Norton's widow.

She wore the clothes and make-up of a grand lady about to attend high tea, complete with pearls, although the truth was that she had the money to pass herself off that way but not the breeding. Her husband, Sir Charles Norton, RIP, was a man who had hauled himself up by his bootstraps and was in the eyes of the world a Labour-supporting, successful self-made man, a knight of the realm by dint of his many achievements. And yes, those achievements were based on a gambling empire of somewhat dubious provenance, but he had been a trusted figure under the Blair government and never really out of favour since, such was his man-of-the-people popularity.

Juliet Norton, though? Born simply Julie Smith – comprehensively educated, the childhood sweetheart of her husband – had never enjoyed quite the same ascendancy nor respect. Juliet Norton, despite the clothes she wore, the accent she affected and, perhaps more pertinently, the money and influence to which she was party, had never really enjoyed that same level of respect from, say, the wives at the golf club and the institutes and societies to which her husband was affiliated. Whether those women genuinely considered her an interloper, a 'competition winner', would never be established for certain, since of course they would vehemently deny the fact. But that was how Juliet had felt throughout her marriage to Sir Charles Norton. It was how she'd felt then and how she felt now.

And that made her dangerous.

Ross, sitting on his sofa in his assistant's clothes, knew it all. He looked into the face of his beloved grandmother and all he saw there was steel and resolve. Ross knew that Juliet and Charles had been devoted to one another and even with his grandfather's love of pranks and gamesmanship, there was one thing of which they could all be certain: Sir Charles Norton would have left the bulk of his estate to his wife, Juliet.

But Sir Charles Norton's estate was worth, not millions, but billions. And even though Juliet might take the bulk, she would take tens of billions, and that still left an awful lot of billions for everybody else.

CHAPTER 9

For a moment the faces on the TV screen waited expectantly.

And yet there was one tile still black. One member of the meeting yet to make an appearance. Ross looked towards Jeffrey Coombs to explain, and when there was nothing forthcoming, looked to his grandmother, Juliet, instead. Her face was implacable. Either she knew what to expect or, more likely, as the long-time partner and now widow of the late Sir Charles Norton, simply knew to expect the unexpected.

It was left to Montana, impatient, to break the ice. 'Mr Coombs? Are we to begin?'

'Just one more member of your family to arrive, ma'am,' said Coombs. 'The late Mr Norton begs your indulgence.'

'He what? He's dead, how on earth can he be begging my indulgence?'

'I would ask that you talk about your father with a little bit more respect,' said Juliet quietly, commandingly.

'I'm sorry, Mama,' said Montana, lowering her eyes.

Ross knew that Montana had always been his grandfather's favourite child, just as he liked to flatter himself that he was the favourite grandchild. With Simon his main competition, that wasn't difficult. Nor was it necessarily a trophy he particularly wanted in the cabinet, but still, you snatched your victories where you could.

He glanced sideways at Kennedy, who stood clear of the laptop's camera. 'You enjoying this?' said Ross quietly from the side of his mouth.

'Positively Shakespearean, sir,' replied Kennedy.

'Something tells me that you're going to relish the next development, then?'

'The missing delegate?'

'Exactly.'

'Wait, you know who it is, don't you?'

'I've got an idea.'

'Well? Don't keep it to yourself.'

'Put it this way, sir, when did you last see your father?'

'Are you having your own private meeting?' barked his mother on the screen. Ross had taken his astounded gaze from Kennedy back to the meeting, knowing that his PA was correct.

As if on cue the face appeared. The face of a man in his early seventies.

He was pasty. His dark, curly hair was unkempt. His eyes wore the same darting, nervy look they wore when seated at boardroom meetings of Norton Gaming.

His name was Clifford Levine. He was father to Ross and Simon. Ex-husband of Montana who had, albeit briefly, taken his name during the marriage but then reverted to Norton shortly after the split, while Ross and Simon had also adopted the Norton name. Sir Charles had given him a place on the board as a wedding present despite always professing to hate him.

Simon gave a sheepish lopsided grin. 'Hi, Dad.' Ross looked at Kennedy, who smirked, and then back at the screen. Juliet maintained her poise.

Montana, however, reacted as though administered an electric shock. 'Mr Coombs, what is *he* doing here?'

'He is here on the express wishes of your late father, ma'am,' replied Mr Coombs.

'He's not blood.'

'Indeed, ma'am, I can only reiterate . . .'

This was it, they all knew. If even in some distant recesses of their minds they had wondered whether things might proceed along vaguely conventional lines, now they knew better. Sir Charles Norton, a man who had built his fortune by pitting his wits against those of the consumer, a man for whom life was a game and games a way of life planned to play with them from beyond the grave.

They would play, every single one of them. The stakes were too high to do anything otherwise.

And now it came time to read the will.

The family sat poised. Every single one of them, apart from Simon was already wealthy beyond the wild dreams of most, but even so, this – this was different. An entirely new stratosphere of wealth. And they were all hungry for it.

'I shall begin,' said Jeffrey Coombs. '*To my wife, Juliet, I leave my share in our house and its contents, as well as our homes abroad, our cars and our private jet. She has access to all of our personal bank accounts so that she may continue to live in the manner to which she has become accustomed.*'

Juliet's shoulders straightened. It was what she had been expecting. Anything less would have been a considerable blow, an undermining of what had been a happy and successful marriage.

'*To my son, I leave the* Clement Attlee.'

'The *Clement Attlee* is a yacht,' exploded Ross. 'I live in Switzerland. What the fuck am I going to do with a yacht in Switzerland?'

'*My son Simon shall receive monies to the same value,*' continued Coombs.

'But that's not fair,' complained Ross, not wanting to give either Kennedy or Coombs the satisfaction but unable to help himself, 'I want the money, not a yacht.'

The grin on Simon's face slid off as Coombs continued, '*But these monies shall only be awarded when Simon is able to provide my lawyer, Jeffrey Coombs,*' he looked up again as though to confirm that, yes, it was he, Jeffrey Coombs, '*with the medical proof of a year's abstinence from any form of hard drugs.*'

Coombs continued. Montana was gifted an estate in Norfolk. She nodded with a look as though to say it was her birthright. Nothing less than she deserved. For Clifford Levine there was nothing. Not yet, anyway.

Now came the main event.

'*As for the distribution of my controlling stock in Norton Gaming, I have devised something unusual.*'

They tensed. Montana's jaw set and her eyes closed as though in anticipation of bad news.

'*First, I should like to make it clear that the controlling stock in Norton Gaming will be awarded to one person and one person only.*'

Their eyes widened, because what they all knew was that

houses and cars and even the private jet was one thing. The big prize, and the reason that they all felt that same hunger, was a controlling stake in Norton Gaming, an empire worth over 100 billion.

Whoever had that share was effectively the head of one of the country's largest companies, which as well as wealth meant influence and power. It meant having the prime minister's private number. It meant the royal family and the president of the United States would take your calls. It meant taking a seat at the top of the table and watching as you bent the world to your own will.

'*As you know, my first passion has always been for games, and so to decide who shall be the one, I have devised a game,*' continued Coombs. '*A game that I trust you will find most diverting.*'

CHAPTER 10

Abbott had planned to spend the rest of the morning drinking and watching TV, but that was before he realised that he'd left his jacket in The Sportsman. Which meant that even though he'd fully intended to offer his apologies for last night's disturbance when the dust had settled, he was going to have to do it sooner rather than later. As in, today.

Now to dress. A few weeks back he'd won the pub's quiz and been given a T-shirt bearing its name as a prize. Partly in the absence of anything else that was remotely clean, and partly in a bid to butter up Nigel, he pulled it on, dragging an unbuttoned black shirt over the top of it.

He checked himself in the mirror. Not good, but then again not too bad. Yes, he looked as though he'd been in the wars, but at least he didn't have the appearance of a drunken wreck.

'You're not fooling anybody, you know,' Cuckoo had said to him, and he was right about that. In the supermarket Abbott had exchanged a glance with another guy buying his daily supply. Nothing was said. No words exchanged. Just that look. The look that told both men, *Here is a fellow traveller*.

'What have you become?' Abbott asked himself aloud,

and when no answer was forthcoming, he left his room and made his way carefully downstairs, trying to ignore the throbbing in his head.

He reached the landing below and there stood the little Somalian kid, the same one from before.

'You look better, man,' said the kid, and Abbott, who had been about to hurry past, stopped in his tracks. As a Royal Marine, he'd spent time in Northern Ireland and joined Operation Desert Storm in Iraq. As a member of the SBS, he had worked in counterterrorism, gone up against drug gangs and carried out counterinsurgency operations.

Then there was his humanitarian work. As part of a four-man team, he had worked with a charity to crack a child-trafficking ring in Thailand, rescuing kids, bringing them to safety.

He thought of the lads. Ward, the explosives expert, who now ran a garden centre in Whitstable. Miller, who had morphed into a personal trainer, and Brace, a full-time mercenary who was also the best sniper Abbott had ever worked with.

Worldwide, over 1.6 million kids a year were sold into sex slavery. Abbott, Ward, Miller and Brace had rescued twenty-two of them on one occasion, and even though it was such a small drop in the ocean, it was those rescues that had given Abbott his proudest moments.

Kids like this one? For a moment, Abbott felt the shackles of his ever-present grief fall away as he cast a practised eye over the boy, taking in the fact that he looked nourished and wore clean, if ageing clothes. Most importantly, there was a light in his eyes.

'How's things with you, mate?' he said.

'I'm very good, man,' the kid grinned. 'Better than you.'

Abbott ran a finger over the scab. 'You like my cut, do you? You ever get any cuts and bruises yourself?'

'If I fall over.'

'You fall over often?'

The kid shook his head, and privately Abbott gave him the all-clear. He reached to ruffle the kid's hair. 'Just you stay out of trouble, you hear?' He pointed to himself. 'You don't want to end up looking like this, do you?'

Abbott let himself out of the front door of the B&B, thinking that maybe all was not lost after all. Perhaps there was enough of him inside, enough of the man from before.

The feeling didn't last long. It lasted about as long as it took to make his way to The Sportsman, knock on the locked door and see the expression Nigel wore when he opened it.

'You're fackin' barred.'

Nigel seemed about to close the door on him but stopped himself. 'And do me a favour, would you, pal? Take off that facking T-shirt.'

Abbott stepped back, flapping open his black overshirt to reveal the T-shirt beneath in all its glory. 'What? I thought you'd be pleased, mate. Flying the flag and all that.'

'It rather depends on who's flying the flag, doesn't it? Because just between you and me, pal, you ain't looking too lively.'

'Yeah, I get that a lot. Listen, look, just give me my jacket. I'll zip it up, nobody will see the T-shirt, I won't darken your door again.'

Nigel rolled his eyes but seemed to soften. 'Nah, it's all right, you can come in, like. There's something I need to tell you, anyway.'

Abbott sat on a stool suddenly feeling very thirsty indeed.

Nigel threw him a disapproving expression but began to pour him a pint anyway, and Abbott thought it was just about the most beautiful thing he'd ever seen.

'Greg collapsed yesterday,' said Nigel, placing the pint down in front of Abbott. 'He was taken to hospital.'

Abbott looked at the drink thirstily, but in a bid to project a sense of being in control of his drinking, did not automatically reach for it. 'Who's Greg?'

Nigel shook his head. 'Greg was the bloke you was about to beat up last night.'

'I wasn't about to beat him up, and what do you mean "taken to hospital"? We didn't even touch each other.'

Nigel looked evenly at him. 'You sure about that? Do you remember anything about last night? Just that I'm hoping that you wasn't quite yourself, like.'

'Why? What did I do?'

'It wasn't what you did. It was what you said. You and Greg sitting here, having an argument about who had it worse. Greg told you he had cancer. You was like, "I'd rather have cancer than a dead son."'

Abbott felt his shoulders drop, his gaze fall away. 'I said that, did I?'

'Yes, you said it. Whole facking pub heard you say it, pal.'

Abbott cringed inside. 'So Greg being taken to hospital, that was nothing to do with what happened outside?'

'No, you're in the clear. Nothing to do with you and all to do with the fact that he was dying of cancer.' Nigel leaned forward. 'Listen, pal, I know when a bloke is on edge. When they're likely to do serious damage to themselves or someone else. I'm looking at it now.'

'It's in hand, mate,' Abbott assured him. 'Believe me, it's in hand.'

He sank the rest of his pint, ordered another. And because that went down almost dismayingly easily, he ordered another.

CHAPTER 11

Walking along Finchley High Road, Cuckoo could hear the noise from The Sportsman. It sounded like a party in full swing at – he checked his watch – just after three on a Tuesday afternoon.

At the door of the pub, he paused. The music was loud, punctuated by shouting and laughter. This wasn't your normal pub atmosphere. This was New Year's Eve or wedding reception stuff. And since it wasn't New Year's Eve, and Abbott had about as much chance of being invited to a wedding as Typhoid Mary, then it seemed unlikely he would even be in there.

Cuckoo was about to turn and go elsewhere when he heard a distinctive voice from inside.

That distinctive voice was Abbott. And he sounded very, very drunk indeed.

Here goes nothing, thought Cuckoo, and pushed open the door.

Inside there were not as many customers as he might have guessed, considering the amount of noise they made. The place was lively but still only half full. As Cuckoo entered, drinkers were raising what seemed to be the latest in a long line of toasts in honour of the memory of someone called Greg.

Cuckoo waited for the toast to end and then made his way to the bar. 'Abbott,' he said, placing a hand to the other man's shoulder. Abbott turned to look at him. His eyes shone, his grin was sloppy, the stink of beer came off him in waves.

'It's Greg, man,' said Abbott. 'Join us. We're celebrating the life of Greg.' He said this last bit loudly, raising the glass, a gesture that was met with a cheer from other regulars.

'Who is Greg?' asked Cuckoo.

'A fallen soldier. A great man. He had cancer. Having cancer is worse than losing a son. I know that now. Yesterday he was sitting where you're standing. Got taken to hospital. Next thing you know he's dead. We have to celebrate *life*, Cuckoo.'

Looking around, Cuckoo saw that what Abbott said made perfect sense. There was a strange sense of wired euphoria among everybody in there. Professional drunks to a man. Broken-down derelicts in waiting. They all knew that they could be next.

'Abbott, are you in any fit state to talk?' he asked and was surprised when that drunken sloppy look on Abbott's face fell away to be replaced by something that might almost have been called alert.

'Come on,' Abbott slid off the stool, 'let's go outside. Nige, is it all right if we go outside, mate?'

The landlord, throwing Cuckoo a sympathetic glance, waved them away, like *mi casa, su casa*. Outside, Abbott went to give Cuckoo a hug, but Cuckoo pulled away, holding his hands up. 'Look, Abbott, I don't want to give offence, but you've smelled better, you know? I thought you were laying off?'

'I was. I mean, I am.'

'Just that Greg died?'

'That's right. Greg died. I mean, great. If you can't get drunk then, I mean, that's . . . when can you?'

'What was his surname?'

Abbott blinked. His eyebrows bunched together. 'I don't know,' he said.

'You don't know but it's still a brilliant excuse to get pissed? And tomorrow there'll be another excuse and then another one the day after that. At least now I know why you haven't been answering your phone.'

'I have been answering my phone.'

'I've been trying you for about three days.'

'Have you?' Abbott looked panic-stricken. 'God, what if she's been trying to get hold of me?'

'She meaning Tess?'

'No. Britney Spears. Who do you think I mean? We left it that she was going to . . . She was going to contact me so I could go over there one night, for a bite to eat.' Abbott winked sloppily at Cuckoo.

'I thought there was nothing romantic between you?'

'We'll see.'

'This is the woman you said lied to you.'

'She lied to me for my own good. That's why I love her.'

'Oh, you love her now?'

'Mate, I have *fucking* loved her since the very first moment I clapped eyes on her as a kid. I haven't stopped loving her. I never will.' Abbott caught Cuckoo looking hard at him. 'Yes,' he said, defensively, 'even when I was with Fiona.'

'Yeah, well, I won't tell her if you won't. Look, how about we get a coffee inside you, eh?'

As they moved off, Abbott fished around in the pockets of his jeans. Triumphantly he pulled the handset from them. He held up the phone. 'See? No battery. How did you find me, by the way?'

'Because you were in here the last time that I spoke to you.'

'We spoke? When? When did we speak?'

'A few days ago. Before you went dark. Come on. Coffee. Now.'

When Abbott stumbled out into the street, he was amazed to see that it was only just mid-afternoon. He moved unsteadily along beside Cuckoo, and without the comforting embrace of the pub, he suddenly felt exposed, aware of the wary looks from passers-by, how he suddenly had so much space on the pavement. Some little bit of him that still fed on self-esteem took hold, and he forced himself upright, taking deep breaths so that by the time they had reached a branch of Costa, grabbed a coffee and sat down, he looked and felt almost human.

Cuckoo had pulled a charging cable and plug from his bag. 'Phone,' he said to Abbott.

'Cheers, mate.' As he plugged in his poor beleaguered phone to charge, he asked, 'So, was I right? Was she lying to me?'

'Yes, she was lying to you. Jason Scutter – the same Jason Scutter found guilty of attempted kidnap regarding your brother and then later imprisoned for that and for possessing child pornography – is alive and well and living in—'

'Not Matlock. Don't tell me he's still living in Matlock.'

'No, he's no longer living in Matlock. He moved all the way to Derby. He's supposed to be living there under a new identity

57

but according to the Home Office, he hasn't been using the new identity, he's been living under his old name.'

'Oh yeah? And why's that?'

'Well, the reason that he might not feel the need to hide is because he has links to organised crime in the area. He is, apparently, related to the Doyle crew, who basically run the crime in that part of the world. Did you know that? Is that why you asked me to look into his associates?'

'Wait a minute. Do you have an address for him?'

'I don't,' said Cuckoo, his eyes flicking.

'Come on. Don't hold out on me.'

'Why do you want his address? You're going to go after him, aren't you?'

'I need to talk to him, yes.'

'Just *talk* to him?'

'There are other people in this, Cuckoo.'

'Dangerous people by the sound of things.'

'I think I can handle a few Derby gangsters.'

'The old Abbott maybe.'

'The old Abbott is in here, mate.'

'This is a bit more like it,' said Cuckoo.

'Don't patronise me. Do you have an address or not?'

'Not until you pull yourself together.'

'I've just told you – that's what I'm going to do.'

'Sure, and when you've done it, give me a call.'

Abbott rolled his eyes. 'You're not going to give me it?'

'Either way, I don't know it yet,' said Cuckoo. And that, surely, was a lie to buy time. 'It'll take me a few days.'

'And don't tell me, I've got to use those few days to dry out.'

'Put a bit of distance between you and your last drink, then we'll talk. I thought that you were getting yourself straight. Last time we spoke I had distinct vibes. "I just need a purpose," you were saying.'

'You don't think getting drunk is having a purpose?'

'I don't think that's what you meant, no.'

'Well, OK then, give me one. Give me a purpose.'

Cuckoo exhaled noisily. 'Christ, it's all on me now, is it? I'm in charge of keeping you alive?'

Now that Abbott's phone had charged, stuff was happening. Alerts appeared. He reached for the phone, but just as he did, Cuckoo snatched it away. 'Listen, Abbott, this is serious. I hear what you're saying. I know that back in special forces you could switch the boozing off at will and pull yourself back into shape when the job required it. But that was before. That was when you were still SF. Alcoholism is a progressive disease. It's an addiction. It's not something you can just pull the plug on.'

'That's OK, then, because I'm not an alcoholic and not an addict so there's no problem.'

'Prove it,' said Cuckoo.

***

Back on the street, Abbott watched Cuckoo depart, knowing that the other man was right. *OK*, he told himself, *let's just cap the day's drinking and then we'll start anew tomorrow.* Inside The Sportsman the wake was still in full swing; if anything, more raucous than it had been before. Even Nigel the landlord was lit up. 'Well, if it ain't The Sportsman quiz champ. Can I get you a beer?'

'Love one,' said Abbott, assailed by a sudden thirst. As Nigel went off to pull the pint, he checked his messages. There was one from Tess sent a few days ago inviting him to dinner. Had he seen it? He couldn't even remember. Either way, there was a second text prompting him. 'Hello? Anyone there? Dinner? Saturday night?'

Abbott fought a wave of panic. Dinner. Tess. Dinner. Tess. Dinnertess.

No fight, no contact, no operation had ever made him feel as off-balance as this. This was the effect Tess had on him.

OK. Calm, calm, calm. So it was only Tuesday. He hadn't missed the date. He texted back, 'Love to. Just give me a time and place and I'm there.'

He thought about Tess. About the two of them sitting together at dinner, not in Kettner's, but in her house. He thought of what Cuckoo had said, and how Cuckoo was right. If he was going to track down Scutter – and if Scutter really was connected – then he needed to be on his game.

He thought about all of that. And by the time Nigel returned with his pint, he was gone.

CHAPTER 12

Saturday night, and a lot had happened since Abbott walked away from that drink in The Sportsman. One thing that hadn't happened, though. He hadn't touched a drop.

Arriving back at his digs that night, he'd poured the last of his spirits down the sink. It wasn't the first time he'd done such a thing, and experience told him that it probably wouldn't be the last. But it was still a significant act. It was still Abbott saying to himself, *Enough is enough*.

Before he'd turned in that night, he'd reached into the inside pocket of his jacket and extracted the real reason that his jacket had been so precious to him. Inside was a colour photograph of himself and Nathan at Nathan's passing-out parade, both in their uniforms, Abbott the proud dad.

Abbott had never wanted Nathan to join up, not when the military had fucked him up, but Nathan had joined anyway – of course he had; he was strong-willed like his father – and once he was there, and when it came to passing out? Well, Abbott had been just about as proud as a dad could be.

And he put that picture on the side of his bed and kept it

there. He kept it there the next day when he spent most of it in bed feeling ill but denying himself the cure. He knew that you weren't supposed to cold turkey on booze. How bad he felt would be a test of how far along the road to alcoholism he had travelled.

The second day, his head was shrouded in a constant fog and his bones ached. There was thankfully no sign of the withdrawal fits that he'd heard about in AA meetings, but even so, it was bad, especially with his alcoholic voice, that AV they always talked about, constantly nagging at him, telling him, *Just one drink, just have the one to sort you out. Buy a small bottle. Set yourself a limit of just two a day, OK maybe three a day.*

No.

Because what else was it they said in AA? 'One's too many, ten's not enough.' He didn't want 'just one', because never in his drinking life had he ever wanted 'just one'. None or many, that was the thing. Preferably many.

At some point he managed to drag himself to the washing machine downstairs, and at one stage he went to the shops, fighting an extra-strong urge to purchase alcohol and coming away with just a pack of sandwiches and a feeling of having scored a major victory.

He got his first decent night's sleep on Friday night. It was fitful, but at least he slept. During the daytime he visited the barber, got a haircut and then invested in a new black polo shirt. It was a bit of a cheap thing, all that he could afford, but he thought it would smarten him up for a first wear.

Saturday evening, and Abbott dressed. He thought that with his new polo shirt and his freshly cleaned Diesel jeans he looked just smart enough without being offputtingly, desperately well-dressed.

His eyes went to the rucksack that he always carried. In the bottom, wrapped in a towel and fastened with a bungee cord, was the Glock that he preferred to keep close, rather than leaving it in the insecure environment of his B&B room. He'd be taking that rucksack with him, of course, but was it presumptuous to stick a new T-shirt and change of pants inside? More to the point, was it weird to turn up with a rucksack?

Tess was used to him carting a bag around; she wouldn't question it. Besides, he could distract her by giving her . . .

Flowers. He took a risk and waited until he reached Notting Hill before he went in search of a florist's. The only one he came across was shut, so he had to make do with a supermarket, combining a couple of smaller bouquets to make one big one.

With an *A–Z* in one hand and his bouquet in the other, he made his way to Tess's house, thinking that for the first time in what seemed like an age, he felt like a member of the human race. Somebody with problems and God knows how many demons to fight, but someone who was going to face them sober.

Tess's house turned out to be a large, white bay-fronted villa in a boulevard lined with other, similar houses. There was a weird mix of cars along the street. Gleaming SUVs and high-performance German cars, as well as the odd dusty and dirty relic that looked like it might not have been moved this century.

Abbott regarded the house, shoving his *A–Z* into his backpack and gripping the flowers, taking deep, nervous breaths. A set of wide steps led from the pavement up to the imperious, shiny-white front door. He climbed the steps, knocked and waited. He heard movement behind the door and straightened.

The door was opened by a tall, handsome, smiling and friendly guy, who immediately proffered his hand to shake. 'You must be Alex,' the man said, 'I've been told so much about you. I'm Phil. Tess's husband.'

CHAPTER 13

They had it drummed into them in the forces. *Never assume.*
Never assume.

Yet, Abbott realised, as he stepped over the threshold and
into the home, still in a state of shock, holding his ridiculous
bunch of flowers and with his rucksack slung over one shoulder,
assume was exactly what he had done.

It was an assumption that he'd made for one very simple
reason: because he and Tess had slept together.

And now, just as it was suddenly apparent that this was an
event that had meant hundreds of times more to him than it
had done to her – and that in itself was enough to make Abbott
want to curl up and die – it had also been enough to dupe
his romantic-fool brain into thinking that she wanted to do it
again. All that stuff about a 'return visit'.

All that stuff? What? One throwaway comment? Christ.
You chump. You turkey.

The reception hall was a vast place of white wooden panelling and stylish wallpapers, old money ushered off to one side
by the tastefully trendy. Abbott felt engulfed by it all. He tried
to pull himself together, still trying as the beaming Phil said,

'Let me take your jacket.' He pointed to Abbott's rucksack. 'Whoa, you're not planning to stay the night, are you?'

Abbott still wanting to shrivel up and die said, 'Just habit.'

'Of course. From the military.' Phil leaned forward and in a pretend-whisper said, 'A little birdie told me it was special forces.'

'Well, the little birdie knows that I'm not supposed to reveal that.'

'So I expect you wouldn't answer my next question, then.'

'Don't tell me. Have I ever killed anyone?'

Phil pulled back. 'No,' he said quickly, an offended look in his eye. 'No, that would be crass.'

At that moment, as Phil reeled, Tess appeared.

'Alex,' she said, coming forward to hold him in a warm embrace – but a friend-embrace, not a lover-embrace. 'How are you? How have you been?' It was all there in her concerned gaze, the reason he had been invited here. Not for the purposes of passion. Never that in her mind. Just out of pity.

Oh, you idiot. You fool.

'Right,' Phil clapped his hands together 'I expect we'd all like a drink.'

'Perfect,' said Tess, leading them through into the dining room. 'Alex, because you're *my* friend and *my* guest, well, I hope you don't mind, but I didn't want to spend all night cooking. His nibs here will tell everybody that he's a dab hand in the kitchen and you know he's not bad as they go, not quite Jamie Oliver and not as bad as my father, but even so, I'm afraid I don't trust him to a prepare a proper grown-up meal for guests, so I've taken the liberty of ordering pizza. Do you mind? I hope you don't mind. You don't mind, do you?'

Abbott mumbled something about not minding. Mainly he was concentrating on Phil, who was hovering with intent, waiting for his chance to say, 'What can I get you to drink, Alex? Beer, wine, gin and tonic?' with Abbott just waiting to reply, 'A beer, please, a beer would be perfect,' wondering if he should have been ordering wine for the extra ABV. Hoping that Phil would be quick on the draw when it came to the refills.

Phil disappeared, leaving Abbott and Tess alone. She put a hand to his arm, a look of concern on her face. 'Are you *sure* you're OK?' she said. She glanced towards the kitchen. 'Phil doesn't know what we talked about the other day. I didn't think that you'd want—'

'And what about the other thing?' hissed Abbott, 'Does he know about that?'

She reared back a little. 'Know about what?' Then dropped her voice. '*That? Us?* No, of course he doesn't know about that, Alex. Fucksake. Don't be stupid.'

'You didn't tell him about it because it meant nothing,' he whispered, and he hated the words. He hated his own needy tone of voice. For a crazy second he wanted to shout, 'The answer, Phil, is that, yes, I have killed people. I've killed plenty. I've caused pain and been hurt in return, but let me tell you that nothing hurt me more than your wife.'

Pull yourself together.

'I'm sorry,' he told her.

'Well, all right,' she said, 'but there's a time and a place, Alex, and this isn't it. For God's sake, my kids are here.'

And as if on cue, giving them both a shock so that they traded a quick glance, the two kids came running in.

They were, of course, lovely. And Phil, as he handed Abbott

a bottle of beer that was chilled to perfection, the kind of beer that Abbott had spent the last three or four days dreaming about, was also lovely. Not threatened by Abbott. Not trying to start a pissing contest. Not feeling like he had to stake his claim.

And better still?

'God loves a thirsty man,' said Phil. 'Let me take your empty and get you another.'

Tess flashed him a quizzical look. There was one thing she didn't know about him. She didn't know how much he drank.

And so, when moments later, the doorbell rang and Tess excused herself to fetch the pizza, calling the kids back down at the same time, Abbott turned to Phil. 'I tell you what, mate, this is going down a treat. I couldn't bother you for another one, could I?' He proffered his empty.

'Man after my own heart,' said Phil, even though he'd barely touched his first. When he returned it was with two bottles, both of which he passed to Abbott. 'Save me the shoe leather, eh?' he said.

By now, Abbott was feeling the booze coming on so that he found himself starting to relax, glugging his beer greedily.

'Now there's a man who needs a top-up,' said Phil, music to his ears, and sure enough, another one came out. They trooped through to a dining room where sat a huge table, the kind of thing you'd expect to see in Bruce Wayne's house. The kids joined them and there was chatter. Abbott began to enjoy himself, asking the kids about school, about their hobbies and which football team they supported.

'Chelsea?' he snorted at one point. 'Fucking Chelsea.' And the kids roared with laughter as Abbott clamped his hand over his mouth, looking theatrically at Tess and Phil. 'Oh, I'm in trouble now,' he said.

When the kids had finished arguing over the last slice of pizza and dashed off back to the PlayStation, Phil offered Abbott another beer.

'Be rude not to,' said Abbott.

With Phil out of the room, Tess's eyes went to Abbott. 'Alex, are you nervous or something? You're drinking an awful lot.'

'Come on now,' said Abbott. 'You only get to talk like that if you're my missus, and as far as I know, I mean, I don't *think* you're my missus, are you?'

Her eyes hardened. 'No, I'm not your missus, Alex.'

'No, you're just someone who cares about me,' he said with a sneer in his voice.

She leaned back, crossed arms, pulled a face. 'Well, you know, that can easily change. I mean, easily.'

'Oh well, yes, it would be awful if we fell out, wouldn't it? Or maybe it would be better for you? Then you wouldn't have to go to all the effort of ordering pizza.'

She leaned forward. 'I was trying to keep it informal, Alex. I thought you'd prefer it that way. I didn't think you'd want me off in the kitchen, with you having to make small talk with Phil, and anyway . . .' She threw up a hand, as if trying and failing to find the right words to say, 'I really am worried about you.'

'Is that why you lied to me?' he said, louder and more sharply than he intended.

Phil had walked back into the room. His expression as he handed over a drink that Abbott too greedily snatched, putting it immediately to his lips, was quizzical. 'Lied to you,' said Phil.

'Lied about what?' His eyes going from one to the other. 'Is everything all right in here?'

Abbott banged his half-full bottle down, sat back and slung his hand across the back of the chair beside him. Opposite, Tess wore a face that he hadn't seen in a long time, a reminder that you were best advised not to fuck with her. But Abbott was too far up the escalator to care. All he knew was that he wanted her to feel anything for him other than the dreaded pity. Even if that feeling were to despise him.

'Alex,' she began to say, because of course she had no idea where he was going with this.

But he stopped her. 'No, I've got something I want to say.'

'I don't think you should,' she pressed, and she stood, as though her standing might draw a line under the matter. Perhaps that worked in her high-level lawyerly meetings. Perhaps that was how she silenced her opponents in court. But not here, not now. Because now, he would be heard.

'Tess told me something about my brother,' he said to Phil and then could not resist letting his eyes slide to Tess, seeing the relief in her face, knowing that even while letting her down and trampling on her hospitality, he had in one respect let her off the hook. 'She told me that my brother didn't die the way my parents told me. She told me that he was taken by a paedophile.'

'I'm sorry. I'm really sorry,' Phil was saying. He regained his seat carefully. His eyes went to Tess, wanting to check that everything was OK, and it was painfully obvious from that glance that Abbott was no longer the amiable guest drinking a little too much and prone to saying inappropriate things in front of the kids. All of a sudden, Phil was a guy who feared that he might have a monster in his house.

'Only she told me that the guy died in prison,' continued Abbott, 'but he didn't die in prison, did he, Tess? You lied to me.'

'Alex . . .' she started.

'Christ, why did you even tell me about Scutter in the first place?'

She shook her head. 'I don't know. Because you deserved to know the truth. You'd been lied to.'

'Look, I'm not sure if this is the best time or place to discuss this,' tried Phil.

'And you thought the best thing to do was lie some more? You thought that would help matters?'

'For your own protection. So you wouldn't get any ideas in your head about going after the guy.'

'So you lied?'

'Yes, I lied.'

'And I'm just supposed to forget that?'

Their voices were rising. Both of them. 'Guys,' said Phil, trying to calm the situation. Trying and failing. 'Guys . . .'

'You're supposed to forgive it,' she insisted.

'Well, I can't,' Abbott roared, and at the same time he stood. The noise of his chair as it scraped back was almost deafening in a room struck dumb by the sudden shock of his outburst. Tess's chin tilted. Her eyes blazed. Phil rose up. Brave Phil, prepared to stand his ground against a guy he knew could beat him senseless with one hand tied behind his back.

And thank God for small mercies, because Abbott, even drunk as he was, was aware that while things were bad they'd get even worse if he stayed, and so instead he blundered his way out of the dining room, heard Tess saying to Phil, 'No, let him go,' behind him as he stopped and retrieved his jacket and rucksack from pegs in the hallway, saw the children on the stairs wearing pyjamas, regarding him silently with a mixture of shock and curiosity, and then turned and piled out of the house down the steps, almost losing his footing and tripping over himself. He slung the rucksack onto his back as he made his way to the Tube and then back to Finchley and to The Sportsman, where the place was like he'd never left it, drinking up, past last orders, Nigel throwing him out, into the all-night off-licence, where he bought more. What happened after that would be for him to try to work out later, because by now he was in blackout, which was not, as some people think, a state of unconsciousness but operating without thought or memory, a state of being that can terrify a non-drinker enough to make them give up for good but to the hardened boozer is just another occupational hazard, something to discuss in AA, which perhaps Abbott would at some point in the future, when he'd talk about the time that he disgraced himself at the home of the love of his life and then later, without knowing how he got there, woke up in Derby.

Because that's exactly what he did.

Alex Abbott got drunk, and when he woke up, he was in Derby.

PART TWO

CHAPTER 14

Lance's real name was Edward, but given that he'd made his home in Malibu and carefully contrived an image as a good-looking, shaggy-haired surfer, inspired in equal measures by the cast of *Point Break* and the actor Owen Wilson, he had changed it to Lance.

Very few people knew that Lance's real name was Edward, least of all his girlfriend. Not that she would have cared, because in the world of Montana Norton, not only was artifice everywhere, but it was also encouraged. Her philosophy in life was to 'be yourself' and 'follow your truth' – just as long as 'yourself' was a controlled and carefully cultivated white-teeth, tanned, surgery-enhanced version of yourself.

Just as long as the truth was in fact a lie.

Lance was there now, of course, lounging around Montana's beachfront home. He had been present for the will reading, though not visible to the rest of the Norton clan. And if prior to the lawyer's revelations he had always thought of Montana's father as 'some old British dude' who was good for little more than keeping Montana and, by extension, him, living in the manner to which she, and by extension he, had become accustomed, then his opinion had performed a 180-degree turn. Having heard of the old man's post-mortem plans for the dispersal of his fortune, Lance now thought that Sir Charles Norton was an absolute total fucking legend.

As if on cue, Montana appeared. She flopped into the sofa beside Lance, but when he attempted to move closer, she waved him away. One of the things Lance had quickly discovered about his girlfriend was that although she dressed, spoke and behaved as though she were a dyed-in-the-wool, 100-percent through-and-through sex kitten, she was in fact nothing of the sort. Any activity that might slightly rumple her clothes or interfere with her make-up was strictly *verboten*, and that included anything south of chaste kissing. But Lance wasn't in the mood to press for affection. He didn't want to give her the satisfaction. Instead, he hopped up. 'Drink?'

She looked at him. 'My father used to ask if the sun was over the yardarm,' she said disapprovingly, since the sun was nowhere near the yardarm.

'I've had our yardarm lowered especially,' Lance told her, with the kind of cheeky grin that used to drive her crazy but now just annoyed her.

Still. Twirling her hair between her fingertips, she nodded. 'Why not? Before he gets here.'

'Coming right up.' Lance left for the kitchen, thinking that if it weren't for this latest development – this *exciting* latest development – then he'd be out of here no matter how much she was fucking worth. Would he be waving goodbye to a life of luxury if he did leave? In many ways yes, but the fact was that he would always be Montana Norton's ex, and that alone was enough to ensure that he would land on his feet elsewhere.

Even so, he had no plans to leave. This new business? This game? Well, that was worth sticking around for. Especially since Montana had charged him with the responsibility of sorting things out his end. 'You're a bloke, aren't you?' she'd said to him. 'This is a job for a bloke.'

Bloke. It was one of her English words that once upon a time he found attractive but now just thought were low rent. Lance could hardly be expected to know the distinctions of the English class system, but even he was aware that the Norton family were not 'posh' in the accepted English sense of the word. Charles Norton might have died a knight of the realm, but he was a man who had come from nothing, and in England it barely mattered how much you had in your account or even what letters you could put before and after your given moniker. What mattered was your heritage. Your lineage. Your family name,

She was right, though. It was indeed a job for a bloke. It was a job for Lance, and he had taken to it like a duck to water.

Montana sat on the sofa, staring at the black mirror of the flat screen TV in front of her as she engaged in one of her favourite activities, which was admiring her own reflection. On this occasion, however, she took little pleasure in it. All she could think about was the challenge ahead.

The thing was that it had always seemed to her something of a foregone conclusion that she would inherit Daddy's business, and had he outlived Mummy, then that is surely what would have happened.

Charles and Juliet had tried for more children after Montana; indeed, Juliet had lost two, one of them almost at term, at which point she had told Charles that one would have to be enough.

So Charles, who had always dreamed of a large family, had poured all his affection into Montana, while she in turn had revelled in her status as the ultimate daddy's girl. Meanwhile, Montana's relationship with her mother had been altogether more complex. Which is to say, a bit shit. No wonder her father had found himself unable to choose between them.

And now, because of his indecision and torn loyalties, or maybe just because he was delighting in being a pain in the ass from beyond the grave, they were stuck with this stupid game.

Lance returned with drinks. He passed one to Montana and then flopped down into a beanbag that he used for gaming, only instead of facing the TV as usual, he turned to her. 'Your visitor is here,' he said, but only after a good long gulp of his Cosmopolitan.

'What? You didn't say.'

'Well, now I have.'

'Where is he? Bring him in.'

'Come,' called Lance over his shoulder, and then to Montana, 'his name is Sergei.'

Their eyes went to the lounge entranceway, where in walked a man mountain. A man who was as wide as the door and almost as tall. His hair was cut short in the military style. His face was square and so was his jaw, the none-more-Russian image only offset by the fact that he wore a light-coloured linen suit with an open-necked shirt underneath.

Lance made the introductions. 'Sergei, this is Montana Norton. Montana, meet Sergei. Sergei is Spetsnaz, isn't that correct?'

Sergei nodded.

'And what is Spetsnaz?' asked Montana.

'Russian special forces. Wherever Russia have fought in the world, you can bet Sergei's been there as well.'

Montana rolled her eyes. 'Like I know where the fuck Russia fight their battles. The information I need is . . .' She turned her attention to Sergei. 'How many kills?'

'Confirmed kills forty,' said Sergei as though programmed.

To Lance, Montana side-mouthed, 'Is that a lot?'

'Is forty a lot?' he said.

'You know what I mean.'

'Then yes. Forty is a lot.'

Montana had stood up. She walked around Sergei, looking him up and down. 'Can I?' she said, reaching to him, asking the question not of Sergei but of Lance.

'Sergei, is it OK if m'lady has a feel of your biceps?' asked Lance.

Sergei nodded.

Montana tried his muscles. Next, she patted his stomach, after which, she stood in front of him nodding.

'You happy?' grinned Lance, who knew she was happy.

'I'm happy,' said Montana.

CHAPTER 15

Abbott took a seat at the bar and cast his eyes around at what was an average, down-at-heel, just-out-of-town boozer in Derby, the kind that served the housing estate around it but not much else. Outside it was the colour of wet, grey cardboard. Inside was a tribute to the colour brown.

It was not the first such pub he'd visited during the two days he'd so far spent in Derby. He was getting used to them by now. Pubs like this had no such thing as passing trade or, God forbid, tourists, but those inside knew the area. They knew their clientele. And that suited Abbott fine.

He had his rucksack with him, of course. One of the disadvantages of making a complete fool of yourself at your ex-girlfriend's house and then clambering into the world's most expensive taxi bound for Derby on a drunken whim is that you tended to come unprepared, but even though mentally his gameplan was not at its best, he at least had the bare bones of his kit with him. Stuff he always kept in his rucksack. His Gerber knife, his Leatherman all-purpose tool, tourniquet with a plastic turning handle, a vacuum-sealed medipack, and of course the Glock. He'd bought his own threaded barrel to

OLLIE OLLERTON

replace the factory one. The threaded barrel didn't look quite as nice – it stuck out more and ruined the gun's line – but he needed it for the suppressor. No factory firearm came threaded. Even the military had to swap out the barrels. One of the advantages as far as Abbott was concerned was that the replacement Glock barrels could be bought quite cheaply.

So that was what he had. The sum total of his war bag.

'You all right there?' said the barman, which was what barmen said these days. Used to be, 'What can I get you?' Now it was, 'You all right there?' He liked the old question better.

'Pint of that,' said Abbott, pointing to a pump that was directly in front of him.

The guy began pulling the pint. He called goodbye to a departing punter over Abbott's shoulder. Abbott let the customer go before he next spoke. 'I'm wondering if you might be able to help me.'

'Landlord's not here now,' said the barman without looking up.

'It's information, actually.'

'Oh yeah?' Quick glance. Finishing up the pint. 'And what's in it for me?'

'I've got a fifty-quid note with your name on it if I think the info's good.'

'Try me.'

'Jason Scutter. Do you know the name?'

The barman looked up sharply, as if taking note of Abbott for the first time. Abbott knew that look. He'd seen a few versions of it over the last two days. For that reason he knew the next words out of the barman's mouth before he even said them. 'Sorry, mate, you didn't say who you were?'

'I'm not police.'

'I didn't think you were. Doesn't make me any less curious.'

'Do you know Jason Scutter or not?'

The barman shook his head. 'Can't say I do.'

'Then it doesn't matter who I am, does it?'

'Well, what if I do hear from him? Who will I contact?'

'I can leave you my number.'

'You do that.'

Abbott looked along the bar, to where another customer regarded him with interest. Over to his right were a man and a woman at a table. Both wore the florid faces of daytime drinkers. Both also looking at him with naked curiosity. He stared them out until they looked away.

The pint was in front of Abbott by now, the barman having moved off. Abbott looked at the drink, his little alcoholic voice, that wheedling AV, insisting that he should drink it. *Just one*, it told him. *Just one wee little dram to take the edge off. You know what? You could maybe just have one drink a day. Why not do that from now on? Just one drink a day. That's a plan.*

And he let the AV have its say. He listened and almost capitulated before that other part of his brain reasserted itself and told the AV to pipe down, because when had one ever been enough?

If one was enough then you wouldn't have a problem, would you?

What did you buy the booze for, then?

Because I like my enemy where I can see it.

So, although the full pint of lager glistened with coldness, and every aspect of it, from the curvature of the glass to the colour of the liquid, called out to him, he moved it away from himself and then indicated to the barman. 'I'll need a pen and paper for my number.'

The barman brought it. Other customers returned their stares to Abbott as he left the piece of paper on the bar and stepped off his stool.

'My name is Alex Abbott, by the way,' he announced, just before he left, addressing not just the barman but the whole pub. 'And if you see Jason Scutter, how about you tell him that I'm looking for him? That I'm coming for him.'

And that was stupid, he thought, as he left the pub. Giving his name out like that. There was something in AA they called being a 'dry drunk'. It meant that even though you were sober, you still carried on with some of your old reckless behaviour. He'd always thought it was a myth. Up until now.

In the car park, his phone rang.

It was her. It was Tess.

Ever since arriving in Derby, she'd been on his mind. Two days off the grog and while his head had not completely de-fogged, it had certainly cleared sufficiently for him to realise that he'd been an utter twat at her house and in doing so had destroyed everything that was good about their relationship. Everything that *had* been good. Everything that *was* good. Everything that might have been good in the future. All of it gone.

He'd been texting her.

'Sorry.'

'We need to talk.'

That sort of thing. Understanding completely that she might want to cut him out of her life altogether. Who could blame her?

And now she was calling him.

'Where are you?' she asked when he picked up.

Abbott might have hoped for concern or maybe even a rebuke. Funny that now he was sober he would quite happily have settled for the pity that he had hated so much when he was drunk. Instead, her voice was totally neutral. Dead.

'I'm in Derby,' he told her.

'And what are you doing in Derby?'

'Something tells me that you know the answer to that question.'

'Oh, we're back to that again, are we?'

'No, no, we're not back to that, I promise. I'm sorry and I'm sorry and I'm so, so, fucking sorry for what happened the other night. Sorry to you, sorry to Phil – he's great, by the way – sorry to the kids.'

'Look, I understand, and Phil understands. It's not like you've made a friend, but he understands, because . . .'

'Because what?'

'God, I don't know, Alex, because you're probably suffering from PTSD. Alcoholism, too, I shouldn't wonder. I mean, I knew you drank a lot, but not . . . that much.'

'I'm doing something about it.'

'Like what?'

'I haven't touched a drop since that night.'

'Good. And now you're sober do you understand why I lied to you?'

'I think so.'

'I did it for your own good. Because I didn't want—'

'Me to come to Derby. Because you know why I'm here, don't you?'

'Yes, I know. And I want you to stop.'

'Stop and just let things be?'

'Why not?'

'Can't do that, I'm afraid.'

'You need to be careful, Alex.'

'What makes you say that?'

'Because . . .'

'Tell me what you know, Tess.'

'Not much. Just that Scutter has links to some dangerous people in that area.'

He thought of the name Cuckoo had given him. *Doyle*.

'I'll be careful,' he told Tess.

'Jesus,' she sighed. 'Spare me the testosterone. Look, I've got to go. I'll speak to you soon, OK?'

The call ended. Abbott thought about Tess. How unwittingly she had set the wheels in motion.

Unwittingly?

Or wittingly?

Was it possible that there was some part of Tess that consciously or subconsciously had intended for all this to happen? Did she like the danger, perhaps? He'd spent years wondering what had attracted the beautiful and intelligent Tess Lacey to him back at school, when she could have had her pick.

Maybe he should take it at face value. She really was trying to protect him. But then why tell him in the first place?

Or maybe, on second thoughts, he should stop trying to figure her out and get on with the job.

He looked back at the pub. Was it his imagination or had there been a figure at the window?

Thinking about what Tess had said. *Dangerous people*.

Dangerous people to whom he might just have given his name.

CHAPTER 16

'Mr Kilgore.'

'Mr Doyle.'

Raymond Doyle lit a cigarette, relaxed into his voluminous leather desk chair and pictured Kilgore at the other end of the line. 'And how is Juliet?' He grinned.

'Mrs Norton is quite well, thank you.'

'Still playing the grieving widow?'

'Mrs Norton is quite well, thank you. Now what can I do for you?'

'There's somebody in town. A bloke asking around after my nephew.'

'I see. And by nephew you mean Jason Scutter?'

'That'll be the one.' There was a silence. 'And I thought that you – by which I mean you and Juliet – might like to know.'

'Some kind of . . . what? A private detective?'

'Search me, but if he's said who he is then it ain't reached my ears, and if it ain't reached my ears, then he hasn't said.'

'And you're sure he's from out of town?'

'If he was from round these parts, then he he'd know better than to be asking after my nephew.'

'Is he staying in the city?'

'Don't know yet.'

'Does this sort of thing happen often?'

'Mate, it happens never. Even more surprising, the bloke's hiding in plain sight. He told one guy his name.'

'Go on.'

'His name is Alex Abbott. And apparently he wants Scutter to know he's coming for him.'

'Leave this with me. I'll be back in touch.'

***

The following day, Doyle's phone rang.

'Hello, Mr Kilgore.'

'Mr Doyle. Does the name Chris Abbott mean anything to you?'

'Something to do with our friend Alex, is it?'

'His brother. I repeat, does the name mean anything to you?'

'Can't say it does.'

Kilgore told Doyle the story of Chris Abbott.

'So now big brother's come looking for payback?'

'Little brother. But yes, it would seem that way.'

'I can only assume that he doesn't know who he's dealing with.'

'Chances are that even if he did know, he wouldn't care. Alex Abbott is ex-special forces.'

'Won't make any difference what he is when I put him through the meat grinder. You tell Juliet that I'll sort it.'

'Wait, Mr Doyle,' said Kilgore. 'There is something I need to discuss with her.'

'Oh yeah? And how long will that take?'

'Remain by the phone. I'll do it now.'

Sure enough, moments later the phone rang.

'We have had an idea, Mr Doyle,' said Kilgore. 'Call off your men.'

'You don't want me to get rid of him? You don't want him dead?'

'Oh, we want him dead,' said Kilgore. 'But we've thought of a way to kill two birds with one stone . . .'

CHAPTER 17

A residential area in the south of the city, and Abbott walked into yet another anonymous, housing-estate pub. More having to resist the temptation of booze. More of that nagging feeling that he was getting further and further into something.

Sure enough, it felt as though the whole pub did *An American Werewolf in London*, the conversation dying, eyes turning his way as he walked in. Was it simply that kind of pub? Or was it him? Either way, he was reassured to feel the weight of the Glock at the bottom of his rucksack. A few days booze-free and he was hardly what you'd call combat ready, but even at half speed, he was still good.

He took a stool positioned in front of a tap, arranging himself. He wore the Finchley Sportsman T-shirt, black over-shirt, the normal drill.

'You all right there?' said the barman, predictably.

Abbott ordered a beer. 'Just a pint of the cooking, please, mate,' he replied, and steeled himself not to drink it. The barman, probably the landlord, lingered, and Abbott wondered if he should read anything into that. In his recent experience, most of them seemed to scurry away as soon as possible.

'Actually, you might be able to help,' said Abbott when he'd paid for the beer, fingertipping the glass away from himself at the same time. 'I'm looking for an old mate. He liked a drink. Might be somebody you know.'

'Oh yeah?' said the landlord. Again, Abbott was used to these guys closing down and going into guarded mode. This one? Not so much.

Abbott told him the name. Jason Scutter. Again, where Abbott had learned to expect a shake of the head, this guy nodded.

'Yes, I know him.'

'He lives round here?'

'He lives the other side of town, two doors down from my sister, as it happens. He's a bad lot.'

'Is that so?'

'The kind who should be in jail or better still in the ground.'

'Well, I guess you won't want to help me find him, then?'

The barman leaned forward, lowering his voice. 'Except that I don't think you're any friend of his, are you? You want to see him for some other reason, am I right?'

'Yes, mate, you're right,' replied Abbott. 'Me and him have business.'

'Thought as much. I'll tell you where to find him, but you need to give me your word that if anybody asks, you didn't get it from me.'

Abbott looked around at what was more or less an empty pub. Just one old guy in a flat cap drinking at a table out of earshot. 'Scout's honour,' he said.

The barman turned away. A moment later, he held out a scrap of paper. 'Good luck,' he said.

If this was a trap, then it was well laid, thought Abbott as he took himself outside and rang for a taxi.

And if it is a trap, then you're walking right into it.

But that guy seemed like he had history with Scutter. And after all, wasn't this why he was here?

If it's true and he was being set up, well . . . let battle commence.

CHAPTER 18

The taxi took him to a newbuild housing estate on the edge of town. Looking around, this wasn't what he'd expected. Certainly not the gleaming blue Audi in Jason Scutter's drive. It hardly fitted with the image of the perspiring, fat and stubbled paedophile that he'd been carrying around in his head.

A man who had lured Chris to his eventual death.

He took a look around. Houses on all sides regarded him with blank-window stares. From somewhere came the hum of a lawnmower, the distant sound of hip-hop from some kid's bedroom. Otherwise, curtains remained in place, nets were untwitched.

Using the rear of the Audi as cover, he stooped, fished the Glock out of his bag, complete with suppressor, and as surreptitiously as possible, unwrapped it and stuffed it into the back of his jeans.

Finishing, he glanced up at the sound of a car arriving, quickly adjusting himself. It was another taxi, drawing up into the road about 200 yards away. A guy got out, paid the driver and then, without so much as a glance in Abbott's direction, trotted off along a driveway towards the houses. He carried a rucksack, just as Abbott did.

Abbott waited until he was gone then went to the door of number twenty-seven and knocked. Soon, it was opened by a tall guy who looked him up and down and then, without surprise or curiosity, said, 'Aha,' almost as though he had been expecting Abbott to come and fetch his ball back.

'Mr Scutter?' he said.

'That's me,' said Scutter, who was well-spoken and not fat, perspiring or stubbled. His hair, thinning on top, was neatly cut, his only concession to the stereotypical image of the paedophile a pair of track pants. Even his black T-shirt looked pressed and fitted well.

'So you're the bloke who's looking for me?' said Scutter, unfazed. 'You're Alex Abbott.'

He knew Abbott's name. Chalk that one up to Abbott's own stupidity. The fact that word had reached him? Well, that proved that what Cuckoo and Tess had said was correct. Scutter was indeed connected.

Even so, this was not going the way Abbott might have expected.

Scutter looked over Abbott's shoulder, out at the estate beyond.

'I think you'd better come in, don't you?'

He turned, walked back along the hall and into his lounge, leaving the front door open.

Still on the doorstep, Abbott tensed, hand going to his waistband, feeling the comforting butt of the gun there. He stepped over the threshold.

'Close the door behind you, would you?' came Scutter's voice from the front room.

He needed no further invitation. He closed the door, making sure to turn the internal deadbolt first, and drew his sidearm.

'Just through here,' said Scutter from the lounge.

Abbott took two smart steps, peered quickly around the door, levelling the gun at whatever was inside.

Just a regular lounge. Armchair, sofa, coffee table.

And Scutter, who sat in the armchair facing the television, although it was off. He sat upright, neck straight, chin slightly raised. In his track pants and T-shirt, he looked like a disgraced PE teacher about to accept with good grace whatever punishment was meted out to him.

Gun held, Abbott scoped the room in sections, checking out likely entry and exit points just in case things got a little turbo. He saw an empty kitchen at the back of the house, and then French doors that looked out onto a patch of green grass with empty, untended flowerbeds either side. A tiny garden waiting for somebody to fill it with love, care and attention.

Abbott turned his eyes back to Scutter. 'I haven't interrupted anything, have I?' he said, indicating the TV, thinking of what Tess had told him about Scutter. The films. We didn't call them child pornography anymore. That was something Abbott had learned during his time in Thailand. We called them what they were. We called them images of child sex abuse.

'No,' said Scutter. He pointed at the coffee table in front of him, on which sat a *Fast & Furious* box set. 'Just that.'

Aside from the box set there was a tin of lager, but otherwise precious few signs of life or personality in the room. Nothing on the neutral-painted walls. No photographs in frames, books.

'This doesn't bother you?' said Abbott, indicating with the gun.

'No, not really. I'm glad it's not a knife or, worse, a garrotte. I often worried that somebody might come with a garrotte. I didn't want to be burned, either, and there was always the fear that somebody might decide to torture me first.

'No, all things considered, and when you take into account how much I deserve whatever comes my way, then I'll take a bullet.'

'Except that I didn't come to kill you, Scutter.'

'I see. Then what did you come for?'

'We'll get on to that. First of all, how did you know to expect me?'

'McGregor called to say you were on your way.'

'Who's McGregor?'

'You've been in Derby a few days, have you heard of the Doyle crew?'

'The name's come up.'

'Head of the family is Raymond Doyle. My uncle, as it happens. McGregor is Ray Doyle's right-hand man. They've been trying to put eyes on you but have so far failed. Lucky for them, you've been chatting up the local barmen. What you have to understand, though, is that if you're here, then the other guy won't be far behind.'

'Other guy?'

'Yes. There's another guy.' Scutter smiled wanly. 'Another hitman.'

Abbott thought of the bloke who'd got out of the second taxi. Could be something. Could be nothing.

He moved to the front window and peered outside. Nothing.

Glanced to the French windows. Same. He turned back to Scutter. 'And this hitman? He's been sent to protect you from me?'

Scutter chuckled. 'Well, that's what McGregor told me. I rather doubt it, though. For one thing, he seemed awfully keen that I should be here, considering his claim to have my best interests at heart. "Oh, there are two gunmen on the way, one of whom wants you dead. Just stay where you are, eh?" Doesn't quite scan, does it? Hmm . . .' Scutter put his finger to his lips, fake-thinking. 'Why might that be? And then the penny dropped that if I were them then I'd want me out of the picture. Basically, any picture – whichever way you look at it, upside down or back to front – is vastly improved without me in it.'

'You seem fairly laid-back about that.'

Scutter sighed. 'I never meant him any harm, you know, your brother. I mean, I *personally* never meant him any harm, but it's true that my aim was to deliver him into the hands of people who would have meant him harm, and for that I fully deserve more than the sentence I served. For that I deserve to die.'

'Who? Who were you going to give him to? Doyle?'

Scutter laughed. 'The Doyles are paid employees, bouncers, enforcers. Nothing more.'

'They seem to command an awful lot of respect.'

'Round here they do. Say my uncle's name and watch them shake with fear. But that's the locals.'

'OK.' Abbott raised his pistol. 'This is the bit where I ask you questions, and you answer them. I need to know about the fat guy.'

'Fat guy?'

'This second guy who was in your car the day you picked up Chris. Who was he?'

'How about I tell you *after* you and I cut a little deal?'

Abbott gave a short, dry laugh.

'I'm holding a gun on you.'

It was as though Scutter wasn't listening. 'You can help me get out of here safely.'

'I don't care about your safety.' He nudged with the Glock. 'Who was he?'

A bead of sweat ran down Scutter's temple. 'And if I tell you?'

'Try if you don't.'

Scutter swallowed. A second bead of sweat escaped his hairline. 'OK, look, as a gesture of good faith, I'll tell you. How about that?'

'How about you tell me as a gesture of wanting to stay alive?'

Another prod.

'OK, OK . . . His name is Sweaty.'

'"Sweaty"? Now there's a name to conjure with.' And something told Abbott that a man who went by the name 'Sweaty' was far more likely to conform to his paedophile preconceptions.

'Yes. I know. You'd say that if you saw him. I think, if anything, it was Sweaty who panicked your brother. He isn't the most savoury of people, if you know what I mean. Sweaty by name, sweaty by nature.'

'What happened to him, this Sweaty?'

'If I tell you more, can we do a deal?'

'Just talk.'

'OK. He left Matlock. He came here, in fact.'

'Both of you from Derby, eh?'

Scutter nodded. 'They set him up nicely.'

'They? Doyle?'

'Something like that. Point being that we can make a deal and I can help you find Sweaty. And if you find Sweaty, you'll find yourself that much closer to the heart of the machine. You'll practically be in the engine room. Would you like to do that? What do you say, Abbott? Do you fancy being my bodyguard?'

Abbott shook his head. 'You are seriously pushing your luck, mate. Nothing changes the fact that you killed my brother.'

Scutter opened his mouth to object, but Abbott stopped him with a sharp jab of the suppressor. 'Shut up. You were *responsible* for the people who killed my brother. And, no, I didn't come here to kill you, but on the other hand, I didn't come here to do you any favours either.'

Scutter had lost a little of his confidence now. A gun barrel at the side of your head will do that. 'All right then,' he said. 'I understand. How about this? You be my bodyguard. You protect me from the hooded claw, and I'll lead you to the men that you really want, the organ grinders, not the monkeys. I'll take you to Sweaty. *And* I'll show you the whole organisation.'

'What do you mean, the organ grinders?' said Abbott. At the same time, he saw a movement outside the French windows and swung to see a guy in the garden, a suppressed MP7 at his shoulder, taking aim.

Abbott dived.

And a bullet that was meant for him blew Scutter's brains out.

CHAPTER 19

Blood, bits of skull and grey brain matter bloomed in the front room. Abbott wheeled, bringing the Glock up in a two-handed grip to see that in the glass of the French doors was a single bullet hole. He was about to squeeze off, but was too late, as the garden guy fired again, this time a short burst that destroyed the glass of the French door, sending Abbott diving for cover and giving the guy enough time to step through the shattered glass and into the lounge.

Another short burst. Dum-dum rounds stitched the sofa behind which Abbott crouched, gun held by his thigh. Rounds tore through the frame, destroyed cushions, dug divots in the carpet, none of them, thankfully, finding Abbott. He shifted position, correctly anticipating the gunman would vary the direction of attack. Sure enough, another burst, furniture mauled by high-velocity gunfire, the whole exchange wildly destructive and yet at the same time strangely quiet, a series of muffled pops, the sound of somebody thumping a pillow.

Traditionally, Abbott had been calm in the heat of a gunfight, and maybe that was because he'd always had a low opinion of his own life. Here the same applied, at least some of the SF training coming back as bullets rained around him, so that instead of being panicked into reacting prematurely, he held fast.

And then when the assault rifle fired dry, he rose fast from behind the sofa, making a quick forty-five-degree motion in order to find his target.

What would a combat instructor have said? Marks for patience. For waiting. For keeping cool under fire.

Points deducted for underestimating the enemy. Failing to anticipate his next move.

Sure enough, the attacker had shifted, expecting Abbott to launch his counter. Rather than trying to reload, he decided to resort to close combat. Pain lanced along Abbott's forearm as from outside of his peripheral vision, the attacker came, using the butt of the MP7 to knock the Glock from his hands.

Abbott let go of the gun but held onto the pain, refusing to be overwhelmed by it and turning to meet his attacker. He found himself staring into the eyes of a guy just like him, almost the same age, probably ex-forces, maybe even SF. A kindred spirit. A man who in another life he might have found himself fighting beside but was now his mortal enemy.

His mortal enemy.

Abbott's arms came up to grasp the MP7 before the attacker could swing it at his skull, and for a moment or two they wrestled until with a surge of strength and a grunt of effort, Abbott shoved the guy backwards. He was gratified to see the panic flare in the man's eyes as the backs of his legs made contact with the coffee table and he was sent off-balance.

The attacker fell, smashing into the coffee table, rolling off and slapping a hand into the exploded head of Scutter. Abbott dived for his Glock and almost got there but the other guy was up and on him. Thoughts of guns were gone now, the guy's hands going to Abbott's face, his thumbs trying to find his eyes.

Trying to gouge them out.

It was an old combat trick. The very act of trying to gouge out your victim's eyes was so barbaric that it could have a shocking, even paralysing effect on them, and the advantage might be just enough to gain the upper hand.

If your opponent was inexperienced, that was. If he wasn't trying to do to you what you were trying to do to him.

They rolled over broken bits of coffee table and brains and blood and beer and *Fast & Furious* DVDs, grappling and both trying to find purchase, not just with their hands but with legs and feet, with moves more intricate than any gymnast, any pair of lovers, reason being that there was more at stake. The guy's thumb found its way into Abbott's larynx, but he twisted away, using Scutter's body as cover and managing to scramble to his knees. At the same time the attacker shifted likewise, and for a second they were at rest, on their knees on the carpet, shoulders rising and falling as they caught their breath.

Guns. The MP7 not far away. Abbott's Glock close at hand. And it was there that Abbott went, diving for it, finger-tips finding it, bringing the butt into his palm, the feeling as welcome as a warm dog and roaring fire in the grate, and swinging it around to bear on his opponent.

It was all the guy could do to stop Abbott pulling the trigger as he launched himself haphazardly forward, crashing into Abbott, who was unable to fire but was able to take advantage of the sudden imbalance, twisting around, bringing his foe with him and using his forward motion against him.

The guy crashed down, Abbott over him, Abbott standing, lifting his foot, stamping hard on the guy's face once, twice and then a third time for good measure. And then, satisfied that his opponent was beaten, rolled away.

For perhaps thirty seconds he lay there, recovering from the battle. Next, he grabbed the guy by the lapels of his denim jacket, grunting as he heaved him onto the sofa. He was out cold for the time being so Abbott rooted through his pockets and came up with a wallet where, according to his driving licence, his name was Owen Flyte.

Like Abbott, Flyte had carried a backpack, just the size to conceal an MP7. Abbott rooted through it. In here were spare mags for the weapon as well as duct tape. There were also two pieces of paper, folded. One was a photocopied photograph of himself, taken from his forces ID. Scrawled on it was the single word, 'Abbott'.

A second piece of paper, a picture of Scutter, again the name.

And then the killer's phone rang.

'Number not recognised.'

He shouldn't answer it, he knew. On the other hand, this might be his best chance at moving forward.

He answered. Held the mouthpiece away from himself, mumbled the word, 'Hello?'

'Flyte?'

'You might be in luck. Who's that?'

'It's McGregor. You haven't replied to my text.'

'I've been busy.'

Abbott tried to piece events together. Evidently Flyte and this McGregor hadn't previously spoken, just communicated by text.

'I'm after an update. Is clean-up required?'

'You might say that. My recommendation is that you come and see for yourself.'

'OK. Stay where you are. Be there soon.'

'Wait,' instructed Abbott. 'The passphrase will be Sasquatch. To which you have to reply, "We always called him Bigfoot in my house." No deviation will be tolerated.'

McGregor paused and Abbott wondered, was he pushing it?

'Understood,' said McGregor. 'Just wait there.'

Abbott ended the call, taking a deep breath. The fact that the enemy knew he'd taken a taxi to Scutter's house meant the pub had relayed that information. Which in turn meant that they would have been provided with a description by the barman or someone else in there.

He took a look at Owen Flyte. At best guess, Flyte was ex-forces like himself, and there were certainly superficial similarities in height, build and age. Flyte's hair was darker but also short. Squint your eyes and you perhaps could mistake one for the other.

He looked down at himself. What might the barman remember?

The T-shirt. The Finchley Sportsman. His quiz champion prize. Never mind what he looked like. What was he wearing?

Which meant . . .

Abbott had never in his life tried or even attempted to try swapping clothes with a half-dead bloke but, if asked, he might have said that it wasn't too difficult a process.

Wrong. Special forces training was less difficult than swapping clothes with the unconscious Owen Flyte. But he did it. Anything else? The picture. He'd just flushed it when the doorbell rang.

He took a hold of himself. Although he'd drawn the line at changing trousers, he now wore Owen Flyte's navy polo shirt and denim jacket, but more to the point, Flyte wore the Finchley Sportsman T-shirt, and if Abbott was right – and him being right was these days a somewhat rare occurrence – then that's the aspect of his appearance they would remember most.

Otherwise . . .

Otherwise he was dead.

As he made his way to the front door, he said to himself, *You are Owen Flyte. Your name is Owen Flyte.* He tried to think like that guy. Tried to put himself in that man's shoes and what went through his mind as he reached for the Yale of the door was that it shouldn't be too difficult because after all, they were both trained killers. They both took lives for money.

'Sasquatch,' he said, when he opened the door and saw the man on the other side.

'We always called him Bigfoot in my house.'

Pleasantries were exchanged. Abbott held the gun on McGregor and then appeared to relax, allowing McGregor into the house and showing him the man on the sofa.

'This guy?'

'Out cold.'

'I can see that, Dr Zhivago. This is Alex Abbott, is it?' asked McGregor. He was in his late-thirties and wore a cheap leather jacket over a shirt that was open by at least two buttons too many, his dark hair in need of a wash.

'Yes.'

'And how do you know that?'

'From his wallet. And the fact that he matches the description I've been given,' said Abbott, surfing a wave of weirdness, as though he was having an out-of-body experience, pointing a gun at himself as he lay, out cold on a sofa, wearing a Finchley Sportsman T-shirt.

'Well, you better finish the job, then.' McGregor indicated the state of Flyte's face. 'Better do it quick, too. Looks like he almost killed you.'

'Sure. He was tough.'

Abbott raised the Glock. *Sorry, brother*, he thought. *You or me. I choose you.*

He double-tapped Flyte, whose body jerked on the sofa, bloody beer bottle-tops appearing on his chest. He wouldn't have felt a thing.

'OK,' said McGregor. 'So now I'm going to take you to meet the boss.'

CHAPTER 20

As they stepped outside the house, Abbott still couldn't get his head around it. The whole Argos-catalogue setting. The carnage within. McGregor had made a call and assured him that the cleaners were on their way.

'How did you get here?' asked the Scotsman now.

Abbott wondered if it was a test. 'Taxi,' he said.

'Well, it's lucky I got a car then, isn't it?' said McGregor, pointing at an electric blue BMW parked at the kerb.

As they left the estate, a white van was arriving, and the two vehicles drew up alongside one another. McGregor's window slid down and he spoke to the guys in the van. 'Thanks to our friend here, there's a lot of cleaning up to be done.'

Three men in the front of the van all looked past McGregor and at Abbott. Strong-arm guys. The kind who worked security, who did odd jobs for the local villains. Right now, Abbott still had his own Glock on board. He had Flyte's MP7 and the extra mags in his rucksack, too, so he was feeling protected, but if his instinct was correct, then he would be relieved of any weapons as soon as he met the big boss.

He was right.

McGregor drove them out of town to an area that was characterised by a series of car dealerships on either side of a dual carriageway. Gleaming cars. Flags waving in a breeze. Unbeatable offers and incredible credit deals giving way to what looked like a series of industrial estates on the edge of town. McGregor took a left onto a service road, where there was no branding, no parked cars, vans or lorries, and just the one sign saying, 'Kemptown. No Entry'.

'Kemptown? What the hell is that?'

'Aye, well therein lies a tale, my friend. Used to be a time when all the drugs in this town were run by a bloke named Ronald Kemp. And they were all run out of here. Kemp had the drugs, Doyle had just about everything else. Well, you can imagine that neither of them was very happy with that, and it was only a matter of time that one of them launched a takeover bid. It was before my time, but apparently there was a lot of blood spilled that night.'

'Grinder?'

'You'll see. The point is that Kemp was moved out and Doyle moved in. What you have here now is a twenty-four-hour operation. Anything that goes on in this town starts here. Drugs. Guns. Prostitution. This is like Derby's crime depot.'

On either side of the service road was undeveloped scratch land. Ahead of them were two white vans parked on either side of the road end-to-end. McGregor, as they approached, flicked the BMW headlights. The doors to the vans opened, two men got out, one of them tucking something into the belt of his jeans.

McGregor stopped. The window glided down. 'Mr McGregor,' said one of the sentries looking into the car, past McGregor. On Abbott's side was the second guy. His hands were behind his back. On the butt of his gun. 'Is your guest armed?'

'Aye, our guest is indeed armed. He is by profession a contract killer.'

Abbott had no idea how much of what was taking place was meant for his benefit but observed with interest anyway as the guard pointed a finger at his own face. 'Scared,' he said. And then looked across at Abbott. 'You all right, mate? Got no beef with you, just that any guns, you have to give them up here.'

'Fine,' said Abbott. 'I've got an MP7 in the rucksack and a Glock in my belt.'

The guy made an impressed face. 'Hand them over,' he said.

'I'll be needing them back.'

'Soon as Mr Doyle says so.'

Abbott did as asked, instantly feeling more vulnerable. They drove on. Abbott saw more men. None had visible weaponry and yet from the way they stood it was clear that all were armed.

They drove on. Abbott looked around, seeing three or four buildings. A main factory building as well as ancillary outposts that in the past might have been workshops or administrative units, now presumably repurposed in order to serve the cause of human misery.

'Open all hours, you say?' he said to McGregor.

'That's about the size of it.'

'And Doyle? Does he live on site?'

'No, he's got his mansion out among Derby's golfing set, but you'll find him here most nights till about seven, eight, nine o'clock.'

'Fond of the merchandise, is he?'

'Not in the way you're thinking, pal,' smirked McGregor, but left it there.

They reached the main factory building.

McGregor led him inside to a series of dingy ground-floor offices. He was invited to take a seat and he found himself wondering if they knew. Was he unwittingly walking into a t rap that at some point would be sprung, armed men guffawing at his pathetic attempts to escape? Not for the first time it struck him that he had literally no idea of what he was getting himself into.

After sitting there a while, feeling like a guy in a dentist's waiting room, they appeared. A phalanx. The Red Arrows, if the Red Arrows were provincial thugs led by a big guy with a navy sweatshirt stretched over a huge belly, who took a draw from a cigarette and said, as though he had been rehearsing it, 'My name is Raymond Doyle. And right now, you're alive because I say so.'

'I came of my own accord,' replied Abbott flatly, still sitting, refusing to be intimidated by the entourage.

'You think, do you?' said Doyle. 'Here, come with me. There's a few things I want to know.'

'I don't know if I can help you,' said Abbott.

'How about we decide that in my office?' He turned to one of his men. 'Have you patted him down?' The guy looked shifty in return, shaking his head, a guilty no. 'Well, then do it!' roared Doyle.

The guy gave Abbott a pat down, but it was so cursory he missed the Gerber knife in Abbott's boot. Amateurs, reflected Abbott as Doyle headed the group out of the reception area onto what had once been a factory floor and then across that to a set of metal steps at the other end. Up they went in silence until they reached a gantry above, close to the mouth of a large, funnelled inlet, which led to a huge machine beneath.

Doyle stopped, took a final drag of his cigarette and then flicked it into the funnel.

Abbott looked at him. 'Expensive ashtray.'

'Meat grinder,' said Doyle. Close by was a large red stop/start button, and he punched it, grinning as the machine started up with a deafening whine. The sound of grinding industrial blades came from below. 'Your friend Abbott will be going in there later. Scutter, too,' he yelled over the sound of the machine starting up. Abbott tensed, wondering if this was it, until just as suddenly Doyle punched the red button again and the machine wound down.

Doyle led the group into an office which boasted views out over the empty factory. He took a seat behind a large desk.

'So you're Owen Flyte?'

Abbott nodded. 'But you already know that.'

'And here's the problem, mate,' growled Doyle, leaning forward and snatching a packet of Benson & Hedges, pulling one out and lighting up without offering them to anybody else. 'That is literally *all* I know. And do you know what? I don't like that. It pisses me off. You staying in the city?'

'Close enough.'

'Where?'

This was good, thought Abbott. Whatever surveillance they'd mounted hadn't extended to discovering his room at the Travelodge. 'I'll be keeping that information to myself for the time being, thank you.'

'Suspicious, eh?'

Abbott shrugged. 'This is the bit where I say that being suspicious keeps me alive.'

'Very wise.' Doyle leaned back. 'All right, we'll let that one go. A man needs his privacy. But just you make sure that I get answers soon, or the next finger you break will be your own, got it?'

Abbott swallowed, knowing that now, more than ever, this was a trip into the unknown. What were they doing? Testing him? Interrogating him? Either way this could end badly if he said something that met with their displeasure.

'What are you doing in Derby?'

'You know what I'm doing in Derby. I'm doing a job in Derby. Correction. I've *done* a job in Derby.'

Doyle's eyes squinted as he took a deep drag, smoking it like he wanted it to kill him. 'I want to know why.'

'Would you believe I don't know?' said Abbott.

A silence hung in the room. Abbott kept his face neutral but his mind raced. Was this the right answer? 'I was given names,' he continued carefully. 'Provided with pictures and told that McGregor would be in touch. That's all.'

Doyle's face darkened. He stubbed the cigarette out angrily in an already overflowing ashtray. He reached for another.

'I'm sorry if I give offence,' said Abbott neutrally, 'the fact is . . . Mr Doyle . . .' At that Doyle looked a little appeased, nodding approvingly at Abbott's newfound show of respect, 'the fact is that the only details I was given are the ones we've already discussed.'

'Well, in that case, I do have the edge on you,' smiled Doyle, losing a little more of his sore-headed bear demeanour. 'I happen to know that what you did today was some form of a test. Reckon you've passed with flying colours.'

'What sort of a test?' said Abbott.

'Kilgore didn't mention it?'

Kilgore? Who was Kilgore? And why did Abbott feel like he'd just been given a glimpse into the higher echelons? He felt his palms moisten. 'Not in so many words, no,' he said.

'You like to play things close to your chest, don't you?' Doyle reached to scratch at his faded sweatshirt. Chest hair sprouted at the collar.

'It's kept me alive so far.'

'How about if I tell you that Kilgore wants me to keep you here for the time being?'

'You might find that difficult.'

'I bet you I wouldn't.'

Abbott's gaze swept the room. To Doyle he said, 'I could take out two of these guys before the other two even had a chance to draw their guns. After that I give myself good odds.'

Doyle held out peace-making hands, cigarette smouldering between two fingers. 'Slow your roll there, chief, there's no coercion involved. The last thing we want is an unwilling employee on our hands.'

'You misunderstand me,' said Abbott. 'I am not and never will be an employee.'

Doyle looked at him. 'I have been asked—'

'I don't care what you've been asked. I didn't get into this game to start working for a small-time gangster in Derby.'

He knew he was pushing it. Why? He wasn't sure. Only that he had a sense of having gained the upper hand and wanted the leverage.

Just don't push it. Just don't push it.

'I was thinking of offering you a job,' said Doyle, with a note of warning in his voice, as though it would be unwise for Abbott to reject it.

'I'm going to decline,' replied Abbott.

Big long drag on the cigarette. Eyes squinting through smoke regarded Abbott impassively. 'Then we have ourselves a problem.'

'We do?' said Abbott.

'Because Kilgore was very keen that you should stay.'

Abbott, still thinking, *Who the fuck is Kilgore?* pretended to consider. 'I tell you what, I need a piss. Show me the way to the toilets, let me have a think.'

'Marky will show you,' Doyle indicated.

'Just directions will do.'

'Indulge me, eh?'

Abbott thought it best to go with it, nodding *sure*. The two of them trooped off to the loo. At the door to the gents, Abbott stopped. He turned to Marky. 'I trust you're not coming in,' he said.

'Happens I need a piss,' said Marky, who in contrast to his boss's estuary tones, had a northern accent. Halifax direction, if Abbott wasn't very much mistaken. One thing you could say about being in the forces: you got to recognise an accent.

In they both went. There was only one urinal, so Marky used the cubicle while Abbott stood, having a piss but also gathering himself, thinking that he somehow needed to extricate himself from this situation, every instinct he had screaming at him to get out before his gossamer-thin cover was blown.

He finished his piss, could hear that Marky was doing

the same in the cubicle. 'Do you want me to wait, darling?' he called.

And then the door to the toilet opened and in came a tiny little girl, maybe eight or nine years old, dragging a plastic bucket and mop.

She looked at Abbott, who looked back, assessing her with the same eyes he'd used for the Somalian boy back at his B&B in Finchley.

But coming up with a very different answer this time.

'Hello, there,' he said.

She looked at him with wariness in her eyes.

'What's your name?' said Abbott. 'And shouldn't you be at school?'

She heard the cubicle door go and her eyes widened only to relax a little when she saw that it was Marky.

'You best get on with it, love,' advised Marky. 'You don't want Mr McGregor getting angry again, do you?'

She shook her head mutely. Abbott had already noticed the bruise at her collarbone, and when he re-entered Doyle's office and agreed that he would stay on to do some work for the organisation, it was that bruise he was thinking of.

That bruise and the look in her eyes.

CHAPTER 21

Abbott sat in the passenger seat of McGregor's BMW. The previous evening, he'd been given his stuff back. McGregor had taken him into town, and he'd made his way on foot to the Travelodge, careful to make sure he wasn't being followed. This morning, he'd met McGregor at the drop-off point.

'I'll drive today,' McGregor told him. 'After that, you'll be behind the wheel.'

'Oh yeah? And why's that?'

'Because I'm the bagman and you're the muscle, pal, and on a normal day, the muscle drives, you get me? That's just the way it be.'

'I'm the muscle. That's it? That's my job?'

'Any problems, take it up with Doyle. He'll tell you what he told me. That you're to accompany me on my rounds.'

'And what rounds is this? Paper? Milk?'

'Paper just about covers it, my friend,' McGregor said, rubbing money fingers at Abbott. 'Only, instead of delivering, we're collecting.'

'And you need me along for that, do you? Big tough Glaswegian like you can't handle that himself?'

McGregor chuckled. 'I'm all about showing you the ropes, Sonny Jim, so that you can fly solo. Then you get to be your own muscle.'

Abbott shook his head. 'I doubt I'll be around that long.'

'That's what the boss wants, and so that's what the boss gets,' McGregor said.

They drove out of the centre and into a residential area, and not the good part either, as far as Abbott could tell from his glances out of the window.

'Looked to me like Scutter was living all right,' said Abbott, breaking a silence best described as 'uneasy'.

'Oh, aye, and what's that supposed to mean, "living all right"?'

'I did my research, McGregor. I know that Scutter spent time in jail, and I know what for. And it's not that common for convicted paedophiles to be living in nice new houses with an Audi slotted in the drive.'

'Ray Doyle does things differently. He looks after members of his family.'

'That includes approving their assassination, does it?'

'What makes you say that?'

'Just that I get the impression that nothing happens in this city without his say-so.'

'True.'

'So he allowed his nephew to be killed?'

At that, McGregor merely shrugged and Abbott let it drop for a moment or so, before adding, as though he'd only just thought of it, 'I mean, it looked to me as though Scutter had been set up there. Like he was being looked after maybe. Payment for services rendered.'

'And what services might they be?'

'I can think of a few. Look, if I'm going to be on board here, then I need to know what I'm getting myself into.'

McGregor sighed. 'Everything is what you're getting yourself into, Flyte. If there's anything going on in this town then it's because—'

'Ray Doyle lets it happen, yes, I was getting that impression.'

'Well, there you go. End of story.'

'And everything includes people trafficking, does it? *Child* trafficking.'

McGregor looked across at him with a sarcastic, patronising expression. 'Aye, Flyte, everything includes that too. Have you got a problem with that? Some kind of noble moral objection that says it's OK to hire yourself out to the highest bidder and kill on their behalf, no questions asked, but you draw the line at dealing in human traffic?'

It was Abbott's turn to shrug. 'So Scutter was being looked after until he wasn't being looked after. Is that what you're saying?'

McGregor drew his fingers across his lips.

'It's just that you and Doyle are making a big deal about how you control the city, like everybody answers to the Doyle crew and yet . . .' He left it, went back to staring out the window.

'And yet what?' asked McGregor.

'Well, there's obviously another player.'

'Like who?

'Kilgore.'

'But you've dealt with Kilgore, haven't you?' said McGregor.

Yet again Abbott wondered if he was pushing it too far. 'I don't know what you think you know, McGregor, but it doesn't work like that. Me and Kilgore didn't meet and never would. All my work is done via an intermediary. I'm talking about the fact that Kilgore can hire me to do a job in this town and Doyle stays in the dark about it. Not only that but the hit is on his own nephew.'

'Well, for someone who values secrecy, you seem awfully curious,' frowned McGregor. 'You want to watch it, pal. You don't want me getting the wrong idea about you and then telling Mr Doyle. You especially don't want me telling Mr Doyle that you think he's a puppet, having his strings pulled by somebody else.'

'I didn't say that.'

'Aye, but it's what you meant.'

'I'm interested in the set-up, that's all. I like to know who I'm working for. That's not curiosity in my game. That's staying alive.'

McGregor nodded. 'Fair enough. But look, Flyte, if anybody's revealing details of the operation, it ain't me. Mr Doyle will tell you what he wants you to know when he wants you to know it. In the meantime, you're my assistant, which means standing around, looking like a hardnut. Think you can do that?'

'I think I can do that.'

Abbott left it as they drew up outside their first port of call, a terraced house in the back streets. Although parked cars lined both sides of the street, there was one particular space free – deliberately so, thought Abbott – and McGregor pulled into it. They got out and Abbott looked around. Across the street an old woman watched them from the window of her house, a look of undisguised hatred on her face. Abbott knew why. He knew that after a career of chasing down drug dealers and people traffickers he had suddenly joined the other side. He saw himself through her eyes.

No, you haven't. You haven't joined the other side. Remember why you're here.

McGregor knocked. A shirtless kid in jogging bottoms answered. He led the pair of them through to the front room.

'May I speak to the drug dealer of the home,' drawled McGregor sardonically. The kid was about to call through when another, older kid – but still a kid – appeared, this one also wearing what appeared to be the regulation outfit of no shirt and jogging bottoms, although he had shown a little flair by teaming it with a flat-brimmed cap.

'McGregor,' said the kid, coming forward. He went to give McGregor a fist bump, but McGregor, to his eternal credit – shooting up in Abbott's estimations at the same time – placed his hands firmly behind his back.

'Money,' he said.

The guy tried to save face by snapping at various under-lings, even clipping one of them around the ear until the money appeared. A sandwich bag was handed to McGregor, who in turn handed it to Abbott. The kids in the house looked at Abbott with new eyes.

Moments later, Abbott and McGregor were back in the car.

'So that's it, is it?' asked Abbott. 'It's drug money?'

McGregor shrugged. 'We've got our fingers in lots of pies.'

'Drugs, prostitution . . .' Abbott paused. 'People? Kids?'

'We're back to that, are we?'

'Just that I saw a kid back at base, a little girl.'

'Just a kid doing a bit of part-time work for us. You got a problem with that?'

'Moral judgements don't figure high on my list of hobbies.'

'Good to know that you're not the squeamish sort. Unless you're just saying what you think we want to hear, that is.'

Abbott gave a sigh. 'McGregor, you don't know me, but you know me better than that. Besides, if I was worried about anyone in the operation where that's concerned, I'd be worried about Marky.'

'Oh yeah?' McGregor looked sideways at him. 'You noticed that, too, did you?'

And if Abbott felt bad, throwing Marky to the wolves like that then, well, he didn't feel *that* bad. He was getting close now, he felt. Close to what, he wasn't sure. Just close.

CHAPTER 22

They made a couple more stops at terraced houses where the clientele were virtual carbon copies of their first stop. Scrotal kids playing at being gangsters, handing over their money, feeling like proper bad men.

'This next one has been coming up short,' said McGregor. 'If I give you the nod, break one of the guy's fingers.'

Inside, McGregor did the count, decided it was light and sure enough, he gestured towards Abbott. 'My friend, Mr Flyte here, needs to give you a message from Mr Doyle.'

The guy whimpered and squealed. Abbott kept his feelings hidden, accepted the trembling hand that was offered and took the little finger.

'Wait.' The kid was sweating, shaking. 'You told me to let you know if the Polish prozzie came. She's been in here, Mr McGregor. She came buying.'

McGregor nodded approvingly. 'Well done. A bit late, mind. But well done.'

The kid looked hopeful of a reprieve, but McGregor shook his head.

'Please,' said the kid quickly, sweating hard now, his hands slick with it. 'It won't happen again, Mr McGregor. I promise it won't happen again.'

'No, pal, it won't happen again,' said McGregor ruefully and nodded at Abbott.

Abbott grasped the guy's wrist with his left hand, tensed on the little finger with his right. He reminded himself that this was a guy who made money off the back of human misery. He told himself that carrying out the punishment might deter him for the future.

Perhaps he was even doing the kid a favour.

He broke the finger.

The kid was still screaming as they left the house without another word.

'Excellent, pal,' said McGregor when they were settled back in the car. 'I don't have the stomach for that kind of work myself.'

Abbott looked out of the window.

***

Their next stop took them to a tatty block of flats and right to the top. Abbott, to his shame, knew a prostitute's flat when he saw one, and he was seeing one now. She sat in the front room, dressed for work, a young Polish girl, not more than twenty-two but old enough to be married with a kid of five or six. He also knew a junkie when he saw one. Two junkies, to be exact. There was a husband on the scene. A jittery guy who loitered, speaking only briefly in Polish.

This, then, was 'the Polish prozzie'.

'You're short,' said McGregor to her, and they waited as she translated for the husband. The kid tried to enter the room but was ushered away. The door to the kitchen shut. Abbott steeled himself, unsure if he could go through with another 'punishment'. The drug dealer was one thing. This pair quite another.

'But business hasn't been good,' she managed, unable to summon the necessary conviction.

'Well, you see, a little birdie tells me that you've been out buying gear. Might be that we have to take our payment in other ways,' said McGregor, who looked meaningfully towards the kitchen. From within they could hear the kid singing to himself and playing, blissfully unaware of what was happening outside.

Abbott felt his heart harden, wanting to reach for his Glock but keeping his face neutral. Meanwhile, the woman was shaking, pleading with McGregor in Polish and English, McGregor merely nodding, letting his threat stand.

They left the flat, stood out in the hall. McGregor held up a finger. *Wait*. Then he pulled out a pen, made a mark on the door, although nothing was visible. 'UV pen,' he explained. 'So the boys know.'

'They don't get another chance to pay up, then?'

'Och, no, those two are never going to pay. We might as well move in before they get their act together and ship the kid out.'

As they left the block, McGregor made another mark. He caught Abbott looking. 'You sure this doesn't bother you, pal?' he asked slyly.

Abbott shook his head. 'Business is business.'

But he thought of the couple upstairs who right now would be living in fear, and at that moment he hated himself even more than usual.

CHAPTER 23

The day of work over, Abbott expected to be dropped in the town centre. Instead, McGregor took them back to Kemptown.

'What's all this, then?' asked Abbott warily. The MP7 was hidden in his hotel room but he carried his Glock and his Gerber knife. Even so, Doyle had the numbers. None of them were likely as fast and accurate as Abbott. But still. Numbers.

'Don't you worry your pretty little head, pal,' smirked McGregor. 'It's just that the boss wants a word, that's all.'

'A bit early for a performance review, don't you think?'

'Maybe. Maybe not. Maybe the boss just wants to get the measure of you.'

'What have you told him about me?' asked Abbott, thinking that if McGregor had informed Doyle about Abbott's occasional information-gathering exercises then Doyle's suspicions might have been raised. And if Doyle's suspicions had been raised, then what might he have in store?

A kid, as it turned out. A kid and a brassy-looking woman, who sat in the factory reception area.

'I don't think you've met Mrs Cynthia Doyle, have you?' said McGregor with an amused air. She wore a furry lounge suit and was completely made up. Once upon a time, you would have called a woman like that 'brassy'. Abbott mentally called her that now.

'I haven't had the pleasure,' said Abbott.

The kid was, what, sixteen? A smattering of teenage acne on his forehead, sullen expression, dressed like a walking advertisement for Nike. 'And this is Finn,' said McGregor, adding, surely in a spirit of stirring the shitpot, 'One day all this will be yours, eh, Finn?'

Finn responded by pushing his hands into the pockets of his track pants and sneering. Abbott saw a large expensive watch on a gold bracelet worn loosely, along with several other bits of jewellery. A gold chain around his neck.

'And may I introduce your father's newest employee, Owen Flyte. Let me tell you, this is the real deal we got right here. A proper bad man, and don't you forget it.'

Finn was looking at Abbott. 'You the SAS man?'

'Something like that,' said Abbott.

'How many you killed, then?'

'Enough,' said Abbott.

Finn rolled his eyes apparently dissatisfied with the answer but offering no real reason why.

'You guys waiting for the boss man?' asked McGregor. Mrs Doyle curled her lip in response. Finn stayed silent. 'Well, I don't suppose you'll be very long. Just a quick meeting with this one here.' McGregor jerked a thumb at Abbott. 'Come on then, Mr Flyte. Let's get this over and done with so these good people can get back home, eh?'

They trooped up to the office, knocked and went inside, where Abbott was surprised to find that Doyle sat by himself, nursing a bottle of whiskey and a bottle of Coke, fixing himself a drink as they entered, the latest in a fairly long line by the look of things.

'Well, well,' he said, sloppily, 'if it ain't my new friend Owen Flyte. How you getting on with the work then, Owen, eh? Hours to your liking, are they? Pleased with the holiday cover?' Before Abbott could reply he had turned his attention to McGregor. 'How's he getting on then, Mack?'

'Oh, aye, he's doing very well. A valuable addition to the team, I'd say. Putting the fear of God into the natives.'

'Well, you can't say fairer than that. That's what you're here for, after all.'

'I thought I was here under orders.'

'Well, you see,' said Doyle, taking a big slug of whiskey and then leaning back in his chair, 'that's what I wanted to talk to you about. See, I'm still being kept in the fuckin' dark here. I want to know why London are so interested in you.' He reached to scratch at his sweatshirt in the usual place. Abbott noticed that the spot was more faded than the rest of his top. A spot close to his heart.

OK, thought Abbott, *play this one carefully.* One wrong move. One thing he said that didn't check out, and his cover, that most flimsy of disguises, was blown. Then again, perhaps he could tease something out of Doyle.

'I've already told you everything I know. Strikes me that you need to speak to Kilgore.'

'You went through a go-between, is that right?'

'That's right,' said Abbott. All his work had been conducted that way. There was no reason to believe that Flyte operated any differently. And one thing becoming clear about the London end of the operation was that they operated very much on a need-to-know basis.

'And you weren't told why you were needed up here?'

'I never am. Ours not to reason why . . .'

'Ours but to do or die,' said McGregor.

'All right, all right,' said Doyle, irritated. 'Come on now, Flyte, you must have some idea why London are so interested in you? You must be wondering why they want you kept here,'

Abbott shook his head. 'There could be any number of reasons. Perhaps they're lining me up for another job. Perhaps there's heat and they need to wait for it to die down. Right now it suits me to stay. I'll be sure to let you know as soon as it doesn't.'

'Lining you up for another job, eh?' Doyle's eyes narrowed. 'I wonder. I wonder if that's it. What does Juliet have planned?' He said this last bit to McGregor. Abbott's ears pricked up. *Juliet. Who was Juliet?*

At that moment, Doyle's phone buzzed. He looked at it then spoke to McGregor, slurring his words. 'Go downstairs, would you, tell them I'll be down in a minute.'

McGregor nodded and left the room.

Doyle drained his whiskey, took a final pull on a cigarette and stubbed it out. He put his elbow to the table, pointing, so that Abbott half expected him to say, 'You're fired.' Instead what he said was, 'You better be being straight with me, Flyte. If Juliet wants to try something, let her try. I've got a safe in there full of all the evidence that I need to put her away for the rest of her life.'

He was pointing to a door off to one side, his finger trembling. He was almost completely in the bag. Probably didn't know what he was saying. Abbott decided to chance it. 'Who's Juliet?' he asked.

Doyle stood unsteadily, grasping onto the edge of the desk for support, the effects of the booze clearly hitting him with more force than he had anticipated. 'Perhaps you'll never find out,' he said to Abbott. 'Better for you that way.'

That night, back in his hotel, Abbott spoke to Cuckoo. 'I got three names for you to look at in conjunction with Doyle. A bloke called Sweaty. Don't know the real name. Another guy, Kilgore. Presumably a surname. Somebody else, the name's Juliet.'

'I'll see what I can do, Abbott,' said Cuckoo. 'How's it going up there?'

'I'm still alive, mate. Only just. But I'm still alive.'

CHAPTER 24

In order to employ a suitable security consultant, which is to say, a security consultant with the necessary ethics, or lack thereof, the ex-husband of Montana Norton, Clifford Levine, had approached the firm retained by Norton Gaming, spoken to his contact there and explained that he needed a more, shall we say, 'specialised' service, a service that was to be strictly off the books.

He had been given a name – Monroe – and a meeting had been arranged. During the meeting, Clifford had looked across at Monroe, who drank a sparkling water as Clifford nursed a G&T. This guy looked like a hard nut made good. He was, in short, just the person that Clifford Levine needed.

Clifford had hired him on the spot.

The two met now, in a branch of All Bar One in Canary Wharf in London, Clifford having dived out of work for fifteen minutes; Monroe looking like a work contact in a smart single-breasted suit.

The only other people in the place were two women having what looked like a business meeting over coffee. Clifford and Monroe took a table well out of earshot.

'What do we know about the proxies of the others?' asked Clifford.

'Nothing. Your opponents have conducted themselves with absolute secrecy, just as we have. All I know is that your mother-in-law, Juliet—'

'*Ex*-mother-in-law.'

'Of course. It appears that her first choice fell through for some reason. I've no news of a replacement.'

'Oh, well, that's good news. Juliet Norton in disarray. Poor old mother-in-law. *Ex*-mother-in-law.'

'Which still leaves you, Mr Levine.'

Clifford nodded. His tongue darted over his lips.

'I trust you have reviewed all the material I sent you.'

It had all been uploaded to a protected hosting site, and, yes, Clifford Levine, sitting in a penthouse flat with the glittering lights of London as a backdrop, had reviewed it all. 'I read everything you sent. Looked at all the videos. I've made my decision.' He slid his phone across. On it was displayed a picture of a woman. 'What do you think?'

'I think that had you tried to choose anybody else then I may have attempted to change your mind,' said Monroe, nodding approvingly. 'Heidi Kavanagh is her name. I should declare an interest because I have, in the past, had a relationship with Heidi, and I can tell you from experience, not all of it pleasurable, that she will prove a very capable operative.'

'I like it. It feels like the left-field choice,' said Clifford, feeling very modern, very progressive.

'You mean because she's a woman?'

Clifford nodded.

'She may be that,' said Monroe. 'I can indeed vouch for

it. She also happens to be the best. Whatever your reasons for making the choice, I can assure you that you've made the right one.'

CHAPTER 25

At night, Abbott struggled, finding it tough to resist the clarion call of the bar downstairs. When he closed his eyes, he heard the crack of the drug dealer's finger. He remembered the looks on the Polish couple's faces. He told himself that the ends justified the means, but it did little to assuage his guilt. It made it no easier to gaze upon his own reflection in the bathroom mirror.

Over the next couple of days, things got worse. Until one afternoon, he and McGregor visited what was clearly a derelict pub in the shadow of tower blocks that according to the various taped-off doorways and windows – not to mention the prominent warning signs – were earmarked for demolition.

Looking around, Abbott found himself reminded of bomb sites in Belfast, areas of the city that had been reduced to rubble and would stay like that for a while. Here the culprit was not bombs but poverty, neglect and misconceived town planning. Not far away was a burnt-out car. Close by, somebody had dumped household rubbish, scorched kitchen units, an incongruous pushchair.

And in the middle of it all, as though mounting a valiant

rearguard action in an attempt to resist the encroachment of the wasteland, was the pub.

The Freemasons Arms was its name. Or had been. Now, though, the windows were covered with metal grilles. The door was reinforced.

McGregor led Abbott to it and knocked. Another incongruity was a modern-looking CCTV camera trained on the door. McGregor looked up into it, smiling sardonically, and moments later, the door was opened for them by a guy with a machete tucked into his belt. He raised his chin in silent greeting, allowed them in and closed the door.

Now they found themselves in what would once have been the bar area, which even though it was unused and derelict, was comparatively habitable considering the state of outside. It even seemed to have a working bar. Sitting on a banquette seat along one wall was a nervous-looking guy whose eyes travelled to McGregor and Abbott. A customer, thought Abbott. What kind of guy was so desperate to get his rocks off that he went to a place where the doormen carried machetes?

Answer? A degenerate.

At a table on the other side of the room sat three men who looked like security. They'd been playing cards but were gazing over curiously, as was a black guy with dreadlocks who stood behind the bar. Along with the optics and pumps were monitors showing feeds from the front and back of the pub.

'Mr McGregor,' said the guy behind the bar. 'Can I get you a beer?'

'Aye, I'll have a beer. And one for my friend here, Mr Flyte.'

'Who is Mr Flyte?' said the barman, dead-eyed. As he

spoke, he drew back the leather waistcoat he wore, displaying the handle of another machete beneath.

'He's providing security for Mr McGregor,' said Abbott, sweeping back his own shirt to expose the butt of his Glock and gratified to see the guy's eyes widen a little in response. Just a touch.

McGregor chuckled. 'Fucking hell, this is like bringing your bird to meet your parents.'

'Excuse me,' the voice was small and came from the guy sitting on the banquette. He had stood up. 'I'm sorry, but I think I've changed my mind.'

'Sit down, your room'll be ready soon,' barked one of the guys from the card table.

McGregor stared at him, waited until he'd regained his seat and then said to the barman, 'Tell you what, I'll leave that beer as long as that's all right with you, Mr Flyte?'

It was. It was more than all right with Abbott, who had been wondering how a refusal might play; indeed, had been wondering whether he wanted to refuse at all, and besides, guilt could take a day off as this was duty, not addiction.

'Where's Sweaty?' asked McGregor. 'Is he in the cellar?'

Sweaty.

Abbott felt his jaw clench, breathing through his nose as the barman nodded. McGregor and Abbott moved off, through a door at one side of the bar and down stone steps into the cellar.

Here, the walls were bare brick, dark and damp.

Here, too, was Sweaty.

It was not difficult to see why. He sat there like Yoda. No, not like Yoda, the other one, *Jabba*, stewing in his own juice – the juice in this case being a mix of biscuits and booze and stubble and cigarette smoke. He wore an old England shirt, three lions on his chest, just to the side of which was a stain that might have been ketchup or blood.

He turned as they entered. 'Mr McGregor,' he said through a mouthful of biscuit. There was a packet of Hobnobs on the desk in front of him, the screwed-up wrappers of several more there, too, while in front of him was a series of monitors, arranged in a wraparound formation, each showing CCTV images.

Some were of outside, front and back, two more of the pub's communal areas. Most, though, were of rooms, the sharp end of the operation.

In one, a young girl no older than nine sat on the edge of a bed in her night clothes. In another was a woman – older, thank God for small mercies – emaciated, sitting at a table, her hands shaking as she rolled herself a cigarette; in the third, a client, a vast sweating hulk of a man, who completely obscured whoever it was he was currently paying to abuse. Another room was clearly some kind of communal area. In here were more girls. Again, very, very young. There were other youngsters, one of whom held a dustpan and brush. Support staff, no doubt.

All told, Abbott counted around ten of them. Not all of them kids, depending on your definition of the word. But all of them trafficked. He had always known that he hadn't needed to go as far as Thailand to face off with child traffickers; he knew that it was happening in this country, too; more and more frequently as more and more desperate people poured in. But to see it up close, having it rubbed in his face? That was different.

Abbott tore his eyes away from the screens as Sweaty spoke. 'This is your new enforcer, is it?' he said, mouth still moving around the biscuit, already reaching for its replacement.

'Meet Mr Flyte,' said McGregor.

Sweaty nodded in greeting at Abbott, taking the opportunity to give him a long, appraising look. Abbott could not bring himself to respond, even for the purposes of his cover. *You helped kill my brother*, he thought. His hands were thrust into the pockets of his Diesels, and he was digging his nails into his palms, trying to control his anger.

'Business good, is it?' asked McGregor.

'Always good,' replied Sweaty.

'I see you got a new customer upstairs. I hope he's been fully vetted.'

'Of course.'

'He seemed a bit nervous to me, pal,' said McGregor warningly.

Sweaty nodded. 'I make sure the boys have a word with him before he leaves,' he said, and grinned, revealing black teeth.

That was it. That was the extent of their interaction. Money changed hands and Abbott left, knowing that he had just stepped into hell.

Knowing that he had to go back.

He needed to pay a special visit to Sweaty.

CHAPTER 26

In his room he stripped and cleaned the Glock. He waited until around 1am, then took the Glock and the suppressor and left.

He found a motor, hotwired it. He drove to the derelict tower blocks, located The Freemasons Arms, and parked.

The front of the pub was dark, but as he watched, a figure arrived and a security light flicked on, illuminating a man in an anorak, who knocked on the door of the pub and then did what McGregor had done earlier, looked up and into the CCTV.

He went inside. The light remained on for a few moments and then flicked off.

Scanning the front of the pub earlier, Abbott had taken note of the security cameras. He'd also clocked the fact that there was a loading door to the pub cellar – a loading door that was bolted from inside. He skirted the pub, confident that none of the cameras could pick him up, and then took a direct line to the loading hatch.

There he crouched, waiting. Around him the desolate urban landscape was still, tower blocks rising overhead, blotting out the moon. Only a tiny sliver of light escaped from the loading hatch.

Was Sweaty down there? Just one way to find out. Gently, Abbott knocked on the hatch. Waited.

From below came the sound of movement. A voice. 'Hello?'

Abbott knocked again. This time the voice was closer. Sweaty had climbed the stone steps to the door itself. 'Who's out there?' he said, sounding as though he was speaking with his mouth full. Abbott remembered the Hobnobs. 'What the fuck do you want?'

'It's me, Flyte,' said Abbott. 'I need to speak to you.'

'Well then, come through the front like everybody else.'

Abbott fixed the suppressor to his Glock. 'No. I don't want them to see me. What I have to say is between you and me only.'

From the other side of the hatch came a dry chuckle. 'I get ya. See something you liked, did ya?'

Abbott shifted a little, going down on one knee and bringing the Glock to bear two-handed. Around him the night was still and dark. The empty tower block cancelled the moonlight. 'You could say that. Now are you going to let me in, or not?'

There was the sound of a bolt being thrown back and then another. Abbott tensed. The loading hatch rose. The top of Sweaty's head appeared, his forehead and then his eyes which found Abbott, adjusting in the dark and then widening at the sight of the gun. 'What the fuck do you think you're doing?' was what he started to say but didn't finish.

And he didn't finish because Abbott pushed the suppressor of the Glock into his mouth.

'Very carefully go back down the steps,' whispered Abbott. 'Don't make a sound, don't make any sudden movements.'

Sweaty, his eyes wide, his lips trembling around a mouthful

of Hobnob and Glock suppressor, inched carefully back down the steps as Abbott climbed inside the hatch and into the cellar, closing the door behind him. Reaching the stone floor now, Abbott positioned Sweaty back on his chair, swinging it around to face into the room. Behind Sweaty the monitors were on, disgusting images only serving to feed Abbott's anger.

'I'm going to take the gun out of your mouth. If you talk louder than a whisper, I'll kill you. Do I make myself clear?' Sweaty nodded. 'Good.' Abbott slowly withdrew the suppressor from Sweaty's mouth. With disgust he noted the biscuit crumbs that clung to it.

Sweaty gathered himself. Beady eyes fixed on Abbott, who watched him carefully. Abbott's eyes flicked to the monitors and their catalogue of torture, and then back to Sweaty's face.

'You're not really Flyte, are you?' said Sweaty after a moment or so. He was keeping his cool. His voice was low. 'You're him. You're Abbott.'

Abbott nodded.

'You killed Jason?'

Abbott shook his head. 'Flyte killed him. I didn't come here to kill him, same as I'm not here to kill you.' Sweaty relaxed a little. 'As long as you tell me what I want to know. Answers. That's all I want.'

Sweaty nodded, jowly flesh wobbling.

'You know who I am. Do you remember my brother, Chris?'

Again, Sweaty nodded.

'What did you want with him that day? And before you answer, don't you dare insult my intelligence.'

'What if it's the truth?' said Sweaty, a stammer in his voice.

Abbott's reply came in the form of a bullet that he put in

Sweaty's desk chair, right between his legs, making the fat man jump. The PVC split. Foam bulged from within.

'OK, OK . . .' said Sweaty quickly, less cool now. 'You've made your point.'

'Keep your voice down. Was it for that?' Abbott indicated the screens. 'Were you taking him for that?'

Sweaty's mouth worked. His face shone.

'Answer me,' said Abbott.

'Yes,' said Sweaty. 'Something like that, yes. But look, not for us. Me and Jay, we were just drones, man. Fucking worker bees.'

'Working for Doyle?'

'Yeah. Doyle. That's right.'

'He into that himself, is he? Abusing kids?'

Sweaty nodded.

'Kids like my brother?'

Sweaty shrugged. 'I don't know. I don't know what his tastes are.'

'You would have put Chris to work somewhere like this? Put him on the payroll?'

'Yeah. Or . . .'

'Or what?'

'Or maybe he would have gone down south.'

'South where?'

'London.'

'London? For who?'

Sweaty shook his head. There were dark stains at the armpits of his England shirt.

'Don't tell me you can't say,' said Abbott. 'Don't you dare.'

'They'll kill me if I do.'

'I'll kill you if you don't.'

'You said you weren't going to kill me.'

'I said I wouldn't kill you if I got the answers I wanted. Am I getting them?' He shook his head. 'Not right now I'm not. Tell you what, let's get you started. Who's Kilgore?'

'You know Kilgore?'

'I've heard the name once or twice. He in London, is he?'

Sweaty nodded furiously. 'He works for them.'

'Works for who? Juliet? Is it something to do with a woman called Juliet?'

A change had come over Sweaty now. Where before he'd been nervous but relatively composed, just about holding on, now he began to tremble. His hands went to the arms of the chair in which he sat, his eyes travelled to the bullet hole between his legs as though trying to make an assessment, attempting to calculate which evil was the greater, the one who stood before him holding a weapon in his face, or the other one – the one he couldn't see but who clearly held him in his thrall.

Abbott watched his thought process with the interest of an anthropologist, knowing what Sweaty would decide. That however scared he was of this other unseen presence, it was the threat before him that was most imminent. And Abbott would leave here with the information he needed.

His eyes flicked to the screens.

Old and empty Hobnob packets. Images of child sex abuse.

And at that very moment, he decided that before he left, he'd put one in Sweaty's brain. He'd put a round in Sweaty's brain and do so without a second thought or backward glance. He'd take no pleasure in it, but he'd do it for his brother Chris and every other poor kid who had suffered abuse because of

Sweaty. And when he was done with Sweaty, he'd get Doyle. And when he was done with Doyle, he'd get whoever it was that Doyle answered to.

'Who are they?' he asked Sweaty. 'Who is Kilgore? Who is Juliet?'

The gun was held steady. Fear in Sweaty's eyes.

Abbott's gaze went up. To the monitors. Seeing the rooms, the prisoner kids, the . . .

Barman.

The barman with the dreads was moving across the floor of the main pub upstairs. He was moving towards the cellar door.

Abbott saw him on the monitor. He watched the guy's hand reach out and saw the door handle on their side begin to turn. With a warning look at Sweaty and one finger to his lips, he shifted his position slightly, ready to take down the barman when he came through the door, eyes flicking to the monitors where he saw that the barman had stopped and his head had turned as he responded to something said to him from across the room. Abruptly, he let go of the door handle, turned and strode off to deal with whatever it was.

Moment over, threat gone, Abbott breathed a sigh of relief and was about to turn his attention back to Sweaty when, seeing his chance, Sweaty launched himself off the chair and at Abbott, one outstretched, clawed hand reaching for Abbott's Glock.

Although his reactions had been dulled by the booze, and although he was, technically, out of shape, Abbott was still a lot, lot faster than an obese child trafficker in the dirty cellar of a near-derelict pub, and he stepped smartly to one side, expecting to reassert his authority as he levelled the Glock. But

Sweaty wasn't finished, and even though his hapless attempt to overcome Abbott had been an abject failure, he had one more trick up his sleeve, and the trick was to open his mouth and scream for help.

He never got the chance. Abbott put a round into his open mouth.

Sweaty's head popped back as the rear of his skull blew out; his body tautened and then he fell in an almost crucifixion-like pose, blood beginning to pool like a scarlet halo around his head.

Abbott shifted his aim to cover the cellar door in case the sound of the struggle had alerted anybody upstairs. Nobody came. Nor was there any sign of alarm on the monitors.

His eyes went back to Sweaty. 'I'm not a hitman,' he heard himself say, but for guys like this he'd make an exception. *You've done the world a favour*, he thought. *You don't need to give this a second's more consideration. In some tiny, tiny way you have reduced the sum total of human unhappiness.*

So why did he not feel better?

He racked the slide back and with the breech exposed, ejected the mag, then plugged two new rounds into it before replacing the mag. He disengaged the slide release catch, pushing a round into the breech of the weapon.

And then he turned and carefully, slowly, quietly climbed the steps, clambered out into the night, and replaced the hatch. He returned to his car, where he made a 999 call, informing the operator that a man had been shot and killed in the cellar of The Freemasons Arms and giving the address. He removed the battery from his phone and then waited, wanting to witness the moment when the cops arrived, and they marched out the guys inside. When the captive kids and girls were brought out and put into vans bound for safer places and happier times.

He waited.

And with a sinking sensation he realised that, of course, the local police, instead of getting in their cars to investigate, would instead have made a call to Doyle, who would have told them to stand down.

Just as he was having that thought, the door to the pub opened and out poured three of the security men, including the doorman and the barman, the security light flicking on, sending light skittering down the blades of the machetes they brandished. He heard voices, shouting.

With a heavy heart, Abbott fired up the motor, drove it back to where he had found it, and then returned to the Travelodge.

Where, to his surprise, he found McGregor waiting for him.

CHAPTER 27

'What are you doing here?' he asked. McGregor was sitting in the driving seat of his Beamer.

'You weren't answering your phone,' said McGregor, cheerfully.

'So fuckin' what? It's the middle of the night. Anyway, how did you know I was here?'

'I'll tell you how I know, shall I?' replied McGregor. 'I know because there is very little that goes on in this city that we don't know about. I know because you've taken somebody's identity, haven't you, ya cheeky bastard?'

Abbott tensed, ready to draw the Glock . . .

But wait, something wasn't quite right here. If Doyle knew he'd been impersonating Flyte, they wouldn't have sent the assistant to deliver the news. He'd either be dead or bundled into the back of a van by now. 'That's right,' he said carefully.

'What happened? You find Abbott's hotel room key and decide that you wanted a free room, did you?'

Abbott nodded, still feeling cautious. No way was he out of the woods. After all, a sharp-eyed receptionist might have put two and two together. On the other hand, it wasn't as though he'd ever exchanged more than a word with anyone. Half the time he'd passed through reception with no one on duty. After dark, forget it.

So it was quite possible that any receptionist would have been none the wiser and unable to shed any light for an enquiring member of the Doyle crew.

And the fact remained that if they genuinely thought that he was pulling a fast one, then they would have taken action, wouldn't they? They'd have come mob-handed.

'You still haven't answered the question of what you're doing here,' said McGregor.

'Aye, well, that's another story. There's been some trouble at . . . Well, you remember where we were earlier?'

'We were at two or three places earlier. Try being specific.'

'The Freemasons Arms.'

'Oh yeah? What sort of trouble?'

'How about you hopping in? We'll get over to the factory, let the boss man explain.'

Abbott's mind raced. Trying to work out what, if anything, the other side had in mind. All of a sudden his cover felt shakier than ever.

'Where were you, then?' asked McGregor as Abbott settled into the car.

'I just took a walk,' said Abbott. 'Sleep doesn't come so easily these days.'

'That's a hangover from combat, is it?'

'You might say that.'

'I see,' said McGregor, nodding thoughtfully. Abbott turned his head to look out of the window, wondering if he should draw his weapon and take pre-emptive action. If they'd worked

OLLIE OLLERTON

out that he wasn't Flyte, then he was walking into the lion's den. If not, then that meant they trusted him fully. And the more they trusted him, the closer he could get.

He checked his watch. It was coming up for 3am. And yet, as they turned into Kemptown and approached the Doyle factory, he could see that the lights were all on, the place already buzzing with men.

They parked, went inside, across the now-familiar factory floor and up the steps to the mezzanine. McGregor knocked on a door. Two of Doyle's foot soldiers appeared from inside, but instead of ushering Abbott and McGregor through they stepped out onto the gantry.

McGregor held out his hand. 'Gun?'

Abbott shook his head.

McGregor waggled insistent fingers. 'Listen, pal, it doesn't look good, does it? You being out like that. At the same time as someone hits our operation. How about you just hand yer gun over, let me check that there isn't a slug missing?'

'I can tell you now that there isn't.'

'Then you won't mind handing it over so we can check. You'll get it back. Soon as I'm happy. Who can say fairer than that, eh?'

The moment hung. Abbott knew that a refusal would invite more suspicion. The guards tensed as he reached behind to the waistband of his jeans. 'Steady, lads. You said you wanted my piece, didn't you?' He plucked it out and with tweezer fingers gave it to McGregor, who handed it off to another of the men.

'Careful with it,' warned Abbott.

'Don't worry. My man Morris here knows exactly what he's doing,' said McGregor.

As Morris left with Abbott's beloved Glock nine, they made their way past the meat-grinding machine and into the main office. There the office was packed. Four men, all of whom stood with their hands clasped, the butts of their sidearms visible. All of them regarding Abbott with open hostility.

And here's you without your gun.

Doyle was there, too, of course. Except that instead of being behind his desk smoking, he stood to one side while in the throne was his wife, Cynthia Doyle. She wore a scowl and Abbott wondered if he should read anything into that. Then again, from his limited experience of Mrs Cynthia Doyle, the scowl was her default expression. Knowing her husband's proclivities, you could hardly blame her.

'Flyte, good to see you,' said Doyle, taking charge. He sounded a little drunk. Not as bad as the other night but getting there. There were pistols on the desk, too. A pair of his 'n' hers Rugers.

'Good to see you, too,' said Abbott.

'Mac tells me that you're at the Travelodge, staying in the late Mr Abbott's room. Is that right?' said Doyle.

Abbott nodded.

'He also tells me that you weren't there when he called to see if you could come out to play.'

'Like I told him just now, I went for a walk.'

'See, that's funny, that is,' said Doyle, 'because earlier tonight, maybe even the exact time that you were out for your walk, somebody paid a visit to The Freemasons Arms and shot my man Sweaty in the face.'

'Jesus,' said Abbott, trying to calibrate his response into something approaching surprised but not *too* surprised. Not overacting surprise. 'Who are you fingering for it? Dissatisfied customer?'

'Well, no,' said Doyle, 'because no customer of Sweaty's would dare.'

'Vengeful father, maybe?'

Doyle's eyes hardened. 'Same applies. We don't have many of them in the picture, to be honest, mate. But I'm thinking that being as you're new to the crew, and that you can't quite explain your whereabouts, then the person I'm looking for might be stood right here in front of me.'

'No, mate,' said Abbott carefully.

'I ain't your mate. I'm Mr Doyle to you.' His men shifted. Cynthia Doyle's jaw moved, and Abbott realised she was chewing gum.

'I'm working here as a favour,' Abbott told Doyle.

'You ain't doing no one a favour being here, believe you me. And it don't matter why you're working here, you still call me Mr Doyle.'

His men bristled. Their eyes darted. Abbott tried to cool the situation. 'I apologise, Mr Doyle.'

'That's better.' Doyle seemed to soften a little. 'Thing is, Mr Flyte, one thing I hate is being taken for a mug. You wouldn't be taking me for a mug, would you?'

Abbott sighed. 'Mr Doyle, you know what I do. You know I'm the best at what I do. If, for whatever reason, I wanted to kill Sweaty – and while we're on the subject, *why* would I do that? – then I wouldn't leave it so everything pointed to me.'

'No, you wouldn't, would you?' agreed Doyle. 'Not if you really were Owen Flyte. But if you were Alex Abbott, then that might be a different story, don't you think?'

Abbott shrugged. 'I fought the man. You didn't. He was a pro.'

'A pro who came here wanting to settle a score. Scutter's dead. But maybe he decided to go on and do a bit more tidying up at the same time, eh? Maybe he found out that Sweaty was involved in trying to take his brother and decided to get a little payback?'

'Look, Doyle, you're barking up the wrong tree, that's all I can say. McGregor will vouch for me. All my work has been in the interests of the business. Your business. You should be thanking me, not suspecting me.'

There was a knock at the office door and Morris appeared, carrying Abbott's gun. He gave it to McGregor, whispering something to him at the same time, impossible to hear.

McGregor nodded. Morris left.

'Gun's fully loaded,' said McGregor to Doyle.

Doyle nodded slowly. 'Well, that's something, then, isn't it? Give it back to him. I'm sure he's feeling only half-dressed without it.'

Abbott took his gun, testing the weight of it in his palm before tucking it into the back of his trousers.

'Johnboy,' said Doyle, speaking to one of the armed men who stood in the room, 'bring Marky in, would you, mate?'

Moments later, two more guards manhandled Marky roughly into the room. 'I haven't done anything, boss, I swear,' Marky was saying. 'Nothing.'

Mrs Doyle spoke now, for the first time since Abbott had arrived. Her voice was high-pitched. 'Only you've always been a bit squeamish about certain aspects of the business, haven't you, Marky?'

'I swear, Mrs Doyle.'

'And you can't seem to account for yourself.'

'I was in bed.' His voice rose. It had a panicked tone. 'Please. You've got to believe me. I've got no reason to put a bullet in Sweaty.'

'Wasn't no secret that Sweaty treated the kids rough,' said Mrs Doyle. Abbott looked into her eyes and saw no pity there. No pity at all.

'I'll be more strict with them from now on if that's what you want,' said Marky.

'More *professional*,' Cynthia Doyle corrected him.

Marky nodded furiously. 'Yes, yes. That's just it. I ain't been strict enough with them. But that'll change, I promise.'

Cynthia Doyle looked across at her husband, who looked at her. She shook her head. Doyle nodded in acknowledgement, as though making up his mind. 'Mr Flyte, do us a favour and put a bullet in Marky here.'

Marky began to wail, struggling against the two guards who stood with their hands on each shoulder preventing him from rising. 'In here?' said Abbott.

'Why not? Here and now,' said Doyle.

'Look, I'm sure you've made your point,' said Abbott. 'Can you really imagine Marky killing Sweaty?'

'Well, at the moment he's the most likely culprit, isn't he?'

'Come on, it only happened a couple of hours ago. It's far too early to say. Have you found out whether there was anybody round at The Freemasons kicking off? Somebody with a grudge?'

But Doyle was no longer listening. His attention went to McGregor. 'A couple of hours ago? Did you tell our friend Mr Flyte here that it happened a couple of hours ago?'

McGregor shook his head slowly. 'No, boss, I can't say that I did.'

Doyle turned back to Abbott. 'How would you know that, Mr Flyte?'

'Well, that's when I was out walking. And if we're back to saying that I'm the trigger man then I refer you to my previous answer.'

'Because you're a loyal and trustworthy employee, aren't you?'

'If you like.'

'Then do what you're being paid to do as my enforcer and enforce. Put a bullet in this man.'

Abbott drew his sidearm.

'Good man,' said Doyle.

Abbott put it back to the back of Marky's head.

'Wait,' said Doyle, 'have you got a silencer for that thing?'

'They call it a suppressor, boss,' said McGregor, 'and yes, he has. I saw it at Scutter's pad.'

'Because it's another funny thing that nobody heard the gunshot. Sweaty was killed in the cellar. I reckon if you fired a gun in that cellar then the whole pub would hear. Unless, of course, it was fitted with a silencer. Or a suppressor.'

'What's the point of all this?' snarled Abbott. 'You seem convinced it's me.'

'I will be if you don't put a bullet in Marky.'

The odds were bad, he knew. He could maybe take out two guys before the rest drew their guns, and if that happened, then he was a dead man. Mission failure.

'I'm not gonna do it here,' he said, trying to buy himself some time.

'Why's that, then?'

'Well, there's the mess for one thing.'

Doyle raised his chin. 'Yes, there was apparently quite a mess when somebody put one in Sweaty. Perhaps that's what you're thinking of.'

OK, thought Abbott, his sidearm still at the back of Marky's head. *What have we got? Four goons in total, all of them armed, guns within reaching distance for Doyle and even Mrs Doyle if she wanted one.* Impossible odds, but what other choice did he have?

Right. He had to do it. The mission would be a failure. At least he'd take some of them with him.

'There was one other thing, boss,' said McGregor suddenly.

'Yeah? What was that, then?'

'His gun. Morris said it was fully loaded, but you know what Morris is like with guns. He also said that it had recently been fired.'

'Did he now?' smiled Doyle, looking at Abbott, who swore he'd never seen a man look so shark-like.

It was time.

Abruptly, Abbott shifted the muzzle of the Glock away from the back of Marky's head, dropping slightly in a two-handed combat stance and squeezing off his first.

Nothing happened.

CHAPTER 28

Idiot.

Amateur.

They'd unloaded his weapon. Of course they had. Taken out the live rounds and replaced them. Or maybe just the top two live rounds.

Either way.

Dead man's click.

Equivalent of standing there with your dick in your hand.

Turkey.

The gun was grabbed from him. Cynthia Doyle pulled a face, shaking her head as though disgusted while Doyle lit the latest cigarette, looking more amused than anything. 'Didn't I tell you, Mr Abbott, that if there's one thing I hate it's being taken for a mug?' His lighter flared. 'Darren, go and start the meat grinder, would you?'

Marky was standing, brushing himself down. His demeanour immediately changing as he dropped the performance. He drew his gun, grinning at Abbott. All guns in the room were drawn now. Even Cynthia Doyle had picked one up. Darren did as he was told and left the room, and a second later, they heard the metallic crunch of the meat grinder starting up, its rusted, bloodstained blades beginning to move.

'How did you know?' asked Abbott.

'Do you know what? It didn't even occur to me that you'd bother to take the dead geezer's identity,' said Doyle cheerfully. 'I mean, it's all a bit spy film, ain't it? It was McGregor who put the idea in my head, like maybe just killing Scutter might not be enough for Abbott, and a way of hitting us harder was to get inside our operation, know what I mean? Soon as the thought occurred to me it was like everything fell into place. I called up London, spoke to Kilgore, who emailed me a picture of Abbott.'

Mrs Doyle flicked over a piece of paper that was on the desk in front of her, poked a pudgy finger at it. 'There's a picture of Alex Abbott,' she squeaked. 'And that's you, ain't it? Unless you're going to tell us that Owen Flyte was your identical twin.'

Hands gripped Abbott. They dragged him out to the machine, the whole posse shipping out at the same time, all of them gathered around the huge, stainless-steel funnel. Looking down it, Abbott swore he could see the bits of the last unfortunates, little scraggy scraps of flesh and blood and bone. Was the real Owen Flyte down there? Was Jason Scutter in there somewhere?

'They've normally shit themselves about now,' gloated Doyle.

His wife stood to one side, her red-lipsticked mouth set, her arms folded across the front of her jogging suit. 'Juicy Couture' it said on the front.

Still held, Abbott was manoeuvred towards the mouth of the machine. Sure enough, he saw the machinery churning.

There was no purchase down there. No living person would be able to prevent themselves being inexorably dragged into the rotating blades. It would be a slow death. A slow, painful death.

And although he was prepared to die, and probably had been since the day that his brother Chris was taken and his life fell apart, Abbott knew that he didn't want to die this way. Better to die fighting.

He went limp, causing his captors to take the strain, altering their equilibrium in such a way that what he did next took them by surprise. He twisted and rotated his arms, bringing his knees up at the same time so that they were forced to bear his entire weight, making himself the slipperiest of eels.

During the months of drinking, his strength had diminished but not completely, and he was able to wrench one arm free of the first man while at the same time dragging the second man forward and rushing him in the direction of the meat-grinding funnel.

Doyle saw what was happening – saw his man about to be deposited into the machine – and came forward with the gun, waving it with no discipline, like a referee trying to deliver a red card. At the same time, Abbott saw his chance to grab himself a weapon, lost interest in feeding the goon to the meat grinder, dropped him and changed the direction of attack, going instead for Doyle, who was caught by surprise and had no time to react as Abbott grabbed his wrist and twisted, easily disarming him and then putting the gun on him.

Abbott was about to pull the trigger.

He was maybe a third of a second from pulling the trigger.

When the lights went out.

PART THREE

CHAPTER 29

Abbott woke up feeling groggy, head throbbing from where he'd been hit.

But alive. Arms and legs intact. No bit of him purloined for an edible meat product. Let's be thankful for that, at least.

He was on the move, lying across the back seat of a large vehicle, probably a Range Rover, travelling at speed. For some moments, he lay still, not wanting to reveal to whoever was up front that he'd re-entered the land of the living. Opening one eye, he was able to get a visual on his surroundings. Surreptitiously, he moved his arm to check, and sure enough, his gun was gone, ditto his Gerber.

As for his company, he could make out a driver in the front seat, and from the back of his head knew that it was McGregor. The passenger seat was empty, which came as a surprise. As far as he could tell, it was just him and McGregor in the car. He considered overpowering McGregor but on the other hand maybe not. Instead, he made a play of groaning, as though he were just waking up.

'Abbott,' said McGregor from the front seat, and Abbott,

having become so accustomed to being called Flyte in recent days, experienced a moment of disconnection.

'McGregor,' he replied, deliberately overplaying his grogginess. 'What the fuck is going on?'

'Well, for a start, pal, you're not dead and this is neither heaven nor hell even though I'm here. Mr Doyle sends his regards, by the way.'

'Right. Great. So how come I'm not dead?'

'Doyle just wanted to give you a scare, that's all. Fact is, you're a protected species. We've been given orders from on high that you're not to be harmed. Not only that, but somebody wants to meet you.'

'Who? Kilgore? Juliet?'

McGregor's eyes flicked in the rear-view. 'Oh aye. You've heard about her, have you?'

'Name's come up.'

'Doyle, eh? Blabbermouth.'

'That's about the size of it.'

'Figures. Fuckin' pisshead. Tell you what, you'll find out everything you need to know in due course. In the meantime . . .' McGregor tossed a phone handset over his shoulder that Abbott caught. It was his own phone. 'Doyle was hoping you might give him a call. There's a matter he'd like to discuss.'

Abbott pulled himself to a sitting position, did as he was asked and dialled Doyle.

'Abbott,' said Doyle.

'You wanted to speak to me.'

'Too right.' Doyle's voice was loud and at a pitch that upset Abbott's poor, throbbing head even more. 'I'll accept your apologies for what you done, shall I?'

'Suit yourself,' said Abbott, feeling behind his ear and wincing. What had hit him? A cosh, probably.

'Good,' said Doyle. 'We'll put any unpleasantness in the past, eh? Fact of the matter is, we're on the same side at the end of the day.'

'I'd really love to know why I've gone from being ingredients for the meat grinder to VIP status,' said Abbott. 'There's definitely a self-help book in this.'

'We all have to answer to someone, mate, even me. And that's the reason you're alive and sitting in the back of my Range Rover, rather than being fed to the dog. What I need to know is this. You came to Derby looking for revenge. Do you now feel satisfied?'

'What does it matter either way?'

Doyle sniffed. His voice dropped an octave or so. 'Look, I don't know why you've been called to London. I don't know what happens next. Whether you stay there or come back to Derby or go wherever the hell you want, I just want to be sure that coming after me isn't next on your agenda. If it is, say the word and it's game on. If it's not then I'll be honest with you, I'll sleep a little better at night.'

'I've done in Derby what I came to do,' he told Doyle, although his thoughts went back to what Sweaty had said. How Doyle liked abusing kids. 'Sure, yeah, you can sleep easy at night.'

'That's all I needed to know,' said Doyle.

He rang off, leaving Abbott to wonder what might have happened had his answer been different. What was the back-up plan?

'Are we all pals, then?' grinned McGregor from the front seat.

'I think so,' said Abbott, sitting back. 'We'll see, shall we?'

CHAPTER 30

'Juliet, then,' said McGregor. They had reached Richmond. They were close now, Abbott could tell. 'Let's talk about her, shall we?'

Abbott still in the back seat, feeling better now. 'I'm on tenterhooks here.'

'Not many call her Juliet.'

'OK.'

'Most people know her as Lady Norton. Name ring a bell?'

Abbott thought. 'Call it a tinkle.'

'You've heard of Sir Charles Norton, right?'

The penny dropped. 'Not the recently deceased Sir Charles Norton?'

'The one and only.'

'And these guys are involved with Doyle?' His mind was already working over what he'd learned. Thinking back to what Sweaty had told him about Chris. *'Or maybe he would have gone to London.'*

'All is about to become clear,' said McGregor.

Lady Norton's house – her mansion, to be exact – was hardly visible from the street. You might even walk past it without knowing, hardly noticing the high wall to one side of you. If you stood on the other side of the street, you could see trees and the top level of what looked like a grand home. But that was it. Nothing to advertise what was going on behind that wall.

And what was going on was gasp-inducing.

They drove in through sober, grey-painted gates that opened and closed electronically in their wake. Abbott saw two wall-mounted CCTV cameras, one of which remained trained on the gate, the other tracking the progress of their vehicle as they passed through the portal. Once inside it was as if they were in a different country, a different world altogether. Richmond, a posh and leafy suburb at the best of times, suddenly seemed almost drab, down-at-heel, and terribly urban compared to the immaculate lawns that lay on either side of a gravel drive leading to the house, sorry, mansion, which was itself modelled on the old American colonial style, complete with balustrades and a long balcony overlooking the front. To his left Abbott saw what at first glance he took to be a gardener. Indeed, the guy was holding a rake. But then, as he turned slightly, Abbott saw the butt of a pistol protruding from his waistband. Two things: Her Ladyship liked her security but she liked her security unobtrusive.

At a front door, they knocked. A man answered.

'Mr McGregor.'

'Mr Kilgore.'

So here he was. The famous Kilgore. He was a tall man, his grey hair in a crewcut, a weathered and watchful look about him, the kind of guy who could play a Nazi in an *Indiana Jones* movie. 'And this must be Alex Abbott,' he said. 'Or is it Owen Flyte?'

'I'll settle for Abbott,' he said.

'Where is she, Kilgore?' asked McGregor.

'She's round the back.'

Now Abbott found himself looking carefully at McGregor, taking note of the change that seemed to have come over him since entering the grounds of the mansion. For someone who was apparently an employee of the poor relations in the Midlands, McGregor was acting very much at home here.

They walked around the side of the house, heading, presumably, towards the gardens. 'You know Kilgore, then, do you?' asked Abbott.

'Aye, I know Kilgore.'

'Feels like you know him quite well.'

'I wouldn't say that.'

'Just that you two seem awfully familiar, that's all.'

'I suppose so.'

Coming around the side of the house, Abbott once again found himself having to restrain a gasp. Beautifully tended gardens as far as the eye could see. In the distance a man on a ride-on lawnmower was cutting an area close to the tennis courts. *You're doing a good job there, mate,* thought Abbott, and then caught sight of the assault rifle sharing the guy's lawnmower seat. Not far away, yet another guy. This one lounging by a tree, making even less pretence at work then the others. *Easy now, fellas.*

They approached where Lady Norton sat on a bench, a black Labrador half-asleep at her feet. She was ageing, and with the bearing to match. Slightly out-of-date but expensive clothes and the kind of white, carefully set hair that was probably attended to on a daily basis.

She rose and offered her hand to shake. The black Lab looked up, regarding Abbott disinterestedly.

'Mr Abbott,' she said, regaining her seat. 'How very nice to meet you.' There was something weird about her that it took Abbott a moment to put his finger on. Although she spoke with the language of a character straight out of Agatha Christie, her voice was just ever-so-slightly at odds with that, as though she were putting on airs and graces.

'That's correct,' he said.

'Can I call you Alex?'

'You may indeed. Can I call you Lady Norton? It's not every day I get to mingle with aristocracy.'

'Aristocracy,' she laughed, a slightly coarse bark. 'Hardly. A comprehensive education and a job in a bookmaker's is what got me here. My husband and I had the titles and the wealth, but we never really got a sense of belonging.'

'Well, I suppose you'd have to say that two out of three ain't bad.'

'You see? A true member of the aristocracy would have no idea that you were quoting Meat Loaf.'

Standing nearby, McGregor chuckled.

'Would you mind leaving us, Peter?' Lady Norton asked him, squinting slightly in the sun.

Peter, thought Abbott. You live and learn.

'Aye, of course,' said McGregor. 'I'll just take a lap around the park.'

Abbott watched him go before he spoke. 'It's not so long ago that Raymond Doyle told me that I was only alive because he permitted it. Sitting here next to you, I wonder whether I'm only alive because you say so.'

Lady Norton nodded. 'Well, that's partly the case. But in fact, I was also responsible for trying to have you killed. In fact, it's far more accurate to say that the only person responsible for your ongoing existence is you.'

'OK, I'll take that. How about we agree to split the difference and we move on to the bit where you tell me why I'm here?'

'God, where to start?'

'Try the beginning.'

She smiled. 'Let me tell you a little bit about my husband. It may not surprise you to learn that he was brought up the son of a working-class man in Derby. As a child he was best friends with a boy who lived two streets away, your friend Raymond Doyle. They would get into the usual kind of youthful scrapes together. You know the kind of thing, I'm sure?'

Abbott, veteran of more than a few 'youthful scrapes' himself, nodded.

'Of the two, I suppose you might say that my husband was the more entrepreneurial, the one who liked to use his head while Raymond Doyle was content to rely on his fists. The dynamic was that Charles was the brains, Raymond the brawn. Charles opened a bookmaker's. Not long after that, he opened another one. Any problems with landlords, or rival bookies or non-paying customers, then Ray Doyle would sort them on Charles's behalf. It was partly – and I do mean partly – thanks to Ray Doyle and the culture of fear that he created that Charles was able to establish a foothold in business. He went on to open casinos and theme parks. Anything with a game at its heart, Charles loved it. What drove him was a love of the game. He was a sports fanatic. A fiercely competitive card player. Any family gathering would be an opportunity for a game. It went to bone deep with him. He had no time for computer games or role-playing. He liked games with a fixed outcome. And like many games players, he enjoyed gambling on that outcome. After his death I fully expected him to spring a surprise, and I fully expected that surprise to be a game of some kind.'

'Not much of a surprise.'

'Very perceptive of you, Alex, no. And possibly that is why he went to such great lengths to ensure that we were indeed surprised.'

'And were you surprised?'

'We were surprised. Charles has decreed that the control of his company shall go to the winner of a very specific game.'

'What did he have in mind?' asked Abbott, wanting her to cut to the chase.

'What he had in mind was a fight to the death.'

Abbott barked a laugh. 'You have got to be fucking kidding me.' And yet even as he had that thought he realised that it all fitted like a glove – the picture he was building of those people – the picture of them being that they were the biggest bunch of sick twists that ever lived.

'I'm not.'

'What? You all get in a ring and duke it out, do you?'

'Not quite. It's a little more sophisticated than that.'

'In a way that somehow involves me?'

'Yes, because my husband, devious though he may have been, did not *literally* expect his nearest and dearest to fight it out to the death. Or perhaps he considered the idea and decided against it for whatever reason. His plan was that we should each choose a proxy. Presumably this is exactly what the other competitors – my family members – are doing right now. In this regard, my associate, Mr Kilgore, organised for me an ex-special forces operative by the name of Owen Flyte. When Doyle was in touch to say that you were – how shall we say? – *disrupting* things in Derby, it was Mr Kilgore's idea that we should set a little test for Owen Flyte.'

'The test being that Owen Flyte should kill me.'

Lady Norton gave a small, embarrassed cough into her handkerchief. 'Yes, yes, I'm terribly sorry about that. You must understand that there was nothing personal intended. It was merely a means to an end. I needed to ascertain Mr Flyte's skillset. The fact that you were in Derby making Doyle nervous, well, it just felt like a case of killing two birds with one stone.'

'Only . . .'

'Only . . . it did not go according to plan. I'm told that you were highly skilled in your dispatch of Mr Flyte. I'm also informed that you managed to pose as him to infiltrate Doyle's operation. And that you did this to avenge your brother. Am I right?'

'That's about the size of it.'

'You are tough. You are resourceful.'

'Meaning?'

'Meaning that in a month's time, when my husband's game to the death is staged and the members of our family each present our proxy, I would like you to be mine.'

Abbott had been expecting it, of course. Ever since she mentioned the death match idea. After all, why else would he be here? Just that the idea – the whole concept – was so incredibly outlandish. 'Where exactly is this game going to happen?' he asked.

'My husband's lawyer, Jeffrey Coombs, is soon to release that information. All we know is that it will be taking place in some kind of suitable arena in an Eastern European country.'

'And it's a battle?'

'It's a battle.'

'An actual battle? To the death. We're not talking paintball or Airsoft?'

'No, Alex. This is a game to the death. Winner takes all.'

'And just so I'm absolutely clear about this, you want me as your proxy?'

'It's the reason you're here today.'

'But if you know so much about me, then you'll know that I drink.'

'Indeed, I do know that. I also know that you managed to defeat my champion, a man I was told was among the best.'

'And that hasn't left you feeling sore?'

Again, she laughed. 'Of course it's left me feeling sore. It's left me out of pocket. But at the same time, I was under the impression that I was hiring the best and if the best can be beaten then . . .' She spread her hands. 'Besides, I'm fairly confident that any drinking issues you have you will manage to keep under control between now and the big day. The lure of £2 million is enough, surely?'

'I'm sorry – what?'

'That's right. If you win, which of course you will, because I have the utmost faith in you, you will be given the sum of £2 million. You may have this transferred into a bank account. You may have it in cash, in gold, in diamonds or in stock. The point is that if you agree to be my champion then you can be £2 million the richer. Do we have a deal?'

Abbot took a deep breath and looked away. That security guy was still lounging by the tree. Light glanced off the lenses of a pair of binoculars. The lawnmower had stopped. Abbott hadn't even noticed the sound drop, but it was now stationary and the driver stood by it, the assault rifle in his arms. Were they waiting? Waiting for a sign perhaps? Why did Abbott get the idea that anything less than complete assent would see him carted out feet first?

'Yes,' he said, at last, 'we do have a deal.' *Because I have no choice*, he thought. *And because of the money. A hell of a lot of money. A life-changing sum. The kind of money you could use to get yourself back on the tracks.* 'Peter tells me that you object to some of Doyle's business practices.'

'I've said nothing to *Peter* either way,' said Abbott, sensing that he was being tested. Sensing, again, that McGregor's position here was different to what he had previously assumed.

'Peter has a nose for these things.'

Abbott decided to go along, see where this particular road took them. 'Well, then, yes, I do.'

McGregor had returned, was lingering close by. 'Peter,' called Lady Norton, and he approached them. 'You were right,' she said to him. 'We may have found our man in more ways than one.'

CHAPTER 31

'And what exactly does that mean?' asked Abbott.

There was something going on here. Something above and beyond sounding him out for the death match.

'Doyle, Mr Abbott,' Lady Norton went on to say. 'He is a blemish. A greasy fingerprint on an otherwise gleaming window. He and his organisation are the trailer park on the edge of town. My late husband had an unfortunate case of blindness where they were concerned. Misplaced loyalty and nostalgia, no doubt. But I have no such qualms. I consider him, his wife, their awful child and all those awful nieces and nephews to be a throwback to a past I would rather forget. Whatever happens concerning the outcome of the game it is my most fervent wish that this company should move forward without Doyle hanging on to its coattails, taking our retainer, trading on our name. They are a loathsome cancer on our business, and I would like that cancer cut out.'

Abbott looked at her. 'And I'm just the man to do it?'

'You are. And you would be handsomely paid.'

'Stop Doyle? That's what you want?'

'I mean put an end to him for good,' she said.

'What sort of end?'

'Cut off the head.'

'You're asking me to kill Raymond Doyle?'

'That's exactly what I'm fucking asking you, Alex.'

Abbott couldn't help but smile as the mask dropped a little more. He was remembering what Doyle had told him about the information in the safe – information that could put Lady Norton away for a long time. All that stuff about Doyle being the trailer park on the edge of town was one thing, but what was the *real* reason she wanted him dead? Because of what he knew?

One thing was for sure. Abbott needed to see what was in that safe.

'What's in it for me?' he asked.

'Well, there is the pleasure of dismantling the people-trafficking operation,' she said, 'would you like to do that?' It struck him that she hadn't mentioned that up until now. Just killing Doyle. She continued, 'Not only that but I'm willing to pay you an extra £1 million for carrying out this job. That's £1 million on top of what you stand to earn during the game. Same as before. You can choose your currency. What do you say, Mr Abbott?'

'I'd say that I'm not entirely comfortable about being used like I'm some kind of one-stop shop for all your people-killing needs.'

'I can see that. But something also tells me that there is a little of the righteous avenger about you, Mr Abbott. Something tells me that you'd like nothing better than to strike a blow at Doyle. For me, they represent my family's last ties with a history that I would prefer to forget. Cut Doyle away from the Nortons and my family can be legitimate for perhaps the first time.'

'You have all this,' he gestured. 'You have a title. You still want to be legitimate?'

'I refer you to our previous conversation.'

'OK, but you know that ordering a hit isn't exactly "going legitimate"?'

'A last unfortunate visit to the dark side before the new dawn.'

'I'll need time.'

'Of course. Take as much as you need. Within reason, of course.'

'I mean that I won't be able to return to work. Doyle is going to wonder what's going on.'

'We'll smooth things over with Doyle,' said Lady Norton. 'We brought you into his orbit and now we're having you back, simple as that.'

Abbott looked away. 'Don't think I've ever been poached before. Fried a few times. Scrambled lots.' He smiled. 'But never poached.'

'Will you be going back to Derby?'

'Not right away. There are things I need to do first.'

'Such as?'

'Getting a team together.'

'Actually, on second thoughts . . .' She held up her hands. 'I don't need or want to know how you intend to go about it.'

'Eminently sensible.'

'In business you learn to let people get on with what they're best at.' She looked across at him. 'So anyway, I take it this is a yes?'

Abbott looked over the rolling lawns. Whatever Lady Norton's motives – and they were surely far more complicated and murky than she was letting on – there was indeed that one very compelling motive where Abbott was concerned: Doyle – the organisation that had spawned Sweaty and Jason Scutter, the pondlife who had tried to kidnap his brother.

Those people would be stopped, and it would be Abbott's finger on the trigger.

'Yes,' he told her. Their eyes met, and Abbott thought, *And when I'm done with Doyle, I'm coming for you.*

CHAPTER 32

They were on the M1 when Abbott broached the subject with McGregor.

'So, today seems to be one for telling the truth. How about you tell me about your relationship with Her Ladyship back there?'

McGregor arched an eyebrow. 'I don't know what you're thinking, pal, but it's not that.'

'You're an employee?'

'Well, you already knew that.'

'Something tells me that being an employee of Lady Norton and being an employee of Ray Doyle are two very different things. Something also tells me that you're much more an employee of her then you are of him. Would I be right about that?'

'Aye, you would,' agreed McGregor, nodding, smiling. His hair was more than usually plastered to his forehead and Abbott wondered if the oft-present smile was in fact a cover for a case of nerves. 'The truth is that it's me who's been reporting back to her. For what it's worth, I'm also the reason that you could very soon be a rich man.'

'According to her, I'd achieve that myself.'

'No, I meant hitting Doyle.' He jabbed a finger at his own chest. 'It was me who put that idea into her head. "We've got the perfect man for the job already inside the operation," that's what I told her.'

Abbott let out a huge sigh. 'What is it with you lot constantly telling me that I'm part of some operation?'

'You know what I mean, Abbott.'

'You seem fairly confident that I'm going to fall into line on this.'

McGregor glanced across the seats at him. 'Come on, Abbott. You can't tell me that you haven't been thinking about your brother. It's why you're here, isn't it? The other night when you wasted Sweaty, it wasn't just about taking him out of the picture, was it? You wanted the whole operation shut down. That's why you called the cops on us. If you just left it at plugging Sweaty then maybe you could have maintained your cover, but you didn't, did you? You wanted to deal a death blow.'

'Maybe.'

'This is your chance to do it. Doyle thinks you're on board. I'll be reporting back to him, pouring all kinds of honey in his ear. He already thinks that he's indispensable to Lady Norton. He won't suspect a thing.'

Indispensable? thought Abbott. But it wasn't that, was it? It was something else. Thinking once again of the safe.

'You're going to make sure of it.'

'Aye, I am.'

'She must be paying you a lot.'

'Aye, she does. But it's worth it to her to have someone

looking out for her interests, keeping an eye on things, you know what I mean? To her, Doyle's like a dog that needs constant supervision.'

'And now she wants to put him down.'

'You gonna lose sleep over that, are you?'

'Just her, is it?'

'What do you mean?'

'What about the rest of the family she's talking about? Who are they anyway?'

'Try Google. There aren't that many of them but for a small bunch they're hardly what you'd call close-knit. There are no alliances there, I can tell you. Well, none that I know about anyway. Naw, I work for Lady Norton and that's it.'

'That really is it? You're up for hire to the highest bidder?'

'That go against your principles, does it?'

'I can't say that it does,' lied Abbott. He felt dirty. As though he wanted to wash. Worse than any shame-filled hangover. He found himself yearning for the pragmatic voice of Cuckoo, the caring concern of Tess.

But then, no.

Pull yourself together.

He had a job to do.

'Look, pal,' sighed McGregor. 'I've got no loyalty to Doyle. The man's a scumbag. Yes, it could be that I'm a scumbag, too, but on a scumbag scale of one to ten, you've got Doyle at ten and then, much lower down, you got me. I know I'm not exactly contributing to the overall sum of human happiness, but I do what I have to do. I don't want you to hate me, Abbott.'

Too late, thought Abbott, but said, 'Why do you suppose she's so keen that Doyle dies?'

'I suppose because she wants to make sure that he can't come back after her. There's no love lost between those two, I can tell you. As far as I can tell, they used to tolerate each other because of Sir Charles, but now he's no longer in the picture . . .'

'That right, is it?' said Abbott thoughtfully. And it could be right, he mused, staring out of the window. But then there were all sorts of reasons that you might want somebody out of the picture permanently. Maybe because you want to shut them up.

'After all,' continued McGregor, 'we're about to smash them, aren't we? Doyle?'

'I am. You're going to stay well out of the way.'

'Then you need to tell me when you plan to do it.'

'I'll tell you when the time comes.'

'Are you going to hit his house?'

'Ray Doyle's got a wife and a kid. I'm not taking the fight to his house. There'll be no families involved.'

From the corner of his eye, he saw McGregor pull a face but couldn't be bothered to take issue with it. Besides which, he thought, the main thing was to make sure that all the trafficked children were safe. He thought back to his time in Thailand, realising that he knew exactly who he needed on this job. 'I'm going to be hitting them where they really live. We'll be taking the fight to the Kemptown factory.'

CHAPTER 33

At Chicksands, Abbott and Cuckoo relaxed on the same bench. A little colder than they had been on the last occasion they met but otherwise unchanged. *Almost* unchanged.

'Looks as though you're still losing weight,' said Abbott, jerking a thumb towards where Cuckoo's belly was – or had been.

'You know Fi. When she gets the bit between her teeth.'

'Or the salad in this case.'

'Yeah. There's a lot of salad.'

'Diets tend to involve salad.'

'Apart from yours, that tend to involve a lot of beer, wine and spirits, although, I've got to say, that was a cheap crack because correct me if I'm wrong, you've either drastically cut down or cut it out altogether.'

'Oh yeah,' preened Abbott, 'and what makes you say that, then?'

'Three things. One, you don't clink when you walk. Two, you don't smell like a brewery. Three, and most important, you actually look well for a change. Almost healthy.'

'Well, you're right, I haven't touched a drop since . . .' He cringed internally to think of the night at Tess's house. 'Well, for a while.'

'How does it feel?'

'It feels OK, no, better than OK. It feels like being out from under its grip, and every day I tell myself that I should reward myself with a drink; every day I tell myself that I don't really have a problem, because if I did then I wouldn't be able to give it up so easily.'

'Has it been easy?'

'Well, no, not actually *easy*, as such. But it hasn't been that hard either. I was lucky. I didn't have withdrawal. Or not the sort where you end up in A&E; not the sort where you hallucinate spiders wandering across your ceiling. I had headaches and sleeplessness and I still have cravings, and I have that weird sneaky voice that goes, "Hey, you haven't drunk for a while, why not reward yourself with a drink?" Or "Hey, you've hit reset. You're a normal drinker now, why not just try one or two drinks? Because now you can moderate!" But if you can recognise the cravings and ignore the voice, if you can play the tape forward then you can get through it. What's the alternative? You either keep killing yourself or you don't. And I don't think it's what Nathan would have wanted, do you? Do you think he would have wanted his dad to drink himself to death in a B&B in Finchley? I don't.'

'Well, I'm pleased for you, mate.'

'Cheers.'

A little throat-clearing followed. A pause before continuing. 'So, I have news for you,' said Cuckoo.

'Ditto.'

'Well, OK, you go first.'

So Abbott told Cuckoo everything he'd learned so far. All about the set-up in Derby. About Doyle's links with Sir Charles Norton. He told him what Sweaty had said – how Chris might have ended up 'in London'. He told him that Doyle apparently had some dirt on the Nortons hidden in his safe. What he didn't say, what he held back, was that he had been hired by Lady Norton. Not yet.

Cuckoo was nodding. 'None of that came as much of a surprise to you,' said Abbott.

'No. Partly my news was that I'd put the names you gave me – Juliet and Kilgore – with the Nortons and put them together with Doyle. Doyle, he barely blips on the radar. But the Nortons – the Nortons are different. Since his death the grapevine's been buzzing and there are fairly credible rumours of connections within the government and security forces.'

'Like what?'

'Contracts. Favours for favours. You scratch my back and I'll let you build your super-casino. That kind of thing. But it is just rumour, Abbott. Nothing on any file. Little more than water cooler gossip. What was most interesting from my point of view was that there were flags attached to any file involving the Nortons.'

'Flags? What does that mean?'

'It means that if anybody is nosing around then it triggers an alert. These flags tend to occur only on cases that apply to ultra-sensitive material. So that departments within departments will be informed if somebody is making enquiries.'

'Does that mean they know you've been poking around?'

'No, it doesn't. Because I know how to circumvent the flags.

I also know how to tell if they've been triggered at any time in the recent past, and in this case, they have.'

'Can you find out who triggered it?'

'It means going a layer beyond my security clearance, but I can call in a favour, yes.'

'Do it . . . please.'

'You think that . . . what? The Nortons were into the child abuse?'

'I'm keeping an open mind. But Charles and Ray Doyle came up together. Maybe they shared certain proclivities. And if they're being protected at the level you suggest then maybe it goes up as well as down.'

'People have been trying to put the finger on some kind of high-ranking establishment abuse network since as long as I can remember, Abbott. What are the chances that you're just going to stumble on it like this?'

'Why must there be one? Why not several?'

'OK, but this all started with your brother's death. Scutter's dead. Sweaty's dead. Is it not time to pull out?'

'And leave it to the authorities? How much good do you think that will do, based on what you know so far?'

'No, just leave it.'

Abbott threw Cuckoo a look. A *shame on you* look. 'No, can't do that, mate,' he said. 'I'm taking down the Doyles. And then I'm taking down whoever else is involved.'

'Oh, you are, are you? "Taking down Doyle"? And how do you plan to do that, Rambo?'

Abbott grinned.

And then he told Cuckoo about the Lady Norton deal.

Both of them.

'You have got to be fucking kidding me,' said Cuckoo.

'My words exactly. But there you have it. I literally have a mandate to take down Doyle. I even have the money to pay for the men I need to do it. Not just one Rambo. Four of the fuckers. And on that note . . .'

He handed over a scrap of paper. 'Three SF operators I used to work with. Ward runs a garden centre somewhere down south, in Kent, I think. Miller's a personal trainer. Tom Brace is still in the game. A mercenary, as far as I know. Think you can do that? I don't suppose any of them have gone off-grid. Well, maybe Tom Brace.'

'I can find them for you,' said Cuckoo. 'And then?'

'If I'm right, and if the Nortons are as dirty as I think, then them next.'

'You've said yourself that they're untouchable.'

'I'm thinking of something a bit better, a lot more permanent.'

'You're planning on hunting them down?'

'Could do that. Or maybe I could get at them when they're all in one place.'

'Wait. You're not going to take part in their game?'

'Where else can I get all the Nortons together somewhere I'll be armed? Where there will already be bullets flying? You've said yourself that they're very rarely even in the same country together, let alone the same place.'

'You're walking into the lion's den.'

'I'm already in the lion's den. And anyway, I'm one of the lions, mate.'

'Are you telling me that? Or are you trying to tell yourself?'

CHAPTER 34

'French Foreign Legion, sir,' said Kennedy.

Kennedy was dressed in his regulation polo shirt and pressed jeans. His boss, Ross Norton, wore baggy surf shorts and a similarly outsized T-shirt. He trailed behind Kennedy like a naughty school kid reluctantly taken on holiday by his parents. He was hungover, having partied into the early hours, and was very keen on banishing that hangover by working on another one. The last place he wanted to be was anywhere that featured loud bangs, which meant that the last place he wanted to be was at this shooting range in Zurich. However, Kennedy had insisted, and Kennedy, of course, could be very insistent indeed.

The bangs were getting louder, making Norton wince. At the same time, he was wondering about the significance of the words 'French Foreign Legion'. Presumably, since it involved loud bangs and shooting, this was something to do with his late father's contest, which, while admittedly was diverting fun and the essence of an excellent future anecdote, wasn't, if he was being totally honest with himself, something that he was taking especially seriously.

Ross wanted to win, of course he did. But at the same time there was something in him, something not in his nature, but rather in his nurture, that was programmed to accept loss. A legacy, no doubt, of the family games that he had grown up playing. Games that were always, but always, characterised by his grandfather's relentless competitiveness. The Nortons were not a family that might go easy on the little ones or let them win in order to build their self-esteem. A generation removed, Ross and Simon grew accustomed to being on the losing side. Theirs was a childhood characterised by loss. An upbringing in which they were constantly reminded of the shame of losing, where coming second was second best while at the same time almost constantly placed in that position. One-on-one, Ross would beat his little brother at whatever games they played, whether it had been football or tennis in the garden, or KerPlunk in the playroom, so at least Ross had that.

Simon? Simon never stood a chance.

No wonder he had turned out the way he had.

In short, Ross had resigned himself to being a makeweight. Just on board to boost the numbers. The winner would most likely be his grandmother or his mother, definitely not him or his brother. And anyway, he had his proxy, his avatar, his champion. Trent Saunders, who Kennedy had informed him was a most capable competitor. Even if Ross didn't win, then he would surely compete with flair.

All of which still begged the question, what was he doing having his headache so mercilessly pummelled in this Zurich shooting range?

They reached an area where ear defenders hung on pegs

and Kennedy wordlessly handed a pair to Norton, who snatched at them gratefully, only to find they made hardly any difference.

'This way, sir,' said Kennedy.

'What do you mean, the French Foreign Legion?' Norton demanded to know.

'I mean, the man we are about to see was trained by the French Foreign Legion.' Kennedy looked at him. 'That makes him among the best in the world, sir,' he said impatiently.

Ross Norton shrugged. By now they had reached an observation gallery where Ross was grateful to take a seat, barely listening as Kennedy talked him through the accuracy of the marksmanship below.

'His name is Scolar,' Kennedy explained.

'I'm very pleased to hear it, Kennedy, but I thought we had already chosen our man. Trent Saunders. Him. He's one of the best, you told me.'

Ross reared back a little when Kennedy turned to him, Kennedy's previous air of irritation having given way to something approaching outright anger. His teeth were bared. His baldness shone. 'As usual, I am trying to help you, and as usual, you are being a snivelling little shit in return.'

'All right, all right,' replied Ross, shrinking away.

'Your grandfather loved gaming. But, more than anything, he loved to stack the odds in his favour. A fan of sports he may have been. Sportsmanlike, however, he very much was not.'

'Are you saying my grandfather was a cheat?'

'Of course he was a fucking cheat, you idiot. Your grandfather never did a straight or honest thing in his life.'

'Christ, you do store things up, don't you?'

'I've often thought that you could have done with storing a few more things up yourself,' said Kennedy. 'Sir.'

'And so I take it this trip is aimed at trying to restore my competitive edge? You're hoping that comparing one with the other will give me a thirst for winning, is that it? I'm supposed to choose between Trent and this Scolar?'

'You haven't been listening to what I've been saying, have you, sir?' said Kennedy.

Ross Norton rubbed his head. 'Give me a break, will you?'

From below the firing had stopped at last. 'Come on,' said Kennedy, 'let's go and talk to Scolar.'

At that moment Kennedy's phone rang and he stood, excusing himself from the observation gallery to take the call. Moments later, he returned.

'I'm terribly sorry, sir, but I have some bad news.'

Ross, who had been dreaming of a drink, looked up at him. 'Go on.'

'It's your brother, Simon, sir. He's been found dead of a heroin overdose.'

CHAPTER 35

So this is what a garden centre in Whitstable looks like, thought Abbott, as he stepped into a greenhouse. He had gone into the shop first, where the air was cooler. 'I'm looking for the owner, Mr Ward,' he had said, gazing around at displays of plant pots, artisan chocolate and craft beer and finding it difficult to reconcile the image he had of Freddie Ward, SF operator and one of the best explosives men he had ever worked with, even being *in* here, let alone owning the place.

'You're not Alex Abbott, are you?' said the lad behind the till. And the penny dropped. Abbott looked hard at him.

'You're his son, are you?' said Abbott.

The kid had stood and offered his hand to shake, but even so, his eyes were wary. 'The name's Graham,' he said. 'And Dad's expecting you but . . . before I show you the way, do you mind telling me what you want with him?'

So polite. So unassuming. Freddie Ward's kid all right.

'It's a bit of business,' said Abbott.

'But something tells me it's not in the garden centre line.'

'No, you'd be right about that.'

'If my mother was here, she would probably tell you to

sling your hook, you know.' The kid smiled like he wanted to offset being rude but wanting to honour his mum at the same time. Abbott's heart went out to him to such an extent that he considered turning on his heel and leaving there and then – leaving Freddie Ward to a new life that he fully deserved to live to the full.

Instead, he said, 'So your mum? She's . . .' He had never met Ward's wife and was only vaguely aware he even had one. It wasn't like he had never been interested. Just that they didn't talk about that kind of thing. You talked about the job. You talked about who was doing what, where and with whom. You talked about music and football and weaponry. But what you didn't really talk about was home. Talking about home jinxed it. Talking about home brought chinks into your armour.

'She passed on a couple of years ago. It's been hard for us since then.'

'I'm sorry.'

'That's all right,' said Graham. 'Thank you. The thing is, I don't know for sure, but I think out of the two of us, Dad's taken it worse somehow. I think that, well, look, what I'm trying to say is that if you're here for any other reason than buying garden equipment, then I can't pretend that I'm pleased to see you. But on the other hand, maybe a taste of the old life is what he needs.'

'I see.'

'And is that it? Is that why you're here?'

'Look, Graham, you seem like a great kid, but I can't say any more.'

'OK,' said Graham. 'He's in the greenhouses. Go through the shop and out the back you'll find them. Dad says the heating there reminds him of the Middle East. You should feel right at home.'

Graham was right. Strolling through the first greenhouse, Abbott stripped off his overshirt, thinking how long it had been since he last saw Ward. Would he even recognise him? A guy in overalls pushed a wheelbarrow past him. 'Is Ward about?' he asked.

'Back there.'

Abbott went on until at the far end of the last greenhouse, he found Ward, who was standing there, hands on his overalled hips, staring out of the window. A droplet of perspiration ran down his temple.

'Ward,' said Abbott.

'Abbott,' said Ward, turning slowly. 'You're early, aren't you?' He checked his watch. 'Oh, sorry, no, you're not early.'

'Well, I think I've seen it all now,' said Abbott as the two of them turned and began to walk together. 'I've never known any explosives expert get sloppy with their timings, especially not the legend that is Freddie Ward.'

'Well, mate, quite a lot has changed, I'm afraid.'

'Yeah, and I heard the reason why,' said Abbott.

'You spoke to Graham, then?'

'He's a good kid.'

'You had one yourself, didn't you? I'm sorry, I forget the name. I mean, I'm not sure I ever really knew it.'

'His name was Nathan.'

Ward looked up sharply at the use of the past tense. 'I see,' he said. 'I'm sorry.'

'Yeah, it happened in Iraq but any more than that I don't want to say. Put it this way, I dearly wish we had been running a garden centre together. Even if he isn't so sure that it's what you want.'

'Oh yes? What did Graham say about that, then?'

'That maybe his dad misses the old life.'

'Ha ha, yeah. One minute you're blowing things up in the Middle East, the next you're selling water features in Middle England.' Ward sighed. 'Look, I know what the right answer is. I'm supposed to tell you that I've never been happier. Never felt more content. And if you came here two years ago, when Lou was alive, then I'd have told you that, and it would have been the truth. Now, I'm not so sure. Put it this way, when you got in touch my first thought was that you needed me for a job. And my first thought after that was that I *hoped* you did.'

'Well, I do,' said Abbott. 'It's a job that requires your skill set. Or will, if everything goes to plan.'

Ward nodded. 'Then I'm in.'

'One thing, though,' said Abbott.

'Yes?'

'I'm not taking you into any danger. You do what you do best and stay away from any bullets, OK? I'm not having Graham be orphaned.'

'So there's real risk, is there?'

'This isn't some soft private security gig.'

'OK, I'm interested. You got my attention. Give me a figure.'

'The job is worth a million. It's a million for what will be preparation then a night's work. A million to be split between you, Miller and Brace, provided they also agree to sign up.'

'What about you? What do you stand to gain?'

'Me? For me this is personal.'

CHAPTER 36

'Miller, are you wearing fake tan, mate?'

It struck Abbott that his old team was a group of guys he knew well enough to trust them with his life and knew that they could trust him with theirs in return. And yet, he had never really experienced the civilian version of them. Freddie Ward's passion for gardening, for example, had come as something of a surprise, and while he had always known that Miller was a little on the vain side – you couldn't hide a thing like that, even in the field – he hadn't realised how evolved it was.

Abbott looked around. Miller's gym – called, appropriately, The Mill – was hidden away in a corner of North London. None of your Holmes Place. This a proper, old-style joint, just short of a boxing gym. But, although it had all the hallmarks of a place where grown men spent hours perspiring heavily – in other words, it reeked – it was well-kept, tidy, properly maintained.

Like its owner. Miller had always been buff, but never quite as toned and sculpted as he was now. And then, yes, there was the question of the fake tan. Abbott suspected that there was quite a bit of depilation involved in the current upkeep of Miller, too. Back, sack and crack, all that.

Still, aside from all that, the same Miller.

Ward had travelled with Abbott, who had raised a surprised eyebrow when he turned up wearing the same overalls he'd been wearing for work. Abbott thought it diplomatic to say nothing, but standing here with Ward in his overalls and Miller looking like one of The Chippendales, it struck him what a strange and eccentric bunch they had always been and clearly still were.

Miller had turfed out the last of the customers and closed up for the evening. They stood in the semi-darkness, surrounded by gym equipment, regarding each other awkwardly. Three men who had been through so much together. Who had killed and seen comrades die before them. Who had saved lives and taken them.

'Ward said something about a job,' said Miller.

'If you're up for it,' said Abbott. 'If you're not,' he lifted his head and looked around, 'because you've clearly got a nice thing going here, then I'll quite understand.'

'Tell him what it's worth,' said Ward. Miller licked his lips when Abbott revealed the figure.

'When do we get to hear the details?' asked Miller.

'If you're on board, then the next step is to get into touch with Tom Brace.'

'This isn't a job the three of us could handle?' said Miller.

'Maybe so, maybe not,' said Abbott, 'but I don't plan to risk it. We did jobs together as a four. Call me superstitious. Call me loyal. Call me somebody who wants the best sniper I've ever worked with at my back. But, yes, I don't want to proceed without Tom.'

'Then you're in luck.' The voice came from the shadows and was followed by the man himself. Tom Brace, who appeared from the dark apparently having lost none of the stealth for which he was famed.

Abbott's eyes travelled from Ward, who shrugged *nothing to do with me*, to Miller, who smiled. Abbott wasn't sure how he felt. If it was a test then, sure, he'd passed it with a show of loyalty. How he felt about having that loyalty tested, and therefore questioned, was another matter.

Clearly his thoughts were displayed for all to see, Brace coming forward to take him by the shoulders. 'Don't read anything into it, Abbott,' he said. He spoke as he always spoke. Quietly. A surgeon mid-operation. 'We just thought it would be a laugh to see your face, that's all. You wouldn't have been asking for me if you didn't want me, right? Nobody ever doubted you, dude.'

Abbott calmed himself a little. Trust was needed. Of course it was.

Where both Miller and Ward had gone on to non-military careers, Abbott and Brace had stayed with the life. Abbott in security, plying his trade in the Middle East and then in Singapore. Prior to the trouble with Nathan, that was. While Brace had become a gun for hire, working wherever the money took him. Not always for the 'right' people, it had to be said. But then, that was the nature of the beast. 'We're going up against traffickers,' Abbott told him. Brace had always nurtured a special disgust for them. One thing Abbott could count on was that.

The guys caught up. Abbott offering a truncated, condensed version of his life since they last saw one another. He accepted their condolences over the death of Nathan, just about managing to keep his emotions under control.

'A little birdie told me that you were drinking,' said Brace. 'I mean, you always liked a pint. We all did. But . . .' His eyes went to Miller and Ward, who were both watching Abbott's response carefully. Brace wore a pained expression, as though he was worried he might have gone too far.

'No, no, it's OK,' said Abbott, addressing them all. 'You're right to ask. I'd do the same in your position. No way you want somebody on the team who's likely to let you down. But you're going to have to take my word for it that, for the time being at least, I'm off it. Just like in the old days. When you hear what I have to tell you, you'll understand.'

He outlined the job, giving scant detail. They nodded, saying little.

'What's the first step?' asked Miller.

'First, equipment,' said Abbott. He looked to Brace as the team member who was still in the game and could lay his hands on what they needed.

'We're going to need NVGs, as well as large dems charges, smaller door charges, solid shot shotgun to take out door hinges and locks in addition to the charges. We'll need shock tube and detonators. Zip ties. And of course we'll need weapons. As well as my sidearm, I'd like an FN Scar.'

After the AR-15, the FN Scar heavy and light was the special forces' favoured weapon. Abbott knew that Brace favoured the SSR – sniper support rifle – which was a marksman version. If Abbott's previous experience of the men was anything to go by, then Ward would choose the Scar, too, while Miller would opt for the trusty AR-15. They wouldn't want to make their decision yet, though.

'What's our objective?'

Abbott nodded approvingly. Just by asking that question, Ward was proving that his head was fully in the game. After the plan, the most important aspect of any operation was keeping that objective in mind. The mission is the goal. And the mission, as he told them, was to infiltrate the camp, locate and terminate Doyle, release the children and extract to safety, neutralising as many of the enemy as possible. That was the mission. The reason that they needed to keep that mission in their heads was because when an operation goes noisy, it needs to follow a process. It's not about feelings or emotions. It's about going into your one metre square, focusing on your immediate environment and moving towards your objectives.

Which was to release the children. Terminate Doyle.

The plan. 'Tom, you're providing sniper coverage.'

'Of course.'

'Ward . . . Sorry, bro, but you're on your own. You'll be responsible for setting the charges. Miller, you'll be my number two. We'll clear the building and locate Doyle. Once that's happened, we can get the kids extracted. Tom, you make sure to take out any sentries and obvious X-rays trying to escape. That, gentlemen, is our DA plan.'

Any operation has two plans. First of all, a Deliberate Action plan, known as the DA, which was the preferred method of execution, in which you commanded the incursion, controlled the situation and, most importantly, decided when it got noisy.

In addition to your DA, you had an Immediate Action plan,

known as an IA. This was for when things had not gone to plan. For when the operation had turned noisy on you ahead of the Deliberate Action plan. It was, in effect, a contingency plan for when things went wrong.

And things always, but always went wrong. No plan survives first contact.

'OK,' said Brace to Abbott, 'what can you tell us about the set-up?'

Abbott told them everything he had learned from his time as a Doyle employee. The sentries, not an especially disciplined rota. The inner sanctum office where on the night of the incursion Doyle would no doubt be located, and the fact that most nights he stayed in the office until at least 7pm, which was when the incursion would take place, darkness having fallen at least an hour earlier. How Cynthia Doyle was often present on a Tuesday and a Friday, when she would turn up with their son, Finn.

'For that reason we'll avoid Tuesday and Friday,' Abbott told the men. 'I want no family members involved in this. Add that to your list of objectives, please. No innocents are to die. Anybody armed then brass 'em up. Anybody else, if they're obviously trafficked children then they're to be extracted. Any persons that you have doubts about, zip-tie them and we'll deal with them before we blow the place. Here . . .' He'd sketched a plan of the Kemptown site, pointing out where sentries might be expected to appear. 'This room here,' he indicated, 'is where the men tend to hang out in the evening. Here,' he moved his finger, 'this is the inner sanctum. This is the site of objective number two. It's where I expect to find Doyle. I anticipate that by the time we reach it, things will have got noisy, thus we can expect Doyle to barricade himself inside. Door is solid, but hinges are on the outside. I can take them out with the charges and use the shotgun as a back-up if necessary.'

'Blow the door, but unless it peels clean, they'll be waiting for us,' said Miller.

'But we know what to do about that, don't we, Ward?'

'Distraction charge?' said Ward.

'Exactly what I'm thinking. If you can set a charge in the car park here, and then blow it, make it loud and pretty, they'll be turned to the window wanting to know what's going on, at which point we'll blow the door, get in the room and take out any X-rays that stand in our way.' He looked at Ward. 'Do you think you can do that?'

'Oh yes.'

'And after that, the dems charges. I want the whole complex totalled by the time we leave. We're sending a message here. Nobody else is going to move in there and take over the operation.'

'It's why I'm here,' said Ward. 'Who's carrying out the CTR?'

The CTR, a Close Target Recce, would be carried out during the planning phase. Abbott already knew the complex well, but experience taught him that you bypassed a CTR at your peril. He didn't dare carry it out himself, instead entrusting it to Ward and Miller while Brace sourced the equipment.

A week later, the team was based in the Welcome Break hotel on the A50 in Derby, where they met in Ward's room and the two operators reported back on the results of the CTR, the results being that there was an increased presence at the factory. More activity than Abbott had suggested. More men on site. More cars coming and going and, perhaps most disquieting of all, more kids. More civilians.

Abbott called McGregor.

'What's going on?' he asked.

'Let's meet,' he was told, and a couple of hours after that they were in a greasy spoon.

'Problem?' Abbott took a sip of tea, set the mug down with a grimace and decided to make it his first and last sip of tea in this particular establishment. Funny, he thought. Time was he would have insisted on meeting in a pub, no matter how dangerous it was.

'Problem? You could say that,' exploded McGregor and then remembered to keep his voice down, leaning forward and keeping his voice low. 'Right now, Doyle thinks you're something close to the devil. He doesn't like the fact that you went to see Lady Norton. He doesn't like that you haven't turned up back for work to give him the skinny on what went on. He is only just – and I mean only fuckin' *just* – buying my story that I know nothing. I tell you, I am *this far* from having my fingernails pulled out. Cynthia's in his ear, giving it all that. He's just getting more and more paranoid.'

'According to Her Ladyship, Kilgore was going to put him back in his box.'

'He's only just in his box and whatever Kilgore's said to him it's done nothing to put his mind at rest. He is convinced that forces are lining up against him.'

'Well then, he's not so stupid, is he?' said Abbott ruefully, at which McGregor pulled a face.

'What are you going to do?'

'Nothing. We're going to proceed according to the plan.

Why is he putting children on site? What good are they at Kemptown?' Abbott thought of the little cleaner girl, but other than that . . .?

'He's talking about some kind of human shield.'

'Jesus.' Abbott shook his head. 'And what about The Freemasons? Has that shut down?'

'Since you wasted Sweaty, you mean? No, I'm afraid not, pal. You remember the barman, the guy with the dreads? He's in charge now. Mind you, they scaled it down. Some of the kids from there are the ones they brought into Kemptown.'

'The Polish couple's kid?'

'Yeah, he's there, too.'

Abbott looked across the table at him, eyes blazing. 'You feel proud of yourself for that, do you?'

McGregor blazed back. 'Do you? Listen, don't go getting any wrong ideas. I'm not the avenging angel in this scenario. I'm no angel at all. My heart is black and it's broken. I've thrown my lot in with Juliet Norton because she pays me more and quite frankly, I'd rather be based at a mansion in Richmond than a shithole factory in Derby. That's it. That really is it. You carry on with your pure motives and if that puts us on the same side then so be it. I've seen what you can do, and I'd much rather be with you than against you.'

Abbott looked at him, thinking, *You're in this up to your fucking eyeballs, aren't you?* But said nothing. Keeping his cards close to his chest.

'Any idea when you're going to do it?'

'You asking for me or because Her Royal Highness wants to know?'

'How about a bit of both?'

'Well, in that case, you both need to remember that I'm not in the habit of sharing status reports.'

'So you're not gonna tell me when you plan to move?'

'I still don't know. And even if I did know, no, I probably wouldn't be telling you when I plan to move. We operate on a need-to-know basis, and I'll decide when you need to know.'

'OK, but here's something that *you* need to know. Doyle's levels of paranoia are going through the roof. He's called on a bunch of guys from Manchester. He wants a larger force down here. They're arriving at the weekend. Does that make any difference to your thinking?'

It did. It meant that Abbott had to move Thursday night latest. 'He didn't like having his hand forced, but on the other side of the coin maybe it was for the best. Perhaps he had been prevaricating, holding off.

'When are we going? When are we going?' Brace was saying that. Impatient.

'I've got a gym to run.' This from Miller.

Ward: 'Those patio sets aren't going to sell themselves, you know.'

The boys wanting him to go. McGregor clearly wanting him to go.

Whatever. None of that really mattered. What mattered was the operation. The objective. And yes, he had to admit that they were as ready as they would ever be. He had to admit that it was time to move.

He told the lads. 'Operation is go for tomorrow.'

He spoke to McGregor again. 'It's tonight.'

'Tonight. OK.'

'Is there any way we can be sure that Cynthia will be absent?'

'I can do my best to find out her movements.'

'Do that. And at the same time, make sure that you're as far away as possible.'

'Will do.'

'Oh, and McGregor? We'll be needing the money as soon as the job is over. Is that clear? I'll need it splitting three ways and transferring to three account numbers that I'll provide to you.'

'I'll be in touch with Kilgore and see that it's done.'

'Excellent. I'll be seeing you, McGregor.'

And I'll deal with you later.

CHAPTER 37

'Mrs Doyle?'

'McGregor. What do you want?'

'Just that me and the lads are planning a bit of a surprise for the boss man tonight, for the anniversary like.'

'What anniversary is that, then?'

'You remember when we took over the drugs business from Kemp?'

'No, not really. Why?'

'Well, that's the anniversary.'

'What? And we're celebrating that, are we?'

'We are now, aye. Me and the boys thought it would be good to mark the boss man's achievement. We are having a little get-together. It'd be great to see you and the boy here for, say, about seven o'clock tonight just before he clocks off for the night?'

'Are you sure about this? Ray doesn't normally go in for this sort of thing.'

'Aye, I'm sure. So we'll see you there?'

'Yes, McGregor. I'll see you there.'

CHAPTER 38

Abbott stole a van and changed the plates. He returned to the Welcome Break, parked up and called Ward. 'I'm in the car park,' he said.

'Roger that. I'll pass the message along.'

Ward was the first to appear. He climbed into the passenger seat of the van and then over the seats into the rear, where he unzipped the holdall to reveal the all-too-familiar black Nomex overalls as well as his chest rig full of the necessary toys for the job: ammo, flash bangs, smoke and a radio with throat mic and earpiece. Last but not least, a balaclava, gloves and NVGs.

From his holdall he took his FN-Scar with suppressor and laser dot sight and began to complete the assembly. Abbott watched him in the mirror, reflecting on how Ward had shed his garden centre, almost farmer-like skin, to become an SF operator again.

Ward pulled on the overalls, followed by the chest rig and placed his balaclava under the flap of one of his ammo pouches, his black Nomex gloves under another, easily accessible. Finally, he threw on his jacket to cover up the fact he was about to unleash hell in the dark of the night. Not a word was exchanged, no thought required. There was no need.

As Ward did that, Miller had appeared from the entranceway of the hotel. Like Ward he was dressed casually, but after clambering into the van began the same drill, prepping so that as soon as they were in position, the operation could begin.

Third came Brace. Again the same routine. But this time, as soon as Tom was in the van, Abbott set off, bypassing Derby itself, going straight to the outskirts and to the industrial estates. He had checked the van, confirmed that all the lights were working and that the tyres were in good order even before he nicked it. Now, driving, he kept to the speed limits, ensuring he did nothing to attract attention.

They drove along the dual carriageway, past the industrial estates and car dealerships and then past the approach road to Kemptown. There, Abbott got a quick visual, the barrier set-up there as always, two vans parked back-to-back, the wasteland on either side.

Further along, they took an exit off the dual carriageway, conducted a full circuit at the roundabout before taking a left, observing to see if any vehicles followed the same manoeuvre, then pulled off onto a service road where a sign said, 'Not Suitable for Motor Vehicles'. Further down was a gate that, two days ago, Ward and Miller had secured with a chain and a padlock. Abbott stopped the van, Ward and Miller disembarked, Ward confirming that the chain hadn't been tampered with and checking that the stick they'd placed in the tracks wasn't broken.

'Clear?' asked Abbott when they returned.

'Apart from us, not a soul has been here.'

'Excellent.'

They drove through, set a sensor on the gate behind them and then moved on until they reached the designated area, a derelict building identified by Ward and Miller during the CTR phase. It had once been some kind of industrial lock-up but was now overgrown with vegetation. An elevated position that overlooked the Kemptown compound, that was hidden from the road and not covered by CCTV. Close enough for Brace to work his magic, for full comms coverage but far away enough not to attract attention from the Doyle crew. All that and a flat roof.

They drove the van inside, got out and made their way up the metal stairway to the roof. Brace took his sniper rifle with its NV scope and positioned himself in the pre-determined location giving the best field of view. Abbott placed his throat mic on and then attached a tactical comms headset, 'All call signs radio check.'

'Mike One, good to me, over.'

'Tango One, good to me over. Whiskey One, good to me, over.'

'All call signs, this is Alpha, good to me, out.'

Communication, they all knew, was the lifeblood of mission success.

The others did the same, tested the link. The voices in his ear sounded familiar and intimate and took him back to his time in SF so that for a second it was like slipping into a warm bath, a world in which he felt comfortable within its constant threat. Was there something wrong with him that he had to pull on a balaclava and an assault rifle on a strap before he felt fully human? Perhaps. Then again, perhaps he should fully interrogate that another time, because right now there was just him, his team, and the objective.

Only the objective.

Abbott joined Brace on the roof with his binoculars. Brace had a good sight of the approach road and the barrier. It was precisely why the location had been chosen. His visual was of the two vans parked end to end. Both men were in the cab of a van that faced them, which right away wasn't great.

They also had the distraction of the flip-up phones they held, thumbs moving furiously, either playing a game or texting.

'They've changed position. CTR had them using the other van, facing away from this position,' said Brace. 'It's one of the reasons we chose it.'

'Change of sentries. This lot probably prefer a different van. It's no reflection on Ward or Miller. No CTR should ever dictate fact over flexibility.'

Abbott kept his cool when inside he was wincing. The oversight – because at the end of the day, and for whatever reason, that's what it was – meant they had to approach from the front. Not ideal, but then again, the SF team had stealth, surprise and the cover of a dark, almost moonless night on their side. Added to that, both sentries were seemingly absorbed in their mobile phones.

'We still operational?' asked Brace.

'Nothing changes,' said Abbott, 'You know what to do.' Pulling his balaclava over his face, he headed down the stairs and made his way back to the ground. 'All call signs, prepare to move.'

CHAPTER 39

'What the fuck is going on here?' barked Doyle. He looked up, angrily stubbing out a cigarette as his office unexpectedly began to fill with people, including—

'Cynthia! What the fuck are you doing here? Finn? McGregor?'

'Today is the day, boss,' said McGregor. He was holding a cake on which was written the words 'King of Derby'.

Doyle lit another cigarette. 'What day?' He was beginning to redden. 'What's going on? Will someone *please* tell me what's going on?'

'Calm down, darling,' squeaked Cynthia Doyle. 'It's just a little surprise, that's all.' Behind her, Marky had entered the room with a platter full of lager and Cynthia needed no invitation to reach out and pluck one for herself. 'Me and Mac decided that we should have a little celebration to mark the fact that it's – how many years?' Brow furrowed, she looked to McGregor.

His eyes darted.

'Och, five years I think, Mrs Doyle.'

'Five years since what?' said Doyle angrily, half-rising from his desk, the cigarette jammed between his lips. There was the crack and fizz as more tins of lager were opened, the sight and sound of which only enraged him further.

'Five years since we defeated the Kemps,' said Cynthia. 'Five years since you became . . .' her hand swept across the cake presented by McGregor, 'King of Derby.'

Angrily, Doyle stubbed out his cigarette in the middle of the cake. 'You have got to be fucking kidding me,' he said. Growing redder and redder.

Cynthia realised that she had made a mistake and turned to McGregor, planning to demand an answer.

Weirdest thing, though: McGregor, far from being contrite or terrified by the sudden volcanic anger of her husband, looked as though he was trying to suppress a smile.

CHAPTER 40

Abbott, Ward and Miller used the cover of darkness to cross a field, keeping to the perimeter until they came to a wire fence. Across an expanse of barren land was the approach road leading to the Doyle factory. They hunkered down. Abbott looked back and could see nothing of the building where Tom Brace sat ready and waiting.

'Confirm visuals,' he whispered.

'No visual on you. Visuals on targets one and two,' came the reply from Brace.

'Ward. Miller. Standby,' said Abbott.

Ward confirmed, pushing himself further into the dirt as Abbott and Miller got to their feet and began to move across the scrubland. Ahead of them was the sentry van, some 200 yards away, the faces of the two sentries illuminated by their phones.

Off to their right, the cluster of factory buildings was a grey against the black night. Even with the darkness as their ally, they still felt exposed, pleased to reach the relative safety of an abandoned sofa that lay about halfway between his original position and the van.

'Visuals,' Abbott whispered into the mic.

'No change,' replied Brace.

Abbott checked his Omega. He wore it always, but somehow it seemed more right here than elsewhere. 'We wait,' he instructed. 'We wait for nature to take its course.'

'Roger that.'

As they lay behind the sofa, the evening growing noticeably colder around them, Abbott reflected on the fact that this was not the first time he had waited for a guard to take a piss. It was not the first time that a guard's need to urinate would spell his end.

Twenty minutes or so he waited, and then Brace whispered in his ear, 'Target is on the move.'

'Which one?'

'Target number one as far as I can tell,' said Brace, which was good. According to surveillance, number one was the more shy of the two sentries and tended to move slightly further away to enjoy a piss.

'OK, standby. I'm going silent. Keep talking to me. I'll signal for the killshot.'

'Roger that.'

Keeping low and moving silently, Abbott and Miller crossed the remaining wasteland with an eye on the cab of the van, where target number two continued to look at his phone. A short distance away, target number one was still having his piss.

Abbott could smell cigarette smoke coming from the open passenger window of the van. Miller held fast in support and carefully, he let the FN-Scar drop to its strap and then crabbed his way around the cab of the van so that he was almost directly below the passenger window.

'Waiting for the signal,' said Brace in his ear. 'He's not going to be all night, Abbott, it's only a piss.'

Inside the van, target number two had responded to the squawk of a walkie-talkie. 'Yeah,' he said.

'Fucking going nuts over here,' came a voice.

Crouched below, Abbott's ears pricked up.

'What do you mean?' said number two.

'I mean, the boss is screaming blue murder in his office. Everyone's in there. Some kind of anniversary.'

What anniversary? thought Abbott. *McGregor never mentioned an anniversary.*

In his ear, Brace sounded a little urgent. 'He's finishing up, Abbott. He's shaking. I need to take the shot.'

Abbott reached into his boot and fingered out the Gerber knife. He took a deep breath, completely in the zone now, thinking only of the operation in terms of its main objectives, its mini-objectives, the targets that formed those objectives.

He gave the signal.

There was no sound. Nothing apart from a soft thump as the bullet made contact, followed by the sound of target number one dropping dead to the dirt with Brace's bullet in his head. A flawless killshot.

At the same time, Abbott stood and brought his left arm into the window of the van, across the front of target two, grabbing him and plunging the Gerber knife through the same window and into his ear.

Target two's eyes went wide, viscous blood and brain fluid leaked from his ear onto Abbott's gloves. He slumped forward.

Abbott withdrew his gloved hands. Objective achieved. Both targets down. What's more, Abbott now had one of their radios. From a compartment in his own headset he extracted a cable that he snapped into the walkie-talkie, able now to hear any enemy comms traffic.

Not that there was any. It was silent. He listened for a while. Number two's mate had obviously gone to enjoy more of the anniversary.

But what anniversary?

'Clear,' said Abbott into the mic. 'Reorg on me.'

In moments, Ward and Miller had joined him at the vans. Abbott pushed the Gerber back into his boot and they pulled the bodies out of sight. He picked the FN-Scar up on its strap and began running along the approach road. To his right, the dark shapes of Ward and Miller, Ward with his bag of magic tricks on his back, both with their rifles in their arms.

The three men reached the unused buildings on the outer reaches of the complex. This was the kind of combat environment in which they'd all trained, and all were comfortable covering angles and working corners as they moved up. To the right was the target vehicle in the car park, and Abbott watched as Ward peeled off towards it, hunkering down by it, and went to work setting the first of his explosives. As well as the main factory building, in which Doyle's office was based, there were three other outbuildings: one that was once offices and administration, one that might once have been a workshop, and one that was probably a canteen. Right now, Abbott was by the canteen. He rose up slightly to peer through the window and saw what looked like a makeshift dormitory for kids. Evidently, they'd been gravitating here to sleep and rest and even though it was relatively early, there were – he counted – five kids in there now, two of whom were lying down probably asleep, two playing some kind of game with their hands, and one who sat with her back to the wall, staring vacantly into space.

'Alpha One,' said Brace in his ear, 'I have a target on the move.'

Abbott's first thought on hearing that was, *At last.* Given that McGregor had warned him about Doyle's increased paranoia, pulling more and more men onto the site, he had been wondering why more of them weren't visible.

'Do you have eyes on me?' he whispered back to Brace.

'Affirmative. Target is approaching your twelve, other side of the building.'

Probably coming to check on the kids. Or for some other reason.

'Alone?'

'So far. Approaching your position.'

'Do you have a clear shot?'

'Better if you can take it.'

Abbott hand-signalled to Miller, identifying the threat. They both crabbed forward, lifting their weapons in the ready position. Abbott as point man peered quickly around the side of the building, establishing a visual on the approaching guard and confirming that he was alone. He withdrew, counting in his head.

At the same time, he saw something else – but something that didn't require his immediate attention. His brain compartmentalising now, as he eased off the safety, slipped a gloved finger through the trigger guard.

'Standby,' said Brace in his ear, and Abbott slipped out of his position, onto one knee, tucking the FN-Scar into his shoulder and squinting through the scope, finding his target, doing all of it in a quarter of a second, squeezing the trigger, two shots in quick succession to the chest followed by a single shot to the head.

The target, spun around by the three shots, folded to the ground. Abbott dropped the rifle to its strap, moved quickly forward and dragged the body into the shadow of the canteen. Miller covered his every move with the precision of a perfectly synchronised dance partner.

The dead guy was a young bloke in his mid-twenties but the butt of a pistol protruded from his track pants and Abbott felt nothing. No sympathy. No remorse. Just the sense of a job completed. The guy was just another kill. Another soul to meet on the other side. Abbott had shot first, that was all.

'Sitrep?' he said to Brace, taking up the rifle again and covering himself, sweeping the barrel around in quadrants, seeing just darkness – darkness and buildings, but nothing else, which meant that either the enemy presence had been drastically reduced since – when was the last recce? – that morning, or all of Doyle's men were concentrated in . . . where?

The main factory building?

And if so, why?

'No further activity,' replied the sniper.

And then he got back to what it was he'd seen.

Parked cars. Two parked cars that weren't supposed to be there. One that he'd spent far too much time in himself, McGregor's BMW. And another, a black Audi TT that he was pretty sure belonged to Cynthia fucking Doyle.

Abbott pulled up his balaclava so as not to look scary and then tried the door to the canteen. It was unlocked. These kids were too terrified to even think of escape. Where would they go anyway? That's what they would have been told. *Try to escape and we'll find you and punish you.* The kids looked up as he entered, their eyes widening in fear. He held up *I come in peace* hands. 'I'm here to help you. I'm here to take you away from these bad people,' he told them.

They regarded him mutely. He was used to that. It's what he'd expected. Experience had taught them not to trust men like him. 'Do you speak English?' he asked, and the little dark-haired girl who sat by herself nodded. 'Can you trans-late for me?' She nodded again, still with the same wary look but prepared to listen at least. 'There will be some explosions, but you'll be safe in here as long as you stay away from the windows. I'll come back for you. How many others are there?'

'Three,' she said slowly, carefully.

'Where are they?'

She shrugged. 'Around. They're around.'

'OK,' he said, 'just stay away from the windows and I'll be back.'

'Charges are set.'

This from Ward. Brilliant, dependable Ward.

'OK, Whiskey One stay back, ready to blow. Mike One, on me,' said Abbott.

'Where is everybody?' This from Miller.

'Good question,' said Abbott. All quiet on the enemy's walkie-talkie. The word pinging around his head was 'anni-versary'. He had this image of them all inside in party hats, McGregor and Cynthia Doyle included. But that couldn't be. That just wasn't possible, was it? McGregor was Doyle's right-hand man. Any celebration and he would have known about it, and if he had known about it then he would have told Abbott. The last thing they wanted was a major concentration of the enemy all in one place, because then it went from being a stealthy incursion to a full-on firefight.

Abbott gave an intel update to the rest of the team over his radio, making them aware of the situation, confirming his intention to carry on regardless. It remained a DA unless the enemy became aware of them. After all, the enemy weren't expecting an attack – especially not one initiated by a former SF team – it was just another night for them.

Together they came up on the factory. The entrance was a large metal roller-door inset with a smaller door. There was a fire exit to the right-hand side of the entrance which would be the entry point, obscured from Brace's field of view. Abbott and Miller moved either side of the door, Abbott provided cover while Miller went to work, confirming the position of the hinges and placing three horseshoe-shaped charges around each, ensuring the detonators were firmly in place. He moved down the side of the building, unravelling the shock tube which would initiate the dems. The other side of that door, armed men. No idea how many. Also, innocents, usual scenario.

And then he heard it over the enemy squawk: 'All right, boys, party's over.' A snigger. 'Get back to your positions.'

At the same time Brace was in his ear. 'Main door's opening.'

'Confirm target,' said Abbott.

'Enemy. Definitely an enemy.'

The main entry roller-door shutter rattled, about to open. Abbott and Miller remained still in the shadows, crouched low. It was time to go.

'All call signs stand by, stand by. GO.'

Ward cranked off the distraction and it did what it needed

to do. A crack and thump followed by the flash of flames as the petrol tank of the car lit up the night sky, illuminating the entire complex.

Almost instantaneously, Miller initiated the door charges, peeling the door clean off its hinges and at the same time blowing the enemy coming out the main door out onto the loading bay.

The complex came to life as doors opened and the enemy started to spill out into the open, confused and in shock, a sniper's dream.

Brace picked them off, men dropping like puppets with their strings cut. Abbott and Miller were now through their entry point and engaging the enemy as they moved through the building, making their way to their objective, in flow and working at ease. *Peace in war*.

CHAPTER 41

In the office above, Raymond Doyle's rage had emptied the room, the men inside piling out and pulling faces at other guys who'd been standing on the gantry listening, bemused, to the events inside the office. *Back to work, back to work.*

Left in the room was a raging Ray Doyle, a ruined ashtray cake, Cynthia Doyle, their son, Finn, and McGregor – McGregor, who wore an odd look. Who seemed unsure as to whether he should go or stay. Acting like a cat on a hot tin roof.

Behaving strangely, thought Cynthia, who said to him, 'What the fuck is wrong with you, Mac?' She was going to have to have words with him, she thought. Find out just exactly what the little toad was playing at by organising a party and making her look like an idiot.

His eyes were darting. His mouth was working. He even glanced at his watch.

'McGregor . . .' she prompted.

And then it came. From downstairs. Shouts. A gunshot. The sound of soft popping and more shouting, running.

McGregor pulled out a gun. He held it on Doyle. 'Get out,' he yelled. 'Out of the office.'

Doyle looked at him, a picture of confusion. His mouth worked, but no sound came out.

'McGregor,' shrieked Cynthia.

McGregor turned the gun on her.

And shot her. Twice.

Finn, the kid – the as-it-turned-out brave kid – gave a shout and leaped forward, but McGregor was quicker, swinging the weapon around and plugging the kid once before he could even reach him.

Two bodies. Mrs Doyle sprawled half on and half off the sofa, a patch of purple blood on the front of her Juicy Couture; Finn, sliding down the wall, his mouth working like a beached fish, dying before their very eyes.

'You're a dead man,' said Doyle.

But McGregor had already turned the gun on him. 'Out,' he said.

Doyle's eyes blazed, but he did as he was told, leaving the office on the end of McGregor's gun. His cheeks were puffed out. He was reddening. Sweat poured off him. A picture of fury and confusion.

Out on the gantry and oblivious to the combat raging below, McGregor punched the big red button to activate the grinder.

'Get in,' he told Doyle.

Doyle looked at him incredulously. 'If you think . . .' he began and then clutched at his chest. The faded area of his sweatshirt was suddenly bunched in his fist. He was gasping for breath, shivering at the same time.

McGregor saw his chance. He stepped forward. Manoeuvred the breathless, convulsing Doyle in front of the chute and was about to shove him backwards when from behind him he heard a familiar voice.

Abbott calling out to him. 'McGregor!'

CHAPTER 42

Tom Brace had taken out the guy leaving from the side door. At the same time, the front entrance to the factory had opened and a Doyle goon appeared. Abbott took him out. One, two, three clustered shots, coming forward at the same time and using the guy's falling body as a shield to step across the threshold with Miller at his rear. Guys inside. Guns being drawn.

'Another one,' said Brace. 'Target acquired.'

'Fire at will,' said Abbott, a target in his own sights, bloke in sportswear, hardly out of his teens, taking him out, *pop, pop, pop*, seeing the familiar landscape of the factory floor but through new eyes now, as a battleground, a plane of combat divided into metre squares.

He went left, indicating for Miller to go right and advance, both finding cover behind industrial equipment and dropping to one knee. *Pop, pop.* Another gunman fell. One of the enemy got a shot off, but it was wild and panicked, the guards in complete disarray as Abbott and Miller moved forward. There were three bodies on the factory floor ahead of them and a general sense of panic in the air. Somebody took a pot shot at them from the back of the factory floor and they both

221

went flat behind cover, searching him out, Miller's suppressed AR-15 chugging.

'Magazine!' Abbott shouted, removing his empty mag and replacing with a fresh one, at the same time moving behind cover and then surfacing to engage the enemy, allowing Miller to carry out a similar drill. On the stairs was another guy. He held his pistol sideways like an LA gangbanger, firing wildly, and it gave Abbott no pleasure to take him out, the red dot laser sight finding its mark in the centre of mass followed by two rounds. A terrified crew member made a dash to their right and Miller took him down.

Two other shooters had taken cover behind machinery to their twelve and were loosing off shots that zinged overhead, splitting the air above them. At the same time, Abbott looked up and saw activity on the gantry, McGregor holding a gun on Doyle. As he watched, McGregor seemed to be leading Doyle out, Doyle wearing a stricken, shell-shocked look.

Two things happened next: McGregor reached and punched the grinder button, the machine instantly leaping into life, and Doyle clutched at his heart, his whole body going taut for a second, face slackening, the classic symptoms of cardiac arrest.

With a signal to Miller – *cover me* – Abbott scooted forward, popping off with the Scar, creating noise and rico-chets, keeping the enemy's heads down as he reached the steel steps leading to the gantry, boots on metal as he raced to the top, where he came up on where McGregor had moved towards Doyle and was surely about to shove him into the funnel of the grinder.

'McGregor,' he shouted. 'What the hell are you doing?'

McGregor turned, saw Abbott, and then returned his

attention to Doyle. Red-faced Doyle. Spasming Doyle. And then, like a man possessed, McGregor did it. He shoved Doyle into the funnel.

Abbott, halfway along the gantry, stopped, not especially wanting to see Doyle dragged into the grinder. But he heard the screams all right. Even a man in the grip of a heart attack knows when his body is being sucked into a machine designed to turn it into mincemeat.

Abbott remembered himself, raised the rifle and took aim at McGregor. 'Switch it off,' he yelled. 'Drop the gun and shut the machine off now, McGregor, or I swear to God I'll put a bullet in you.'

'Abbott, we're on the same side,' called McGregor over the pulverising sound of the grinder. 'I mean, did you see that, pal? I just did you a favour. You should be thanking me, not threatening me.'

Even so, he did as he was told, dropping the gun, which fell with a metallic clank to the gantry and reaching to slap off the grinder.

Abbott glanced into the chute and the sight was as bad as he had feared. From below came more of the *pop pops* of Miller's AR-15. He took a step back, sweeping the barrel of his own weapon across the floor below. If there were any enemy left, they were keeping a low profile.

'Abbott, I've got two guys surrendering down here,' called Miller from below. 'What you want me to do with them?'

'Zip them,' he replied over his shoulder. 'Find out if they know where any of the kids are, then tell them to get out of here. We're about to blow the place.'

He turned his attention back to McGregor. 'You and me are

OLLIE OLLERTON

going to have a talk about this at some point. Right now, I need you out of my sight.'

To Brace he said, 'Tango One, I have a guy coming out. Hands raised, unzipped. He's a friendly. He's getting in his car and leaving.' Back to McGregor. 'Later,' he said warningly, 'now get out,' watching as McGregor made for the steps.

Abbott was now on the lookout for friendlies. Gun raised, he entered the office, saw the bodies of Cynthia Doyle and Finn, checked for signs of life, and found none. McGregor's doing, no doubt.

'Downstairs clear,' he heard from Miller. 'They've either legged it or they're hiding.'

'Sensible,' said Abbott. 'They know when they're beat. Make a final sweep, would you? We're leaving now.'

Next, he called for Ward, who in a few moments had joined him on the gantry, Miller covering his quick journey across the factory floor.

'The safe's in there,' Abbott told him when he arrived, and Ward already knew the drill. They'd been through how Ward needed to blow the safe but preserve whatever was inside. Ward did as asked, and in two minutes the door to the safe was hanging off, Abbott clearing smoke with his hand to peer inside.

What was he expecting to see? He had no idea. Even so, it caught him by surprise. The sole contents of the safe was a CD. He grabbed it and then together with Ward clattered back along the gantry and down the stairs, covering himself as he approached the factory floor. No sign of Miller.

'Tango One, be advised Mike One and I are exiting the building,' reported Abbott.

They emerged to see Miller close by, packing off a guy who

224

was zip-tied, all but slapping him on the rump, yelling, 'Get out of here,' sending him darting off away from the site.

At the same time, Abbott saw two children cowering by one of the buildings. He recognised the bruised cleaner girl. 'You two,' he shouted to them. 'You need to get out of here. This place is about to go *boom*.'

Not far away, Ward shrugged off his rucksack and set to work on the charges. The kids, seeing him at work and knowing for sure that the men in balaclavas meant what they said, emerged from their hiding place, allowing Abbott to hand them off to Miller.

'Tango One, we need the van down here for extraction,' said Abbott into his mic, looking around for the one more kid left, needing to find the child because if they didn't then he couldn't risk blowing the factory, and if he didn't blow the factory then as far as he was concerned the job was incomplete. His message was not as powerful as he wanted it to be.

And then he saw him, the last one, the Polish couple's kid, who like the first two, was hiding in the shelter of a nearby building. Abbott held up his hands, ran over and spoke to him. 'We're here to rescue you. You see that man there?' He gestured towards Miller, who was returning. The kid nodded. That was a relief. At least he could understand English. 'Go to him. He'll take you to the others and then we'll get you out of here. This place is about to explode.'

Miller left, Abbott covering Ward. 'That's it,' he told Ward over the comms. 'All the kids are accounted for. You're safe to proceed.'

'Any enemy remaining?' said Ward, already working, thumbs pressing a detonator into C4.

'If there are, they'll have to take their chances,' replied Abbott.

An expert and a fast expert at that, it took Ward just five minutes to set dems charges on the four buildings.

'Ready,' he told Abbott. 'Place is rigged.' The two of them joined Miller at the canteen, where the eight children were gathered, and Abbott did a headcount. The little girl he'd spoken to earlier was there, the other three; the Polish couple's child, the cleaner girl and the last one. All accounted for. He and Miller ushered them into the back of the van, which had arrived with Tom Brace at the wheel, Miller covering them, swinging the barrel of his AR-15 left and right, showing good muzzle discipline even after all these years.

'We have someone out there,' he said all of a sudden.

'You back there,' called Abbott. 'You need to come out into the open now. You won't be harmed.'

The guy appeared. One of Doyle's flunkies. Another kid in track pants and a sweatshirt. As Abbott covered him, Miller moved forward, relieved the guy of his gun and zipped him up. 'Go,' he said, and the guy began running, hands behind his back. That was four altogether, zipped and sent on their way. Aside from that, plenty of fatalities inside the factory, as well as the sentries taken out on the approach. As a plan, it had not been carried out flawlessly, but so far each objective had been achieved. Abbott wasn't complaining.

They drove, putting the factory to their back. At the dual carriageway they stopped. Abbott saw the final zip-tied guy still running across the wasteland behind them, but the guy was out of the blast zone by now, and besides, the police would be here soon.

'Whiskey One, blow it,' he said.

They opened the rear doors of the van but motioned for the kids to stay inside. 'Watch,' he told them. 'The place is about to go up.'

Ward gave the small handheld detonator to the bruised cleaner girl, inviting her to press the button. She did the honours, and the children cheered as in the distance came the crump of the explosion – one, two, three, and then a final fourth as the main factory went up, the skyline suddenly orange, the fingers of a huge blue-black plume of smoke reaching to the heavens.

Time to leave, and Abbott provided Brace with directions to The Freemasons Arms. Arriving about ten minutes later, they pulled up out of sight of the pub. Shards of light blazed beneath the boarded-up windows.

'Do you need back-up?' asked Brace.

'No,' said Abbott. 'Anybody who comes out that front door can take their chances.' He swapped his Scar for his Glock, left the van, and took a familiar route to the cellar hatch, discovering that it had been padlocked since his last visit. He put a round in the padlock. Another one until the lock hung loose. Carefully he raised the hatch, pointing the gun below, into the cellar.

Empty.

The screens were on, just as they had been during the Sweaty era. The operation was clearly still a going concern. Abbott trod carefully and quietly down the steps into the cellar with the Glock held two-handed. He glanced at the screen, where he could see that the rooms upstairs were currently not being used. No customers, thankfully. In the communal area were three kids; sitting in the bar area on the ground floor were two men playing cards as usual, while behind the bar sat the guy with dreads.

Abbott reported the sitrep back to the van.

'Do you need support?'

'Negative,' said Abbott, 'I can do this myself.'

He climbed the steps at the other side of the cellar, keeping an eye on the monitor downstairs. The men were still in the same positions. Quietly, Abbott opened the cellar door and stepped out, staying in the shadows. He raised the Glock.

The two men at the card table were first to go. The barman was reaching for his machete, but he looked up. He saw Abbott. He saw the face of the man who put a bullet in him.

* * *

It wasn't long before Abbott was leading the three kids out of the front door, then to the van. Some ten minutes after that, they were pulling up outside the flats where the Polish couple lived, and Abbott, having done his best to wipe the camo paint from his face and look as normal as possible, took the kid upstairs.

It was the father who opened the door, perhaps expecting a customer. But when he saw his little boy, he dropped to his knees and took him in an embrace so enveloping Abbott worried that he might do the kid a mischief. At the same time, the husband was calling over a shoulder, and the mother appeared, her eyes going from Abbott to her little boy and in the next moment she joined her husband on his knees, hugging the child, fussing over him, all three of them speaking quickly in Polish.

Abbott wasn't sure what the kid said, but in the next moment, the father had risen to his feet and seized his hand to shake it. 'Thank you, thank you,' he said, tripping over his words, pumping Abbott's hand. 'I will never be able to thank you enough.'

And later, when Abbott and his team had dropped the kids off outside a police station, instructing them to go inside and tell their story, and then left to dump the van and take themselves back to the Welcome Break, finally falling exhausted into bed, it was that 'thank you' that Abbott thought about just before his eyes closed for the night.

PART FOUR

PART FOUR

CHAPTER 43

Inside RAF Chicksands – the HQ of the British Army's Intelligence Corps – was Cuckoo's office, and inside the office was Cuckoo, or Alan Roberts as most people knew him, who right now was staring intently at a computer monitor but not really seeing what was on the screen. Looking but not seeing. Waiting, in fact, for a knock at the door.

There came a knock at the door.

'Sir? You wanted to see me, sir?'

The guy's name was Johnny. A member of Chicksands' human resources department. Cuckoo had never knowingly clapped eyes on Johnny until this very moment, his only contact with human resources having been with the department head when making new appointments, such was Cuckoo's exalted position in the operation. Now, however, he directed the HR guy – age? What? Mid-thirties? – to take a seat and let the silence between them settle and marinate, regarding Johnny, who looked back nervously.

'Is this a human resources matter, sir?' enquired Johnny meekly.

'Not really,' Cuckoo shook his head. 'This is a matter more, well . . .' He looked away. 'For the moment, let's just say this is a matter that should stay between you and I. Something to do with extracurricular activity.'

'Sir?'

Cuckoo leaned forward. 'You've been nosing around on the network.'

'Have I, sir?'

'Indeed. Your terminal has been used for searches on the system. Searches conducted when you, and you alone, were using it. They were unauthorised searches and you made them in an attempt to find military intelligence on a high-ranking civilian family.' He paused, enjoying the queasy look that had taken Johnny's face hostage. 'Now, why would you want to be doing that?'

'I don't think I understand, sir,' stuttered Johnny.

Abbott would not have recognised Cuckoo now – Cuckoo, the man who roared, '*Do not* lie to me, son. You're not at fucking school here. I'm not playing games. I want to know why you were making those searches.'

Johnny withered. 'I was making them on behalf of somebody else, sir.'

'Who?'

'I'd rather not say, sir.'

Cuckoo did a bit more shouting, but this time, although he cringed away slightly, Johnny didn't completely crumble. Almost, but not quite. He took a large gulp of air, straightening his shoulders as though to give himself strength. 'Respectfully, sir, I will need to speak to my supervisor regarding your request.'

This, thought Cuckoo sourly, was what you got for trying

to turn the thumbscrews on a member of the human resources department. 'Of course,' he said. 'I would expect nothing less. But I want to see you back here this time tomorrow – with an answer. Do I make myself clear?'

'Yes, sir.'

CHAPTER 44

Abbott had said goodbye to the lads at the Welcome Break. He'd assured them that McGregor would be transferring the money into their nominated offshore accounts, and then, before they left, said one more thing: would they be interested in a second mission at some point in the near future, the date yet to be decided? A rescue mission.

'Who will we be rescuing?' Tom Brace had asked.

'Me,' Abbott had told them, thinking that their money would come out of the cash that Lady Norton was to pay him for the death match. If they all came out of it alive, and provided she continued to hold up her end of the bargain, then he was good for it.

Now Abbott was back in his room at the Travelodge, looking at a 700-millilitre bottle of vodka on his desk and talking to his AV, which was calling to him with a louder voice and even greater urgency than it had in some time, his poor neglected reward centres shrieking at him: *come on, you did a good job. You deserve it. You deserve a drink. Just one.*

But no. Because while the operation had indeed been a success, in the sense that Doyle was dead, most of his lieutenants were dead, his operation was at an end and, most importantly, the trafficked children released, it was only the beginning, the tip of the iceberg. There was much more to come. More to do.

Perhaps he'd have a drink when it was all over.

Perhaps.

And in the meantime, you, shut the hell up.

As his AV fell silent, not beaten just temporarily quelled, he turned his attention to the CD, pushing it into his laptop to watch it.

There were dozens and dozens of movie files on the CD. He picked one at random. Double-clicked. The image that greeted him was of an empty room, a dirty mattress on the floor. And even though Abbott's exposure to scenes of abuse was thankfully rare – he had done far more rescuing than he had ever done witnessing – he knew what was coming next, and he steeled himself for it, finding himself forming strange hopes. *Please let it be a grown adult. Not a kid. Please, not a kid.*

His heart sank when the door opened, and a woman led a child into the room. She held the boy's hand like a mother would, or a protective older sister, and with a smile she directed the child to the bed. Her lips were moving, the film silent – thank God for that, at least – no doubt bidding him to take a seat, for that's what he did. He was just a little kid, no more than eleven years old, that age where you can't hide your emotions even if you try, and right now what Abbott saw on the kid's face was rank fear. Heartbreaking fear.

Abbott tipped back his head, taking his eyes from the screen as he thought of the kids they'd saved last night. He wondered how many of them had gone through their own version of this particular scenario. He thought of The Freemasons Arms and how he'd left it standing for the simple reason that he wanted the cops to find evidence of abuse there, hoping that one of the kids would lead them to it.

Right now, though, he fervently wished he had burned it down to the ground.

He looked back at the screen. The woman had returned, smiling reassuringly at the boy, holding out a can of Fanta. Again, her lips were moving, trying to put his mind at rest, no doubt.

And then Abbott gasped, because for the first time he saw her face properly, and she was a lot younger than the woman he had met in Richmond, but it was still unmistakeably her.

It was Juliet Norton. *Lady Norton.*

Had he ever doubted that she was in it up to her eyeballs? Not really. But that was one thing. It was quite another to be confronted with the evidence, to see with his own eyes that any involvement she had was far from peripheral; that she did, as they say, get her hands dirty.

Worse was to come. The door opened and two men entered. One of them was a man he had last seen reduced to his constituent parts in a meat-grinding machine, Raymond Doyle, wearing a dressing gown and a smile, wiping his nose.

Behind him came another man that it took Abbott a second or so to recognise, until – of course – it was Charles Norton. Would he have been *Sir* Charles Norton then? Difficult to tell. The footage had to be around ten years old. Abbott's next thought was to wonder who had set up the camera. And then he saw Ray Doyle's eyes flick up, as though checking for it, which of course made perfect sense. Even if Norton had been plain old Charles back then, he was no doubt on the way up and Doyle had seen a means of making sure that his own fortunes were linked to Norton's ascent. Chances are he had never needed to use his insurance. Norton's loyalty had ensured that he had continued to live in the manner to which he had become accustomed. Possibly Doyle would have been reaching inside that safe soon, had Juliet not employed Abbott to take pre-emptive action on her behalf. She wanted Doyle out of the picture for the reasons she had told him at Richmond, but also because of what he knew about her and her husband.

What she hadn't told Abbott was that if his brother Chris had lived and been delivered into the hands of Doyle then he might well have suffered the same fate as . . .

The kid in the video.

Norton and Doyle had both removed their robes. Both had gone to their hands and knees on the mattress, approaching the boy, who cowered away as Juliet Norton stood back with her arms folded across her chest, her lips moving, saying what, Abbott had no idea, but whatever it was, it did nothing to put the kid at ease, because his emotions were written all over his face, a little boy who should have been loved and cared for and treated to days out and marshmallows in hot chocolate by loving parents. Who instead . . .

Abbott watched what happened next. Not all of it. Enough. Until he could take no more. And when he'd finished, he sat for a while, only just managing to control the anger and hate, the sheer vindictive energy within himself. He didn't need to watch the other files. He knew what they contained.

And then he called Cuckoo.

'Hello, mate,' he said, when Cuckoo answered, his friend's voice a reminder that a better world was out there.

'Abbott, you're still alive.'

'Apparently.' He updated Cuckoo, telling him about the previous night's operation.

'I saw the fire on the news,' whistled Cuckoo. 'I had a funny feeling that it all had something to do with you.'

To Abbott it was already ancient history. 'Listen. I've got evidence that can put Juliet Norton away.'

'Right,' said Cuckoo carefully. 'What kind of evidence are we talking about?'

'I'm talking about films of Juliet Norton, her husband and Ray Doyle abusing children. Dozens, maybe hundreds of children.'

'You know what this means, don't you?' said Cuckoo, when Abbott had finished.

'It means we have the evidence we need,' replied Abbott.

'Sure, but more than that, it means you can pull out.'

'Pull out of what?'

'You don't need to participate in their bloody game, that's what I mean,' insisted Cuckoo.

'Does it? It fingers Juliet, but that's all.'

'Well, maybe she's the only one who's guilty?'

'Guilty of what?'

'What do you think? Child abuse.'

'They're all dirty, mate. Maybe they're not abusing kids. But they're still all part of the game, aren't they?'

'And that means they deserve to die?'

Abbott stayed silent.

'Either way, but you don't need to risk your life going into the game. Not now you have this. Take down Juliet this way. Hunt down the surviving members of the family individually.

Creep into their houses late at night, put bullets in their heads. Honestly, if that's what you want, I won't lose any sleep over it. Just don't play their game.'

Abbott mulled it over. Cuckoo was correct. Perhaps there was a part of him prepared to go along with the idea because he wanted the risk and got off on the danger and knew that it kept him away from the bottle. And yet any upsides were surely outweighed by the risks. Even with the insurance policy of Ward, Brace and Miller, there were still far too many variables. There would be no IA. No DA. Maybe going up against the Nortons that way fulfilled a deep need in him. Maybe it was also a dumb thing to do.

Two things could be true at the same time.

'OK,' he said to Cuckoo after a long pause, 'what then? What instead?'

'You make a copy of the CD, and you send one of them to me.'

'And what do you do?'

'I blow the gaff.'

'Wait a minute, the last time we spoke, you told me that there were internal flags on the files. We already know that the Nortons have influences far and wide. Why won't they just use that power to keep a lid on it?'

'Because if you or someone else tried to blow the gaff, then sure, that would happen. But if I do it? Let's just say that in the same way that I know how to circumvent their flags on the system, so I know how to sidestep the fingers of influence.'

'Reminds me. You were going to find out who'd been nosing around.'

'To cut a long story short, some bloke called Johnny from

human resources was the one who triggered the flag, but he was making enquiries on behalf of somebody else.'

'When do we find out who?'

'Good question. He's due in my office in about ten minutes. Watch this space.'

'OK, in the meantime, we'll do it your way. I'll get you the disc and I'll make myself scarce.'

'And going after the Nortons individually?'

'We'll see,' said Abbott, who was already beginning to feel a little flat, his eyes going to that bottle of vodka as his feeling of sweet purpose slowly dissolved. 'We'll see.'

Abbott finished the call then left his room, found a member of staff, and cadged a Jiffy bag from her. Back in his room, he slipped the CD inside the envelope and ordered a courier, telling them that the bike was going to Bedfordshire and that he'd provide the specific address to the rider.

The phone rang. Cuckoo again. 'Johnny from human resources came back. He was doing a favour for a mate at GCHQ.'

'Right,' said Abbott. 'Which mate? What's his name?'

'Hold your horses. I'm getting there. It's just a random drone at GCHQ. I've already spoken to him, and it turns out that I'm not the first person wanting to know who's been asking after the Nortons. He's had a visit from MI5, and he told them what he told me.'

'Which was?'

'That he was making enquiries on behalf of a lawyer by the name of Teresa Oakley.'

'*Shit*,' said Abbott, and ended the call.

CHAPTER 45

Cuckoo wasn't to know, of course, but Tess's given name was Teresa – Teresa Lacey. Her married name, however, was Oakley.

Right away, Abbott dialled her.

No reply.

Another call was coming through. 'Hi, I'm your courier. I'm outside.' Abbott stood, picked up his Jiffy bag and made his way to reception, trying Tess again at the same time, preoccupied as he handed over his package to the courier.

'Cheers, mate,' said the courier, his voice muffled by the helmet he wore. He turned and left reception, past the vending machines they had there, out into the car park, where Abbott could see his bike was parked. Again, he tried Tess. Again, there was no reply. Straight to voicemail. 'Hello, you have reached the voicemail of . . .'

'Come on, Tess. Come on . . .' he was muttering to himself.

At the same time, he realised that he had forgotten to provide the courier with the full address. Looking out into the car park, it seemed that the courier had come to the same conclusion at the same time. Seeing Abbott still in reception he hailed him and began to trot back towards the building.

Behind him, two Range Rovers glided into the car park.

A warning bell in Abbott's brain went off as from the Range Rovers stepped several men wearing black cargo pants and T-shirts, polo shirts and sunglasses even though they were not needed. Abbott watched as they swarmed over the courier. He saw a Sig Sauer produced. Suppressed, of course, the sign that these guys meant business. And if there was any doubt in his mind, then the next gun he saw sealed the deal. A CZ 75B, the Czech-made pistol that was famed for its reliability and accuracy. Posers didn't bother with it; it was one for the professionals. In the next second, the courier was being clubbed to the ground, the Jiffy bag was snatched, and in Abbott's ear he heard, 'You have reached the voicemail of . . .'

The men had all drawn their weapons. They were advancing to the hotel entrance. Abbott swung and saw that the receptionist had appeared. Their eyes met and he saw the betrayal in her face. He'd pushed his luck staying here in the first place, let alone remaining here after the Kemptown job. Now it looked like they'd come to make him pay.

But this wasn't Doyle's men, he knew. This was worse. This was Juliet Norton's people.

And that was much, much worse.

CHAPTER 46

With an afternoon appointment on her schedule, Tess had left the office and was on her way to her car, which was parked beneath her building. She'd been thinking how she might engineer it so that however long the appointment ended up being, it would take her to the end of the working day. She fancied an early one tonight. Perhaps get home sooner than 8pm for once, maybe even have dinner with Phil and the kids. The thought buoyed her as she came down the grey-painted steps at the back of the building to the car park entrance, where she plugged in the code and pushed open the door.

Just as she opened the door, a man appeared. She didn't recognise him, but that wasn't unusual; it was a big building, plenty of people used the car park.

He thanked her for opening the door with a quick nod of his head and held it for her, letting her pass before hopping inside himself.

And she knew, of course, that the correct protocol was to challenge him, ask to see his building pass or perhaps even establish that he knew the door code, but correct protocol was hardly ever followed, and after all, he was courteous, seemed businesslike and in a hurry, so she let him go and began to make her way across the concrete apron towards her Mercedes, parked on the other side of the low-ceilinged car park.

The air was thin and warm, but worse than that was the feeling down here, the tomblike sense of somehow being encased in concrete. She didn't like it at the best of times and today, for some reason she couldn't quite put her finger on, she felt more than usually nervous. Just a feeling she had, but an insistent one. A sense of something having changed. As though that thin, warm air had been displaced, its chemistry altered.

Something not right.

Or was it just her mind playing tricks on her? After all, having told Alex of her fears regarding the crime organisation run by Raymond Doyle in Derby, Tess had learned that Doyle had links to the recently deceased Sir Charles Norton. There had always been rumours about the Nortons and the level of their influence, so she'd asked a friend at GCHQ to investigate it for her.

'I can't help you,' he'd told her at first.

'Oh? Why's that?'

'I'm not sure. Something to do with the security classification.'

'Is that it, then?'

'All I can suggest is that I have a friend who works at RAF Chicksands.'

'What's RAF Chicksands?'

'Military intelligence. Johnny's in human resources so in theory he has much higher-level security clearance than I do. This is a guy who's on a team that can literally vet anybody.'

And so she had asked him to contact Johnny, all the while wondering why she was doing this. Was it *for* Alex? It wasn't like she owed him anything, and in fact every sensible and settled-down fibre of her body told her that having anything further to do with Alex Abbott was very bad news indeed. He had all kinds of problems. He was a dangerous man. Dangerous literally and dangerous metaphorically.

And yet . . .

Johnny at RAF Chicksands would look into it, she was told. But a couple of days later her contact had been back in touch sounding somewhat discombobulated. 'Who are these people?'

'Um, I was hoping you could tell me.'

'Well, no, I can't. And nor can Johnny. According to him there are all kinds of clearances needed. Levels he didn't even know existed. He says he's leaving well alone and reckons you should, too.'

Which was enough to spook anyone.

She stopped, right there in the car park, halfway to her car, with something having occurred to her. The absence of something. The absence of a sound.

She swung about and sure enough, the door to the stairwell had not clicked shut. Either the mechanism was faulty or something on the other side was stopping it.

The man who had passed her? Had he remained there for some reason, preventing the door from shutting? From her position she could see that the door rested in the door frame, just not quite fully closing, although it was impossible to tell if there was anything – or anyone – on the other side.

Her mind went to something that Alex had told her once. *Listen to your instinct.* She swallowed. Her eyes went back to her car. Her keys were in her hand and she activated the clicker, although why, she wasn't sure. The car unlocked with a comforting clunk. Sidelights came on. The internal light glowed. There was no sign of anybody there.

Or was there? Did she imagine it, or was there a movement in the shadows simultaneously accompanied by a shuffling sound? In the office it was occasionally joked that there were rats down here but somehow she didn't think that was a rat.

Listen to your instinct.

Smartly, she turned, and although her first thought was to go back up the stairs into the sanctuary of her office, that door still had not shut, and so instead she headed quickly for a narrow pedestrian walkway to the left of the exit ramp, trotting up it fast towards the rectangle of daylight at the top.

She reached the street and was about to turn right to head for the main entrance to her building when she saw a man approaching her from that direction. Like the first guy she had encountered, he wore a smart single-breasted suit. Almost exactly the same kind of suit, in fact. Same build. Same look about him.

Their eyes met.

She was in danger. She knew it. She actually felt the adrenalin inside her as though it had been administered via hospital drip.

At the same time thinking of the number of things she'd watched where she was screaming at the screen, 'Why doesn't she just call the police?'

So she turned, quickly, jabbing out 999 on her phone.

'Emergency services, which service do you require? Fire, police or ambulance?'

'Police, please.'

'Putting you through.'

Through to force control. 'Police, how may I help you?'

'I think I'm being followed.'

'OK, let's start with your name and your location.'

She went through it. She told them who she was and what she did, and if she exaggerated the extent of her criminal work, well, that was just to ensure that they took the threat seriously. She was asked to stop and wait for a squad car.

She glanced behind. The guy still there. 'I'd prefer not to stop right now,' she told the call handler. 'Can I just keep on walking? Are you able to track me using my number?'

'Yes. We can do that. We've got you. We can get a squad car to whatever is your current location.'

'Thank you, thank you.' Something was happening on her phone. 'I've got a call coming through,' she told the call handler, and then saw who it was. 'This might be something to do with what's happening.'

'OK, well, you should see a squad car soon.'

She took the incoming call. It was Alex.

'Alex,' she said.

'Tess.'

And she'd never been so glad to hear his voice.

CHAPTER 47

Abbott, with the phone glued to his ear, was making his way along the corridors of the Travelodge and back to his room. He needed his laptop on which he'd copied the CD just prior to giving it to the courier. And he needed his Glock.

And finally, Tess answered.

'Alex.' The voice like nectar in his ear.

'Tess,' he said, still hurrying, reaching for the key card from inside his Diesels. 'Are you all right?'

'No, I think I'm being followed.'

He stopped in the corridor, thinking, *Oh God, what have I brought down upon her? What have I got her into?*

'Do you have any idea why?' he asked her, even though he knew the reason. Still wanting it to be something else. An angry client maybe.

'I was looking into the Doyles and because I was looking into the Doyles I got looking into the Nortons, and—'

'I know, I know,' he said, feeling immediately wretched. 'What do you see?'

'I called the police,' she said with an almost distracted air. From the sound of her voice she was walking fast.

'That's good,' he said, thinking, *The police. Did he want Tess in the hands of the police?* 'But I need to know what you see.'

At the other end of the line she took stock. 'OK, well, there was a guy in the car park. He was behaving a bit strangely. So rather than go to my car, I headed for the street. Up there, I saw another guy looking a bit like the first guy. It's all too much of a coincidence. That's why I called the police.'

'Do you see him now?'

She glanced behind. The street was not busy but some way back she could see him. He was on his phone, just the same as she was, but not looking her way. Not for the first time in the last ten minutes or so she wondered if she were simply having an attack of the heebie-jeebies. 'The guy's still there, Alex,' she told Abbott.

'What's he doing?'

'Just on his phone.'

'But he's still following?'

'I mean, in the sense that he's behind me, yes.'

'They'll have more than one man on you,' he told her. 'Look to your front, probably on the other side of the street. Look for either a guy by himself or in a pair.'

She did, and sure enough, across the road were two men, both in suits, one on his phone and the other . . .

Looking right at her.

Quickly averting his gaze.

'Yes,' she told Alex. 'Two of them up ahead.'

'OK, the chances are that they were planning to take you in the car park.'

'*Take me?*'

'We can assume that's what they want to do. They're not following you for any other reason.'

'Oh my God,' she said, and she heard the shake in her own voice. 'Should I just approach a random stranger? Get him to help?'

'No, because you'll have to stop. If you stop then they'll move in. They'll have medical or law enforcement credentials and they'll have you out from under the nose of the Samaritan before he even knows what's happening.'

'What if I go into a shop? A pub? A restaurant?'

'Same. For now, until I say any different, just keep moving. If they break into a run then you do too. Head for a Tube station. If you see a police car in the meantime, flag it down. But listen, Tess. Only a uniform. Not a plainclothes copper with a badge. Just a uniform.'

That was her best chance, thought Abbott, still on the move himself. Get her in the back of a patrol car being her best bet. Get her in the system. Once she was in the system he could contact Cuckoo and get him to pull strings before they could reach her.

'Don't worry, Tess. We'll get you out of this,' he reassured her, but on the other end of the phone he wasn't so sure. What's more, he had his own problems. He came to the lifts, thought to himself, What would he do if he were them? He'd be covering the lifts, and switched direction.

He pulled open a door and took the stairs, came round a dogleg, and there stood a guy on the steps.

It was one of them. Same look. Abbott had taken him by surprise, but he recovered quickly and his hand whipped inside a black denim jacket to what Abbott could see was a shoulder holster, snatching out the sidearm. Abbott leaped up the three steps that separated them and went for the gun arm, twisting his body across it, jamming down on it and snatching the weapon from fingers rendered suddenly useless by pain, turning the guy's own gun on him.

Down went the gunman, folding awkwardly to the steps, gunless and pathetic all of a sudden, his hands going up in wanton surrender. 'Don't shoot,' he pleaded, but Abbott was in no mood to take chances; he put one in the guy's leg, and then, as he screamed and writhed, reaching his hands to the wound, blood bubbling up from his trouser leg, did a quick frisk and found a walkie-talkie.

'Who are you working for?' he demanded to know.

The guy didn't answer, too absorbed in his own pain. Abbott helped him with that. He pressed the suppressor into the wound. 'Who are you working for? Is it Juliet Norton?'

The guy shook his head furiously. 'No, no, I don't know that name.'

'Kilgore? Is it Kilgore?'

'Yes, yes, that's him.'

'Then you work for Juliet Norton,' Abbott told him. He left the guy writhing on the stairs – hopefully he'd black out – and dashed up the rest of the steps towards his floor.

'Any sightings?' he heard over the walkie-talkie. 'I'm closing in on his room.'

Shit.

'Alex,' he heard from Tess, 'are you still there?'

He cradled the phone between his shoulder and his cheek, checking the weapon he'd taken from the guy on the stairs. He had a full clip. He put one up the spout, checked the suppressor was secure and then stepped smartly out into the hotel corridor, swinging left and right.

The passageway yawned at him, empty, with at least two fire doors between him and his room.

Over the walkie-talkie he heard activity. 'Back entrance clear. Front entrance clear. Ground floor clear.'

'Receptionist says he was going to his room.'

'Number three? Any sign?'

'Negative.'

He adjusted the volume and spoke to Tess. 'Yes, I'm still here,' he told her, keeping his voice down and beginning to move along the corridor, gun held low, ready to either hide it or use it, depending on who might make an appearance. 'What's your sitrep?'

'Still the same. One guy behind, two up front, one on either side of the road.'

'Are they aware that you're alert to their presence?'

'Yes, I think so. Our eyes have met.'

'OK. So they'll know you're calling for back-up.'

But, he thought, they don't seem too bothered about it. The sort of not-bothered you might be if you thought yourself untouchable. And that's significant. 'What they'll try to do next is box you in.'

'Box me in? Oh, box me in before they snatch me.'

'Yes,' he said. 'Sorry. Look out for a van. An SUV. Anything with blacked-out windows.'

'Oh God, Alex.'

'Don't worry. If something like that draws up to the kerb, that's when they'll make their move. Start screaming. Stay as far away from the road as possible. In the meantime, have you got anything on you? Rape alarm? Pepper spray? Uzi 9mm? Anything like that?'

'No, sorry, sorry.' He was trying to put her at ease, but she still sounded on the verge of panic, as though her failure to be in possession of pepper spray might somehow prove a deciding factor.

'It doesn't matter,' he tried to reassure her. 'They're useless anyway. Just a deterrent really. Do you have your car keys on you?'

'Yes.'

'In that case get your keys out of the bag, hold them in your fist with the keys themselves poking out between your fingers, like knuckle dusters, do you see what I mean?'

'Yes, I think so.'

'OK, where are you now?'

'Right now, I'm on Farringdon Road,' she said.

Abbott had gone through the first of the two fire doors, was approaching the second. He could see his room door through the glass. Still, he had the corridor to himself.

The walkie-talkie crackled. 'Number two. Report. Report. Nothing from number two.'

'Number two located. He's on the stairs. He's bleeding out. We need to get an ambulance.'

'No ambulance. We don't have time. He knew the risks.'

'Wait a minute. His walkie-talkie is missing.'

'Number three, he must be on his way to you. Everybody else. Everybody else, converge on his room.'

'Tess,' said Abbott, 'stay on the line. There's something I have to do.'

He was coming up on his room now. The expected

convergence hadn't quite happened yet. But it would. He found his key card and very, very gently inserted it into the slot, trying to remember the sequence. At some point there was a bleep, but was it when the key card was first inserted or afterwards? Very, very gently in with the key card.

Bleep.

* * *

She didn't like it. The fact that Alex was no longer there and talking to her. Even though he was miles away and physically unable to help, just having him on the line and being able to act as her eyes and ears had reassured her. And for a moment or so back there she'd almost found her predicament thrilling. Stupid woman.

She looked to her right and saw a side street, which she knew led up to Hatton Garden. It would be busier than her current location. Busier being better in this case.

The only problem being that she had to take the side street.

Ahead of her the two men, both of whom had their backs to her. One was on his phone, or pretending to be; the other was simply walking with his hands in his pockets. He glanced quickly behind himself, most likely to check she was still there behind them. She pretended not to notice. Pretended to be absorbed in talking on her phone.

Now she did the same. She glanced behind to check if she was still being followed, thinking, *Lone Suitman, are you there?* and finding that . . .

No. He wasn't. He was gone.

Gone.

He had been there. Now he wasn't. OK. Try not to think

about it. Try not to wonder too hard where Lone Suitman had gone and instead take advantage of his sudden absence. As quickly as the thought occurred to her, she turned hard right and began half-walking, half-running up the street that led up to Hatton Garden. A narrow one-way street on an incline, there were no other people beside her. Just Hatton Garden at the top, where pedestrians moved to and fro across the entrance to the street, people going about their late-afternoon business, the sight of it reassuring, like a prize, a pot of gold at the end of the rainbow. All she had to do was reach it.

And then, at the top of the street, moving in from the junction with Hatton Garden was one of the guys. No, not just 'one of' the guys. It was 'the' guy – Lone Suitman. The guy who'd been following her. Well, at least she knew where he'd got to, she thought. He was on his phone, and she heard the words 'here, she's here, moving in' and she knew that she'd made a terrible mistake.

In a panic, she swivelled around, about to reverse direction and return to the safety of the main road below, but there had appeared the other two men.

She looked back at the top of the cut-through where Lone Suitman had broken into a trot, was coming down towards her, quickly narrowing the gap between them.

'Alex,' she said into her phone. 'Alex, can you hear me?'

* * *

Bleep.

Abbott reacted at once, flattening himself against the corridor wall. A third of a second later, three bullet holes stitched their way down the hotel-room door. He waited, waited, holding his nerve. From his phone he heard Tess calling him, 'Alex, Alex, can you hear me?' But said nothing, outwaiting the guy inside, the guy who would surely need to know whether any of his three shots had met their target.

'He's here,' he heard from the other walkie-talkie, the words much louder in the corridor. How would the gunman inside interpret that? The answer came as the door opened an inch, the gun barrel appeared, and Abbott acted at once, shoving the door open at the same time as he put the barrel of his weapon to the wood and pulled the trigger multiple times. There was a scream as the guy inside was hit and as Abbott shoved his way into the room, he saw him clutching at his wounded arm at the same time as he tried to level his gun. Abbott had been lucky, and he knew it. He wasn't about to push it any further. He put two rounds in the guy and put him down. *One for housekeeping to deal with*, thought Abbott crazily, as he snatched up his laptop and retrieved his Glock from its bottom-of-the-wardrobe hiding place. Now he had two weapons.

'Number three, number three,' the walkie-talkie was saying. And Abbott couldn't help himself. He took up the walkie-talkie and said into it, 'Number three is dead.'

'You fucker, Abbott,' came the reply. 'We're coming for you.'

'I'll be waiting,' he said.

'Go radio silence,' came the command. Next, the line went dead. Going to the door of his hotel room, Abbott cycled through different frequencies. Nothing. But they would be coming. He tossed the walkie-talkie away and returned his attention to the phone.

'Tess?' he said. 'Tess?'

* * *

She wheeled around. At the bottom of the street, the two men had also broken into a run. Probably couldn't believe their luck that she had chosen such an idiotic path to take. *Oh God, she was thinking. You idiot. You absolute idiot.*

And then she reeled back again, and what she saw was that the guy running towards her from the Hatton Garden end was almost there, about to reach her. His eyes were wide, his teeth were bared. And he thought he had her. He thought he had his quarry.

But he didn't. Because if Tess knew one thing, it was that if they managed to get her off the street then she belonged to them. And whatever the cost, she could not let that happen. She could not let them take her.

And so it was with a scream that she used the momentum of her turning body, bringing up her right hand at the same time – right hand complete with makeshift knuckle dusters that slashed across the face of her attacker just as he reached her.

It was a flailing, ill-timed shot, but luck was on her side, the key catching him below the eye and sending him yelling in pain, hands going to his face as he spun off, self-preservation keeping him away from a second blow.

For a second, she considered taking off, trusting in the fact that she could probably outrun him.

Except: heels.

So use them.

As the guy reeled, she stepped forward and dragged her foot down his shin, stamping down hard with her heel on his foot, so hard that she broke the shoe, but gratified to hear him shout

out in pain in response. And now she took off, ripping her shoes off as she went and leaving them behind. She had always hated to see people in bare feet in the city. Couldn't stand it. Just the thought of it turned her stomach. But all of a sudden it didn't matter, she didn't care. She just needed to reach the sanctuary of Hatton Garden. And she did, coming up to the junction with Hatton Garden and throwing a look behind her she saw her attacker pulling himself upright, his two accomplices reaching him at the same time, and she knew that she had pulled victory from the jaws of defeat, because now she was on Hatton Garden – busy, familiar, comforting Hatton Garden – and all she needed to do was find a policeman.

'Tess,' she heard from the phone she still held. 'Tess?'

'Alex, you're there?'

'Are you all right?'

She was better than all right. She was adrenalised, overjoyed, a feeling coursing through her like nothing she'd ever felt before, a feeling that despite everything she had to admit to quite liking, as though for the first time she understood the attraction for men like Abbott. Why they did what they did.

'Yes, I'm all right,' she said. 'Lots of people around now. I'm in Hatton Garden. I'm going to try the police again. I'll get back to you.'

* * *

At the other end, Abbott felt some small measure of relief all the while knowing that they weren't out of the woods yet. Neither of them. Least of all him. He peeked out into the corridor and could see a figure through the frosted glass of the nearest fire door. He squeezed off a shot, the suppressor reducing the gunshot to a mere plop, making the hole that appeared in the glass into something approaching a magic trick. The guy on the other side fell.

Anticipating back-up from behind, Abbott ran towards the door, shoved it open and found the guy rolling in pain on the other side, Abbott's round having wounded his shoulder. Abbott kicked his gun away and kept going, through the next fire door and to the steps, and next to the steps the lift. They would be expecting him to take the steps. Looking down the stairwell, he saw shadows, decided against, and sprinted past the door, past the lifts and to an emergency fire door at the other end.

This one, he could see, opened out to a set of steps that came down the outside of the building. He knew about it, of course. But then again, he'd been staying in the hotel; he had made it his business to know where all the exits were. His attackers? Not so much. They would have conducted a quick CTR of the place before launching their attack, if that.

Or, at least, that's what he had to hope. He had to hope that this particular exit wasn't covered. Hope number two: that the door wasn't alarmed.

Both hands on the bar, steeling himself against what might happen next, he pushed.

There was no alarm. The next thing, he was on the steps outside, clattering down to ground level and trying to work out his next move. His handset was ringing. He raised it to his ear as he descended.

'Tess?'

'Alex. It's OK. I've got a squad car on its way. They'll be here any second.'

'Remember,' he told her, 'only . . .'

'Uniforms,' she finished for him. 'Got it.'

'OK, I'm going to ring off and speak to Cuckoo.'

'Cuckoo?'

'Never mind. Just go with the copper. Everything's going to be sorted out. You're going to be OK.'

'Thank you, Alex – and Alex?'

'Yes.'

'When I next see you . . .'

'Yes?'

'When I next see you, hopefully I'll get the chance to thank you properly.'

'Sure,' he said. And despite everything – despite the situation, despite his need to remain cool and perhaps even more importantly *sound* cool, his heart sang. 'I'll hold you to that.'

* * *

She had reached the Tube station now. She heard sirens and wondered if they were for her. Hoped they were.

She looked around. There was no sign of her pursuers. Perhaps they'd decided to give up for the moment. To regroup and try again later.

'Later' being the operative word, of course, because of course they'd try again. Whatever can of worms she'd opened, she had a feeling that it wasn't easily closed.

And then she saw it, a badge. Behind it a man in plainclothes, and she recoiled, thinking purely of the one instruction she'd been given. Only surrender to a uniform. But this guy was significantly older than the men who had been following her. From his suit onwards, he looked a little more careworn.

Even so, she backed up, head swinging this way and that and just a little panic creeping back.

'No,' she said, 'I need to see a uniformed officer.'

'Of course, of course,' he smiled, holding up his hands and staying in place. 'You hear that?' he pointed. 'That siren? That's for us. That's the uniforms arriving *literally any second now*. How about you stay there, and I'll stay here, several paces away, and we just wait? Would that be OK?'

The police car had appeared now, was climbing up the road towards them. She relaxed a little. She looked at the plain-clothes guy. 'Thank you,' she said, with true gratitude.

'That's quite all right, Mrs Oakley,' he said. His smile widened. 'That's quite all right.'

***

Abbott jumped the last few steps of the fire escape, reached the ground and took a look around.

Not a soul to be seen. He jogged forward fifty yards or so, so that he was able to see around the hotel building. Visible was a border hedge, after that the car park. In the car park two Range Rovers. Enemy Range Rovers.

He moved around and then heard the voice. 'Hold it there, Abbott.'

Appearing from the door of the hotel was one of the goons. He held the receptionist. Had a gun to her head. 'Drop your gun and put the laptop on the ground,' he said. 'Do it now, Abbott, or I'll put a bullet in her.'

The receptionist was staring at him, petrified, the skin on her face taut with tense muscle. 'I'm sorry,' she said, almost whispering the words, mouthing them.

'Are you serious?' said Abbott. 'I mean, this is the woman who sold me out, yeah? I'm supposed to give a damn about her?'

'I'm sorry,' she said again. Louder this time. Tears ran down her cheeks.

'Yeah, whatever,' sneered the guy. 'You think you're one of the good guys, Abbott. I know you do. Now put the gun down. Lay the laptop on the ground and step away.'

'Mate, you have got me all wrong,' said Abbott, and he put a round into the receptionist. Although maybe the goon was right because he put the round through her shoulder and into the guy behind, the guy shouting in pain and surprise as he peeled off and to the ground, holding onto his wounded upper arm in agony.

Abbott wondered briefly whether he had been captured on CCTV and then decided that it didn't really matter. Things had gone beyond that; they had overtaken the usual social and legal boundaries, and he had a feeling that everything here would be wiped from existence, the receptionist either killed or paid off, same for any witnesses. He had the feeling that his enemies were people who could, if they wished, control the world.

The receptionist was alive. Injured but not fatally. She groaned and then, thankfully, lost consciousness. Now, thought Abbott, it was time to leave.

And then he felt the gun behind his ear. A voice that he recognised. 'Looks like I'm doing you another favour, pal.'

'McGregor.'

'The one and the same.'

'You really are Lady Norton's star pupil at the moment, aren't you?'

'How about you drop your weapons and get in the motor?' said McGregor.

'How about I don't?'

They both heard it at the same time. The sound of sirens in the distance, getting closer. Abbott grimaced. It was the last thing he needed. 'We don't have much time, Abbott,' insisted McGregor. 'Listen, pal, I can't afford to leave you alive. Come with me, get in the car, we'll get you away from here. We'll get you paid. Turn the clocks back. Come to an arrangement. Or you die here in the car park. It's up to you.'

Abbott's fingers relaxed. His sidearm dropped to the ground. It wasn't surrendering, he told himself. It was living to fight another day. 'And the other one,' insisted McGregor. 'Lift it out carefully, finger and thumb, drop it to the ground.'

With the sirens getting louder, Abbott did as he was told. He still had his knife in his boot.

'I'll be having that knife, too,' said McGregor, as if reading his thoughts, and Abbott felt the Gerber leave his boot.

From the hotel came two gunmen, men that Abbott hadn't previously seen. One of them came to Abbott, looked at him with hate-filled eyes and dragged his arms behind him in order to zip-tie him.

'Thanks, pal,' McGregor told his associate. He leaned forward, speaking to Abbott. 'Time to take a trip, Abbott.'

A moment later, he was in the back of the Range Rover with the hate-filled zip-tie guy at his side. Another had appeared from the hotel and Abbott recognised him as Morris from Doyle's set-up. That was interesting, Morris turning out to be a second Norton mole. Morris gestured for Abbott's laptop before clambering into the second Range Rover with the other guy. They were leaving three men behind. Soon, the clear-up would begin.

Meanwhile, McGregor took his place in the passenger seat. Beside him sat a figure that Abbott recognised. 'Hello, Mr Kilgore,' said Abbott.

'Hello, Mr Abbott,' said Kilgore, 'look what I found.' He held up the Jiffy bag then tore it open. From it he took the CD. 'Well, well, well . . . Looks like we arrived just in time. This, presumably, is the compromising material that Doyle used to boast of having. We often wondered if he was bluffing, but it turns out not.'

He turned slightly to regard Abbott in the back seat. Those hooded eyes taking him in as though assessing prey. 'And you, supposedly our employee – a man about to be in receipt of a great deal of money from Lady Norton – were about to let it go into the wild.'

'Watch it,' said Abbott. 'Watch it and see what kind of woman you're working for.'

'What kind of woman we're *all* working for,' corrected Kilgore. 'A woman who pays handsomely, as you well know. So tell me, Mr Abbott, who were you planning on sending this to, and why?' asked Kilgore.

'Look, why would I want to endanger my fee, eh? It was just a bit of insurance. You think I'd want to blow the gaff?'

Once again Kilgore turned in his seat to regard Abbott. 'Well, this is the thing. We know very little about you. One thing we do know, for example, is that you turned up in Derby wanting to deal with some red in the ledger regarding your brother. Perhaps what I might take from that is that you are a man of principle. Perhaps the money is of no interest to you.'

Abbott shook his head. 'Well, imagine how much good I can do with all that money. I mean, that's a lot of principles I can work out, yes? A lot of charities I could donate to. Plenty of folk I could help out of the gutter. Is that what you mean?'

Kilgore turned back. 'No, I don't think it's what I mean. Where were you planning to send it? Address in Bedfordshire, according to the courier.'

Abbott reflected on how lucky it was that the Norton men had made their play before he'd had a chance to brief the courier. Chain of events was that the receptionist, having been paid off by the Nortons and told to report back if Abbott did anything unusual, gave them a call when he ordered the courier. Sure enough, they'd turned up mob-handed but showed their hand too early.

'My own address,' said Abbott. 'I was going to post it to myself as a form of insurance.'

He saw Kilgore's eyes in the mirror. Saw that he didn't believe him. And yet somehow it didn't seem to matter. Abbott had the distinct feeling that things were moving forward whether he liked it or not.

McGregor's phone rang. 'Aye?' he said, and then, 'Thank you.' He ended the call and said to Kilgore, 'Abbott made a copy of the movie but according to Morris he hasn't sent it anywhere. Not from that laptop anyway.'

Kilgore turned again. 'Did you?'

'Would I tell you if I had?'

'Probably not.'

'Look,' sighed Abbott, 'I did the job on Doyle. I found this CD. I realised it was a useful thing to have so I decided to mail it to myself for insurance. Now, let's talk about that money for doing the Doyle job. I've provided McGregor with a list of—'

'That money has already been transferred,' retorted Kilgore impatiently. 'Your men have been paid.'

Abbott had a moment or so of experiencing a deep sense of satisfaction, thinking of his guys getting their reward.

'OK, well, I guess that makes us even.'

'Apart from the fact that you still have a game to compete in.'

'You can't be serious.'

'I'm deadly serious. Never been more serious. This –' he brandished the CD, 'this and whatever your motives surrounding it, changes nothing. You will still compete for Lady Norton; you will still win, and you will still be paid what you are owed. As for whatever loyalties you may have, they are for you to know and us to guess at. The simple fact of the matter is that Lady Norton needs a proxy and the more I know of you in action, the more convinced I am that you are the right man for the job.'

Abbott's mind was racing. Was it time to revert to plan A? Compete in the game willingly and try to take them down then? But no. He was being set up. There was no way he was playing their game, literally, metaphorically, any other -ly.

'I'm sorry, mate, you're nuts if you think that I'm going to go out and kill for you.'

'Oh, you are,' said Kilgore, sighing pleasantly. 'The reason is that two weeks ago we cloned your phone. Turns out that one of your contacts is the same woman we noted was conducting her own research on us.'

So that was it. They had put two and two together to make four.

That was what had brought them to . . .

Tess.

Kilgore had opened a laptop, angling the screen. 'Can you see this?' he asked Abbott.

'Yes.'

'Good,' said Kilgore, and he punched a button.

The image that appeared was Tess. Just Tess. She had a piece of tape across her mouth. Her hands – which were up, almost in front of her face – were zip-tied, just as Abbott's were.

And Abbott knew three things. First, it was all on him that she was in this predicament. Second, he was going to get her out of it. Third, he would have to play their game. He would have to play their game and win.

'What happens now?' said Abbott.

'You take a nap,' said Kilgore.

Abbott was aware of a movement from the man sitting beside him and turned his head just in time to see the hypo-dermic needle but too late to do anything about it – nothing but fall into unconsciousness as the needle went into his neck and the sedative did its work.

And when he woke up, he was in Poland.

CHAPTER 48

He knew it was Poland from the language on the signs, but as for whereabouts, he had no idea. Not the nice bit. Not Krakow or Warsaw. What he saw mainly was motorway with barren fields on either side, scenes that seemed eerily familiar from his time at Kemptown.

'Why do I seem to make a habit of waking up in Range Rovers?' he said groggily. Except, he realised somewhat belatedly, he was no longer in a Range Rover. At some point, they had changed cars. He was now in a Mercedes people carrier.

Otherwise, everything was the same. Still the same companion next to him, a guy they had been referring to as List, or maybe it was Liszt, while upfront sat Kilgore in the passenger seat with McGregor driving. The difference being that McGregor, driving, was now on the other side of the car.

'Not a Range Rover, now,' said McGregor redundantly.

'Yeah, I just worked that out,' said Abbott. 'You know, if you're wanting me to take part in your game, I mean, just a thought, but it might be worth *not* drugging me beforehand.'

Kilgore and McGregor shared a look. Kilgore was the older of the two, taller and clearly the most senior in the relationship, but of the two of them McGregor knew Abbott better. He wondered which of them had suggested drugging him and which of them had been against it.

'OK, well, how do you feel now, then?' asked Kilgore. It was him, Abbott decided. He was the one who had wondered about the wisdom of drugging Abbott. He could imagine the conversation. McGregor telling Kilgore, 'No, it's too dangerous, pal.'

'Groggy,' said Abbott, which was an accurate reflection of how he really felt. 'When do the games begin?'

'We'll be arriving in a couple of hours,' said Kilgore. 'Just get some rest.'

He sat back, partly because it really was in fact the world's dumbest idea to drug a guy you were expecting to go into battle for you, and so, yes, he could use the rest, and partly because he needed to think.

His plan for the game had always been that he would have the back-up of Ward, Miller and Brace, but the situation had gone FUBAR (an old military term meaning Fucked Up Beyond All Recognition) before he'd had the opportunity to set those wheels in motion. And to say the situation had moved rapidly was understating it. In the space of what felt like a few hours he'd gone from a Travelodge in Derby to what felt like the back of beyond in Poland.

So you're on your own. What are the odds? What are your chances? For the first time possibly since Lady Norton's proposal he thought seriously about it.

OK, so what did he know? Well, he knew that the battle-ground was to be somewhere in Eastern Europe, and here he was. He also knew that the five immediate members of Charles

Norton's family – his widow Lady Norton; his daughter Montana, her ex-husband Clifford Levine and their two sons, Ross and Simon – had each chosen a proxy. So that meant five of them in the battle. Presumably each of the other competitors would have a similar skill set to him; presumably they would all be highly motivated and carefully chosen.

That said, Lady Norton and her lieutenant, Kilgore, seemed especially keen that Abbott should represent them, even though he had incriminating evidence on her.

Despite that fact? Or because of it? Did it mean that Lady Norton could feel justified in getting rid of Abbott when it was all over? Was it better to keep him close at hand? Either way, there was very little point in worrying about imponderables.

So it would be Abbott versus the other contestants. He had faced worse odds. Would any of the Nortons cheat, that was the question? After all, he had been busy putting plans into place himself. Then again, he had no designs on *winning* the contest. For them, cheating was a far riskier strategy.

But that wasn't the whole story, was it? Because if he was going to do the job properly – and he fully intended to do the job properly – then he was taking out the Nortons at the same time. And that would mean going up against whatever private army they had on site.

What did he know about those guys so far? They were in a convo of two people carriers. In his: Kilgore, McGregor and beside him in the back seat, the hate-filled one they called Wilson. Was Kilgore a combatant? He couldn't be sure. He had the appearance of a hard nut but perhaps in more of a corporate sense.

McGregor? McGregor had no training, but he wasn't squeamish, he was prepared to have a go and that counted for a lot.

In the other vehicle was Morris, again probably not a combatant. Even though he was a weapons expert, he was more of an IT guy. Abbott had come across the type many times. Guys who knew all there was to know about guns, who always wanted to – so they said – 'pick your brains', which was really just an excuse for them to show off their own detailed weapons knowledge. Guys who fell asleep at night dreaming of combat, but if you put them in the field would shit their pants.

As well as Morris, there was another guy, Liszt or List? A large bloke. Abbott found himself thinking of the three guys he'd accounted for, back at the Travelodge. Wishing he'd managed to take out more.

And then, of course, was the impossible-to-know. The guarantee that not only would there be more security at wherever they ended up – guys in cargo pants and polo shirts and Aviators – but that the individual Nortons were likely to have their own guys on board. PAs probably, but maybe security experts, too. After all, whoever was finding their proxies for them had to be in the game. The fixers wouldn't necessarily be on site. The fixers of Abbott's acquaintance liked to steer well clear of the action. But who knew? If the money was right, then why not?

One thing was certain: they were either underestimating Abbott or overestimating him. And either way that was a mistake for which they would pay.

And then, of course, was the question of Tess's location.

Would they have brought her to Poland? If he was right and they intended to get rid of him whatever the outcome – and after all, any other option didn't quite make sense – then the answer was yes, they would bring her to Poland and deal with her, this loose end, at the same time as they dealt with him.

After that? What? Go through his phone, of course. Cuckoo was in his phone as Cuckoo and not his real name, but if you had their kind of resources, it wouldn't be too difficult to put him at military intelligence and military intelligence at Bedford, the destination of the CD. Another loose end they'd want to tie.

Which meant that Cuckoo's was another life he needed to save.

He settled back in his seat. Trying to keep his mind clear. Trying to stay present and focused on the job at hand. As he knew from years of drinking and then being on the wagon and then drinking again, there was one thing to be grateful for, at least, and that was the fact that he was neither drunk nor hungover. His condition could be better. But on the other hand, it could be a lot, lot worse.

He dozed, conserving his energy, reaching for a state of total focus by clearing his mind, until he heard the word 'Abbott' and opened his eyes. 'We're here.'

And the first thing he saw was the fact that they were entering what looked like a vast construction site. His brain struggled to make sense of what his eyes could see. A theme park, by the looks of things. Half-built theme park, the skyline a forest of cranes and scaffolding providing a strange and surreal counterpoint to the attractions.

But what kind of attractions? He had his answer when they

drove beneath an arch surely designed to welcome visitors to the Norton's latest entertainment venture.

An arch on which was emblazoned the words, 'Welcome to Murder World!'

CHAPTER 49

Abbott saw CCTV cameras but thus far, no guards, armed or otherwise.

That was interesting, he thought. It indicated that any security presence at the site might not be quite as large as he had feared. The two people carriers drew up together in a car park. A car park that was intended for the park's visitors. Lines were painted, while already positioned were several other people carriers of the same make, as well as a large Humvee. Not far away was a sign with blood-dripping words saying, 'This Way to Murder World' in English and – he assumed – Polish.

The men assembled. From the boot of the people carrier, List took two M-16s, one of which he handed to Wilson. Taking the weapon, Wilson's eyes were on Abbott. Abbott wondered if one of the dead or wounded back at Travelodge was big pals with Wilson. He'd have to watch that one.

Now Kilgore swept his arm around as though introducing Abbott to the place. 'What do you think of it so far?'

'I think it's a car park, mate. It's a nice car park, but I'll be honest, it's not the first car park I've ever seen.'

Kilgore chuckled. 'This is Norton Gaming's latest attraction.

It's due to open next year. The world's first murder-themed theme park. Adults only, of course.'

'Got to protect the children,' said Abbott pointedly. 'What's next? Sex World? Drug World?'

Kilgore almost smiled. Almost. 'You're closer to the truth than you might imagine.'

'Sex World. I knew it. You'll be opening that one in Chipping Norton, no doubt.'

'Oi, Billy Connolly,' said McGregor, 'let's get a move on, shall we? People to see.'

They moved off with Kilgore and McGregor at the head of the pack, List and Wilson covering Abbott with the M-16s, Abbott's hands still zip-tied in front of him. He had thought about trying to work at the tie and loosen it, but then again, why waste energy? He had no plans to escape. Not yet at least. He wanted to give every indication of playing ball, going along with the scheme. So he went willingly with his captors, and instead of plotting escape took stock of his surroundings.

There was no danger of Norton Gaming underplaying the 'murder' theme. Everywhere he looked there were billboards on which loomed top-hatted killers wielding bloodstained knives, hooded figures with axes, old-timey gangsters with Tommy guns. Just off to his right and currently sectioned off by constructors' wire fencing was a huge spiked metal ball. Not far away was another. Across from that, a mechanised hand holding a meat cleaver, chopping, chopping, a victim screaming. In one area were a whole bunch of figures presumably intended for distribution around the park. Men in boiler suits carrying machetes. Misshapen axe-wielding monsters. Surgeons with scalpels. Evil nurses with hypodermics. Supplies of red paint in Poland must have been severely depleted by the building of Murder World. Literally everything was liberally doused in blood.

The other thing that Abbott saw in abundance was CCTV. Everywhere he looked were cameras, sometimes whole nests of them fixed, he noticed, rather than oscillating but as he cast his eye around, he realised that they were positioned in such a way that every inch was covered.

Now they reached a pedestrianised area, either side of which were what were no doubt intended to be concessions stands. Empty, of course. A short walk led to a quadrangle. In the middle were picnic benches covered in plastic while on all four sides were more units intended for refreshments and souvenirs, but here, one storey above, was a balcony that ran around three of the four sides. The group approached a door. 'Staff Only' said a sign, again in English and Polish.

Kilgore pushed open the door, on the other side of which was a set of austere stone steps leading upwards. They ascended to the balcony above and here at last was another guard. He carried an M-16, same as Wilson and List, and greeted his two colleagues by name, waving them on to a room further along. Through another door, into a staffroom with a line of lockers on one side, a row of pegs on the other, and a piece of elaborate graffiti. 'Killer Crew'.

'So,' said McGregor, 'today has been an interesting morning for the Nortons. They've been meeting each other's proxies for the very first time.'

'But we proxies don't get a look at each other?'

'Where's the fun in that?' said McGregor. 'Come on, you're the last. As soon they see you, the game begins.' He indicated a set of overalls. 'You're green. The competing colours are yellow, orange and bright blue.'

'Just four of us? I was expecting five.'

'Simon Norton has recently expired of a heroin overdose. Consumed by his grief for his inspirational grandfather, no doubt,' said Kilgore drily. 'As a result, we have one fewer competitor and therefore one fewer proxy.'

McGregor indicated the overalls. 'You need to put it on now.'

'Green's not my colour.'

'We're not going the full *Reservoir Dogs* on this, are we? You're green. There's no discussion.'

'Sure,' said Abbott. He raised his zip-tied hands. 'You're going to need to get me out of these first.'

'Aye, that's true,' said McGregor, almost ruefully. 'Here,' he produced Abbott's Gerber knife, 'I'll use this, shall I?'

I'll be taking that off you later. 'Sure.' Abbott proffered his hands. 'Be careful, though, it's very sharp. The last thing you want to do is give me a nasty nick. I'd hate to have to retire with injury, especially when I've come so far.'

'No danger of that, pal,' said McGregor. He glanced behind himself to check that Wilson and List were paying attention. In return they shouldered the assault rifles, watching Abbott carefully. To one side stood Kilgore, looking on with an almost bemused expression as McGregor reached forward and – *snick* – slashed the zip-tie.

The plastic dropped to the floor. McGregor stepped smartly back, already holding the knife away, as though concerned Abbott might make a sudden grab for it. Abbott's eyes went from him to Wilson and List, to Kilgore. He rubbed his wrists. He turned, went to the pegs and reached for the set of green overalls.

'Now,' said Kilgore, 'if you'd like to try on your overalls I shall go and check to see whether the competitors are ready for you.'

He walked to the staffroom window where the blind was drawn. 'Perhaps you'd like to survey the battleground while you wait.'

The blinds ascended. Kilgore left the room. Abbott zipped up his overalls, moved to the window and looked out over Murder World. He saw bloodied clown faces, presumably entrances to attractions. There was a large automated knife sculpture, the hand moving up and down. He saw a large meat cleaver. More of the spiked metal balls. The park's centrepiece was a huge under-construction rollercoaster, part of which passed through a gargantuan noose.

'There are four areas.' McGregor had moved across the room to join him at the window. He pointed. 'See that bit over there? That's Horror House. Over there, you've got Nightmare Alley. And there you've got the Fear Palace and next to that is Mutilation Mansion. Pretty good, eh?'

'Whatever turns you on,' said Abbott, casting a practised eye over the terrain, seeking out areas of good all-round vision. Places you might put yourself to achieve a height advantage. 'When do I get to choose my weapons?'

McGregor chuckled. 'If only it were as easy as that.'

'What's the process, then?'

The voice came from behind them. Kilgore. 'All will be revealed. They're ready to see you now, Abbott. Follow me.'

'Wait,' said McGregor. 'Should we zip-tie him again?'

Kilgore seemed to consider.

'Yeah, that's right,' said Abbott, 'better consider the optics on that one. Tied up or not tied up? What do you think will give Lady Norton's opponents the right idea?'

'Sharp, Abbott, really sharp. This is exactly how we want you for the game. It's good that the sedative didn't take that out of you,' said Kilgore.

As it was, no zip-ties were produced. Instead, the five of them trooped out of the staffroom and back along the balcony. Kilgore knocked on a door, which was opened by another guy touting an M-16, who nodded them through into what looked like a small anteroom, the kind of place that a nervous job applicant might sit prior to an interview.

But nobody took a seat at the small sofas lining either side of the room. They were taken through to the next room, a big conference room. In here sat the Norton family.

CHAPTER 50

'Thank you very much, Kilgore,' said Lady Norton. Abbott looked at her and tried to square the image before him, the one of the slightly elderly but still very elegant multi-millionairess with the person he had seen on the video, presiding over the very worst sort of depravity.

And found that he could not. Because even though she was evidently a person capable of something so terrible – and indeed by the simple act of being here and competing in this sick charade was participating in something also quite evil – he still could not compute. That look. That Agatha Christie way of expressing herself. It didn't fit. Even though he knew it to be true.

He cast his eye across the other members of the meeting. Next to Juliet Norton was a spare seat that Kilgore now took. Beside him was Clifford Levine. Next was a surprise. Sitting beside Levine was a fixer that Abbott knew from The Circuit, that collection of commercial security operators who worked all over the world but mainly in the Middle East.

The Circuit was where Abbott had gone after SF. It was where guys like him went when they couldn't bear to leave the life behind. They either joined big security firms or they relied on work which mainly came through fixers, people like this guy here. His name was Monroe. He and Abbott were hardly what you'd call buddies. As far as Abbott could remember, they had once exchanged a few words in Baghdad, of all places. But still, he knew Monroe and Monroe knew him. Their eyes met across the room, but Monroe's gaze slid away, and if Abbott had been looking for help in that direction, then he was looking in the wrong place. Monroe's presence told him something else. That whoever his opponents were – his true opponents, the 'proxies' – they would not be paid thugs off the street. They'd be the cream.

Next to Monroe was a man that Abbott recognised as Ross Norton.

Norton was slouching. He wore an open-neck shirt and an air of relaxation shared by nobody else in the room. That was interesting, thought Abbott. Did that mean anything? Should he read anything into that?

Sitting beside Ross was a man older than him, who Abbott took to be his PA, or perhaps his security consultant. He wore a similar air to Kilgore, almost a Kilgore mini-me.

Beside the Kilgore mini-me sat Montana Norton, who if anything was even more attractive in the flesh than she'd looked on the news. Next to her a guy who could only have been her boyfriend. A surfer dude, for want of a better description. Probably not as laid-back as his normal state of being, but still comfortably the second-most relaxed person in the room.

There was another man present. He sat slightly apart from the others. An older man around Lady Norton's vintage, healthy-looking but nevertheless seeming distinctly uncomfortable and out-of-place. Was this the lawyer she had referred to, perhaps? Coombs?

Behind them all was a wall of screens and Coombs used a remote control to switch off the screens as Abbott entered. Abbott was just in time to see images being broadcast from what looked like the entire park before the wall of flickering pictures went to black.

And then Lady Norton stood up and with a grand sweep of her hand, said, 'Everybody, can I introduce you to Alex Abbott, my proxy?'

CHAPTER 51

They were looking at him carefully, each one of them wondering why he had not cropped up during their own process of selection. Why had their security consultants not proposed this 'Alex Abbott'? What was so special about him that he was to represent no less a figure than the family matriarch?

The answer was twofold. First, the fact that instead of following the tried-and-tested path of leaving The Circuit and then moving into close protection work, Abbott had gone solo, taking himself off to Singapore to nurture his drinking problem and deal with his PTSD. His son had died. He had suffered the betrayal of former comrades. He had gone back to the bottle. As a result, and because word spreads fast in their industry, he had been considered a bit of a burnout among those in the game. Second, the events of the last two weeks, during which time this burnout had got himself back on track.

'Green looks less than enthusiastic,' said Montana Norton, who had been assessing Abbott as though he were a racehorse.

'Whatever makes you say that, darling?' smiled Juliet.

Abbott's eyes had gone to Montana, to Ross, to Clifford.

Had they any idea what Sir Charles Norton and his wife had got up to in their spare time? And assuming that they were ignorant, did that make them innocents? Did that mean they should escape Abbott's wrath?

No – no, it didn't.

'Well, it's the fact that these two men are holding guns on him,' said Montana sweetly.

'Yes, that is a bit of a giveaway, Grandmama,' smirked Ross. 'Are you sure – I mean, are you absolutely *certain* – that he's here of his own accord?'

'It's true that I have had to use a little persuasion on Green,' admitted Lady Norton.

'Hang about, is that in the rules?' argued Ross. 'Won't he have an extra incentive to win?'

His mother, Montana, seemed to be agreeing, nodding at him vigorously. 'Yes, darling, yes.' Abbott wondered how she felt, this mother who had just lost her son. There was no reason why a bereaved mother should not be dolled up as she was. Far be it for him to give a shit, much less dictate how a woman should dress, whatever the circumstances.

But a bereaved mother competing in something like this? That was different. That was just further validation that this lot were scoring high on the psycho scale.

'Well? Mr Coombs?' Ross demanded to know.

'There is nothing in the rules that prevents proxies from being coerced,' Coombs said blandly, in response.

Abbott wondered if this was what Coombs had envisioned doing at law school, all those years ago. Defender of the dispossessed? No. Legendary criminal lawyer? No. Plaything for a bunch of sick millionaires? *Sign me up*.

Their eyes met and like Monroe, the lawyer's gaze slid away. There was one thing to be said for his position, thought Abbott. Impossible though it seemed, tough as the odds were, it felt great to know you were the good guy for once.

'Well, now that we've got that sorted,' said Lady Norton, 'how about we tell you what happens next?'

Abbott looked at her. 'That would be grand, Lady Norton,' he said with just a trace of irony.

'Excellent,' she sniffed. 'In a moment we shall be randomly selecting for you one of our four areas. Shortly, you will be transported to your given area, where the game will begin. You will find a weapon in the area. Unless, of course, you would prefer to use your fists.'

'Wait,' said Abbott, holding up a hand.

There was a slight shift in the room. Nobody was accustomed to hearing Grandmama addressed that way. Nor, judging by her face, was she. 'I suggest you remember your place, Green,' she said.

Abbott cocked his head. 'Oh, yes? Or . . .?'

She tilted her chin, as though letting this latest act of defiance ride. 'Go ahead. What is it that you want to say?'

'I want to know about weaponry. What will I be using? What will the others be using?'

'My understanding is that you have all been issued with a Sig Sauer and thirty rounds of ammunition. Is that correct, Mr Kilgore?'

'That's correct, ma'am.'

She smiled wanly at Abbott. 'Is that all you need to know . . . Green?'

Abbott looked at her.

Green, he thought. Not wanting to show his hand, reveal his intentions but unable to help himself.

'I saw that video,' he told her.

The words dropped like a stone in the room.

'A video taken a very long time ago,' she replied tartly.

'Does that help you sleep better at night?' asked Abbott.

'What video?' said Ross. 'It wasn't a dirty video, was it, Grandmama?'

Abbott looked along the line. They didn't know, he realised, but – and this was maybe worse – nor did they care.

Lady Norton was regarding him icily as though she at once pitied and resented his hapless attempts to invoke family disapproval. 'I do hope that you are not going to be any trouble, Green.'

'I'll play your game,' he told her. 'First, though, I need to see proof of life.'

'We are referring to Mrs Oakley, are we? You seem awfully attached to her given that she is, as far as we can tell, happily married with two children.'

'You're right. I'm awfully attached to her. Which is why I won't be doing any death matching until I know that she's safe and well.'

Lady Norton nodded at Kilgore, who leaned forward on the table and nodded at the lawyer, who stood and raised his remote control.

Abbott noticed that his other hand shook slightly and that he disguised it by shoving it into his trouser pocket.

The screens flicked on. When Abbott had entered the room, they'd showed different images, now they showed just one. It was Tess. She sat on a sofa, unaware that she was being watched. Not far away stood a guard with an M-16.

'Not good enough,' said Abbott. 'That could be anytime, anywhere. I need to see her.'

'And how on earth do you expect that to happen? How do you know she's even here?'

'I think she's here,' said Abbott. 'I think she's here, and I want to see her, or the deal's off.'

'I do not appreciate being spoken to like this, Green,' snapped Lady Norton. 'There is no *deal*. There is simply you doing what you're told if you want her to stay alive.' Her colour was up, the carefully cultivated cut-glass accent slipping. Her family were looking on, fascinated.

'I think I want this guy,' smirked Ross. He turned to his companion. 'Kennedy, is it too late to change our minds and have this guy instead?'

The man called Kennedy shot him an if-looks-could-kill glare but said nothing. To Lady Norton, Abbott said, 'Call it what you want. But you've just hit the nail on the head. There's no point in me doing it if I don't know that she's alive.'

Lady Norton turned her head to whisper into Kilgore's ear. He nodded and left the room. For two minutes or so, Abbott stood watching the Norton clan watching him. The amusement of Ross, the barely restrained anger of Juliet, the curiosity of Clifford and Montana. *Didn't expect this, did you? Fireworks before the fireworks.*

Kilgore returned. He motioned to List and Wilson, who hefted their weapons and then indicated Abbott to the door.

With a final look at Juliet Norton, Abbott left the main conference room, crossed the smaller reception area outside, went to the door and out onto the balcony beyond.

He stood at the rail, List and Wilson taking up position on either side of him, guns trained on him. His eyes went to the balcony on the opposite side of the quad where Tess stood stock-still, staring across the quad at him, her face impossible to read. It struck him how unusual that was. How normally she wore her emotions on her sleeve, written all over her face. Had the terror of her predicament forced her into herself, he wondered. Had the trauma shut her down?

Needing to speak to her, needing to reach out, he called across, 'Tess . . .'

'Watch it,' said Wilson, the muzzle of the M-16 coming forward. 'Nobody said anything about having a chinwag while you're out here.'

Abbott didn't take his eyes off Tess but said to Wilson, 'Go ahead, put a round in me. Should be fun explaining that to the boss, eh?' And he didn't need to turn to look and see the thunder on Wilson's face as he tried again, calling across to her, 'Tess, I'm going to get us out of this.'

Her feet were shoeless, the result of a struggle perhaps, and she wore what was presumably the same suit she'd been wearing for work the day she was snatched – just yesterday, in fact. Dark circles beneath her eyes. Eyes that seemed flat to him. Lifeless. And yet he could have sworn that his words brought a little light to them, and although she said nothing in return, she slowly raised her arm, a clenched fist of strength and solidarity.

A second later, she was being bundled away, back into the room in which she was being kept, the door slamming behind her. 'Guest Suite' said a sign on the outside.

List motioned with the muzzle of his weapon for Abbott

to return likewise, but Wilson stopped them, bringing his face close to Abbott. 'Me and you are gonna have words this day, Abbott,' he said.

Wilson pushed open the door and went back inside. To Abbott, List said, 'The guy on the stairs you shot . . . He ended up bleeding out.'

Abbott looked at him. 'You could have called him an ambulance.'

'That guy was Wilson's brother.'

'Well, you could have ignored whatever orders you were given and called him an ambulance,' repeated Abbott.

'I don't think Wilson sees it like that,' said List. 'Come on. Let's go.'

'Are we happy?' said Kilgore flatly when the three of them had returned to the conference room.

'We're happy,' confirmed Abbott, eyes going to Lady Norton.

'Then,' said Kilgore, looking along the table to the lawyer, the uncomfortable lawyer, Coombs, for confirmation, 'I do believe that it's time for the game to begin.'

CHAPTER 52

Almost exactly one mile away, the French sniper known as Scolar was scaling a ladder that ran the height of a water tower. On his back was a rucksack as well as his rifle case. He reached the observation deck, where he used an ultraviolet light to check that the spray he'd left the last time he was here had not been disturbed. As expected, it was just as it had been before.

From his rucksack he took a blanket that he folded lengthways and laid down on the concrete walkway that ran around the circumference of the tower. Next from the rucksack he took his spotting scope, then lay down and focused it on Murder World, finding it, seeing the odd figure moving around, guards with assault rifles, but no activity yet.

That was good. He was in plenty of time. Exactly twenty minutes before the game was due to begin.

Scolar had selected his weapon carefully. During his time in the Middle East he had liked to use the old faithful Steyr SSG 69 or the more modern Barrett M95 as preferred by the US military. For quick jobs, the Steyr was the one. A standard sniper rifle that worked well in the desert. The Barrett M95, with its pistol grip and tripod, was a rifle for the patient man.

For this job, however, Scolar had selected the McMillan TAC-50. This was a rifle designed for long-range antipersonnel work. Its manufacturers claimed it could take out a target at over two miles, though this had yet to be proven in the field. It, too, had a bipod and a pistol grip and was fed from box mags, each holding five rounds, as well as a muzzle brake to cut down on recoil.

He set it up now, attaching the butt stock, the Schmidt & Bender telescopic sight, and unfolding the bipod. He lay down, pulling the stock into his shoulder, lifting the weapon slightly and adjusting it to the right, squinting through the sight to match the visuals with those of the spotting scope, adjusting it for distance and wind speed. He worked the bolt, slowly and then fast, enjoying the feeling of it in the palm of his hand.

With that done he delved once again into his rucksack, drawing from it a photocopied picture of the operative called Trent.

Scolar didn't think he'd forget that Trent's colour was yellow but he liked to be sure. As a member of the French Foreign Legion, he had served in the Gulf War, in Rwanda, the Congo, Afghanistan, the Ivory Coast and more. He understood at moments of high intensity, the brain had a habit of switching into battle mode, when salient facts, small though they were, defaulted to the instinct of training in combat. He preferred to have something to refer to.

Next, he sat up, loosening his shoulder muscles. He pulled an energy bar from his rucksack and munched on it as he used the spotting scope to monitor activity below.

In the centre of the park was the huge execution-themed

rollercoaster, while to one side was an area apparently desig-nated for souvenirs and food, complete with picnic tables and concession stands, a set of balconied buildings on three sides.

As he watched, he saw activity. A man in green overalls moved out to the balcony. Across the quad was a woman. The two of them were looking intently at one another, words were exchanged, and she raised her fist.

Scolar thought nothing of that. Whatever was happening there fell outside of his remit.

He sat, munched on his energy bar and continued to wait.

He glanced at his watch. The game was very shortly to begin and so it was time. Time to go to work. He pushed the wrapper back into his rucksack. Same with the spotting scope. Next, he stretched out and then lay down on the blanket, pulling himself to the weapon, rather than the other way around. The first thing he saw was a motorcycle making its way to the far end of the park. It was carrying two people. Neither wore helmets. The rider wore a black denim jacket, the pillion passenger was a figure in an orange boiler suit.

He took a good look at the guy in the orange overalls. Accepting the job, he'd wondered if he might recognise any of the proxies. The strange assistant, Kennedy, had told him that each competitor was operating in total secrecy and that none knew the identity of another's proxy. Even so, Scolar had wondered. It might well be that he would see somebody he had dealt with in the past. A fellow traveller. Their world, after all, could be somewhat insular. But not the guy in orange.

'Enemy,' said Scolar to himself, finding the guy's head in his crosshairs and tracking him as the motorcycle moved across the park. It would be so easy to pick him off now, but Scolar had his instructions. He was to use gunfire as cover. Under no circumstances should he give himself away.

Tracking to the side he saw a second bike. This one's pillion passenger wore the yellow boiler suit. 'Friendly,' said Scolar to himself.

He felt the first drops of rain.

CHAPTER 53

'It's just a final precaution,' Abbott was told as he was zip-tied with his hands behind his back. He looked at the motorbike, rider already in the saddle. 'And how am I supposed to get onto that?'

McGregor pointed to the pillion handle. 'Passenger rear grab. We used to call it a sissy bar back in Glasgow. Back in the day, when I was just a wee boy.'

'Did you indeed?' Abbott motioned with his head for support as McGregor helped him aboard. 'It's good to have you on the team,' said Abbott sarcastically.

'I'm glad you feel that way, pal,' replied McGregor in kind. 'Your area, by the way, is the Fear Palace. I'll see you on the monitors, eh? Don't let us down, Abbott.'

'Oh, don't worry, I won't,' he said.

And then something odd happened.

McGregor's eyes flicked behind Abbott, to the rider, who sat astride the bike with his back to them. He said, 'Your lace is untied. Do you want me to get that for you? Rather than have to unzip you?' He was looking significantly at Abbott, who went along with it, knowing full well that his laces were fine.

'Thank you, that would be much appreciated. Not too tight, please.'

McGregor knelt and, as Abbott watched, quickly hoisted up Abbott's trouser leg and shoved his Gerber knife into his boot, giving it back to him. McGregor stood, looking meaningfully at Abbott. 'There . . . That should be fine.'

'Thanks, Mum,' said Abbott. Though he was glad of the knife, the gesture made him wonder what measures other players would be taking to help their proxies. It made him wonder, too, about McGregor's loyalties. Could it be that McGregor was trying to send him a message? To show him where his allegiance lay? Difficult to know. Best not to ponder it. Abbott had more immediate things to worry about – like the fact that he was about to go into battle.

They took off, and although Abbott had been half-expecting to hang on for grim life, in fact, his driver took it easy, presumably not wanting to risk harming the precious proxy by throwing him off the back of the bike.

When they stopped, the rider was similarly careful in helping Abbott dismount. Soon, the zip-tie was cut, and moments after that, the rider was back on his bike and racing away.

Abbott looked around. A couple of feet away was a brown hessian bag, the kind of thing people took to health-food shops. Abbott moved quickly to it. The choice of weapon was fundamental. It would dictate how he played the game.

It was a Sig Sauer. Great. Not only was Abbott familiar with the weapon, but it suited his favoured tactic. He didn't have the patience for a Tom Brace-style wait. Never had. He liked to go on the hunt. Search and destroy. Master of your own destiny.

There was a full mag in the Sig, three more mags in the

health-food shop bag. He pulled the slider back, put one up the pipe but left the safety on.

Now what?

Presumably the other proxies would be moving around the park. It began to rain. At the same time, almost as though the two events were timed to coincide, there was a general noise of motors starting up, and the attractions – those that were built, anyway – rumbled into life. Lights blinked. Malevolent laughter rang out. Knife hands rose mechanically up and down. There was the distinctive sound of a gallows being sprung, a guillotine and several different species of scream. Not far in the distance was the familiar clanking sound of a rollercoaster beginning its inaugural circuit. Abbott, suddenly robbed of one of his senses, went to full alert, bringing the gun up close to his chest and taking a 360-degree look around himself.

OK, he thought, *this changes nothing. You're still the hunter. You're still well advised to head for the centre of the park, because that's where your opponents will also be going. You're convinced of your combat superiority, but so are they. You think you're the best, but so do they. We all think it. Now's the time to find out for sure.*

Across the park in the conference room, the Nortons, their assorted assistants and right-hand men, watched each of the proxies begin their game.

'What's all this about a video, Mother?' asked Montana. 'Something incriminating, is it?'

'Indeed it is,' replied Lady Norton. 'It's footage that simply cannot be allowed to get out. It would mean the end of our family.' She looked across at Montana warningly. 'Our *whole* family.'

Montana paled slightly. 'Well, what was it? What sort of footage?'

'It all happened a long time ago,' said Lady Norton as though hoping to dismiss the matter. 'An unfortunate expression of your father's more base desires.'

And that was it as far as Lady Norton was concerned. Subject closed. Lance nudged Montana, looking at her, whispering, 'What base desires?' Montana shrugged, not wanting to go there, no desire to dig into her family's unspoken and unexplored secrets. Their darkest most disturbing truths.

She thought about Simon, his lifelong history of drug abuse. Her eyes went to the screen where Sergei, the Russian special forces operative, was beginning to make his way through the park, and she willed him on, her thoughts starting to wander. What if she won and were to wield absolute power?

What would she do with her mother then?

'Well, well, what's this?' said Ross, his attention drawn to Clifford's proxy, Heidi, who wore the bright blue. Except that she was, at that moment, stripping off her overalls.

'Um . . .' said Ross, looking towards the lawyer Jeffrey Coombs, 'invigilator? Is that allowed?'

'I see no reason why not.'

'Shouldn't this have been confirmed prior to the game beginning?' said Lady Norton.

'The rules of the game are that I should invigilate as I see fit,' said Coombs, doing his best to meet the glares of the Norton clan. He was feeling far less secure in this environment than he had before, when he had addressed them from behind the safety of his desk. The presence of all these weapons was making him feel very nervous indeed. 'If any of the other proxies decides to remove their overalls then the same leniency shall apply.'

Underneath her overalls, Heidi wore a T-shirt with the name 'Sweaty Betty' across the front. A short little rah-rah skirt. Never had anybody looked less like an ex-special forces operative.

Clifford Levine leaned towards his security consultant, Monroe, whispering, 'This is either very clever or very fool-hardy. What do you think?'

'She knows what she's doing,' said Monroe loyally, but concern was etched on his face. Some remnants of his relation-ship with Heidi remained, clearly.

Below them in the park itself, Sergei moved stealthily, skirting a lake area with a pier that featured an automated crum-bling effect. Tethered boats featuring skulls on poles bobbed on water dimpled by raindrops. He felt vulnerable, exposed. He was grateful when he came up on a small, sheltered area below a sign that said, 'Rest in Peace'.

He heard a voice. 'Hello? Hello? Is anybody there? Can anybody help me?'

Sergei lifted his weapon. 'Hello?' he said. 'Who is that?'

The voice came again. 'Who are you? What am I doing here? I was in a bar. I was talking to a guy and the next thing I know, I'm here. What's going on?'

'Show yourself,' demanded Sergei. The voice was coming from the other side of the Rest in Peace shelter. He edged care-fully around, only just resisting the impulse to put a round through the side of it. It could be a trap. But then, on the other hand – if this woman was genuine – it could simply be a stunt dreamed up as part of the game, just to make things more interesting for the competitors. What's more, he could use the girl. Use her as a hostage. He came round the side of the shelter quickly, catching her by surprise. She was crouched and, as soon she saw the gun, put her hands up, trembling.

'Stand up,' he told her.

She did as she was asked.

'Lift the T-shirt.'

She did.

'All the way,' he told her, motioning with the gun. She did. Just a bra. Just a bra and the rah-rah skirt.

'Lift the skirt,' said Sergei.

'Please,' she whimpered. 'I don't know what's going on . . .'

'Just lift the skirt, lady. I need to check you're not armed.'

'What do you mean "armed"? I'm not armed. Do I look like I'm armed?'

'She's not armed,' said Clifford out loud in the conference room. There was a brittle, tense atmosphere in the room, each of them riveted by a spectacle that they had helped to create, a spectacle in which they were so invested, thinking, *This was what got the old man's juices flowing*, and now they could see why. The game.

'She's not armed,' Clifford repeated indignantly to Monroe, as though it were somehow Monroe's responsibility. 'How the hell is she going to pull the switch on him if she's not armed?'

'She's very resourceful,' said Monroe, almost to himself.

Down in the park, Sergei said to Heidi, 'OK, you're clean. I'll get you out of here.'

He was trying to sound reassuring, even while wondering how he might best capitalise on his hostage. Was it even prudent to take one? Perhaps he should just put a bullet in her now.

After all, she might simply be a liability. On the other hand, he could use her as a human shield . . .

All of which thoughts served to distract him from her, so that he missed the fact that her head had moved quickly from left to right to check that there were no other competitors in the vicinity. How she almost imperceptibly tensed.

And then struck. Launching herself from her left foot, climbing almost impossibly high at the same time, she looped her right leg around his neck, bringing her left up to join it, snatching him into a scissor hold, yanking him to the concrete, and then, as he writhed, rotating from the hips to bring pressure to bear on his neck. Pressure that was impossible to withstand.

That killed him.

He made a sound. A death rattle. His gun discharged. And in the final few seconds of life, he had time to marvel at the skill of the woman who had bested him and realise with regret how completely he had been duped.

CHAPTER 54

From his vantage point, Scolar watched the action unfold. Had it been Trent then he might have needed to step in. He pondered this new development. After all, his understanding of the situation was that combat would be conducted using firearms.

'Well,' said Clifford Levine in the conference room, showing an even-more-than-usually-pronounced lack of tact. 'That went very well.'

In response, Montana Norton glowered. Her fists slammed down onto the tabletop and she stood up, unsure where to direct her anger. Towards her boyfriend – soon to be very ex-boyfriend – for having fixed her up with the games' worst competitor? Towards her ex-husband for being the one who had inflicted the loss? With her mother, just for being her mother?

All that she could hope for now was that either Ross or Clifford went on to win. Otherwise . . . if her mother won? It absolutely did not bear thinking about.

Clifford, with years of his ex-wife's tantrums under his belt, remained oblivious. Quietly, he said to Monroe, 'My God, did you see that? The woman's a genius. You're a genius. *I'm* a bloody genius.'

Beside him, Monroe made *simmer down* gestures with his hands. 'We're a long way from being out of the woods yet,' he told his employer quietly.

What he kept to himself was the fact that Heidi wouldn't be able to pull that same trick with either Yellow or Green. As Monroe knew well, she and Trent were acquainted. Ditto she and Abbott.

Meanwhile, down below, Abbott heard the gunshot and scooted for cover, finding it in the shadow of what looked like a wave swinger, except that instead of bearing the usual colourful, carnival colours, it was decked out in black and Murder World's signature blood red.

He waited for more shots. None came. An accidental discharge, perhaps? One combatant taking aim on another, a pot-shot?

Maybe so. Either way, it was the first real proof he'd had that there were indeed other players in the game. He peered around the side of the wave-swinger base.

In the conference room they watched as Abbott approached the trundling rollercoaster from one angle. Their eyes went from that screen to another, where Heidi and Trent were also making their way towards the park's centrepiece, but from a different angle. Heidi had retrieved her overalls and gun and was carrying them.

Their breath was held. Even Montana, who had gone from entertaining thoughts of simply storming out to regaining her seat. She no longer had a stake in the outcome and yet remained enthralled by the spectacle.

'It looks like Heidi and our man will be the next to meet,' said Ross, who seemed to have lost some of his sardonic demeanour along the way. Perhaps he was thinking what Kennedy was thinking, which was that their man Scolar needed gunfire to act as a cover for his own involvement – and so far the only bullet fired had been an accidental one.

Certainly, that was exactly what Scolar himself was thinking, perched in his bird's-eye view, watching the woman come together with the friendly, Trent. Which order outweighed the other? he wondered. Should he still save Trent, even if she attacked without her gun?

Getting closer now. There was a half-built structure of some attraction between them. 'Acid Bath' it said. Some kind of underground ghost train, where the riders travelled in old-style baths. The building above, mostly constructed though still shrouded in scaffolding, was clearly meant for visitors to queue up in. Small windows, yet to have glass fitted, allowed a view through from one side to the other.

From his vantage point, it seemed almost impossible to Scolar that Heidi and Trent wouldn't see one another, but he knew that things would look very different at ground level.

And then.

Heidi froze.

'She's seen him,' said Ross in the conference room.

Monroe's hand went to his mouth. She'd seen him. That was good, wasn't it? Because if she'd seen him, then she surely would have recognised him.

Sure enough, they watched as Heidi ducked down, moving away so that she could not possibly be spotted, at the same time pulling her Sig from her boiler suit and dropping the bundle.

In the conference room they watched.

'She's there,' said Ross, half-standing. 'Trent, you idiot, she's just there.'

'He can't hear you,' snapped Clifford.

Ross bit back. 'Oh, do shut up, Dad. What are you even doing here, anyway?'

'I beg your pardon,' roared Clifford, 'I am still your father, you know.'

'Shut up and sit down, both of you,' roared Juliet, every inch the Norton matriarch, waving a hand at the screens where Heidi was continuing to creep up on an oblivious Trent. They watched as Trent, almost seeming to sense the presence of danger, brought his gun to shoulder level, his elbows crooked, rotating his upper half slowly as he shifted forward in degrees.

Up in his perch, Scolar kept Heidi in his crosshairs and then abruptly shifted his aim slightly to the right, finding Trent.

Careful now. Very careful. He shifted slightly. Just a tiny bit. Finding the correct spot.

And then fired.

'What was that?' asked Clifford Levine.

'What you mean?' demanded Ross.

'Your man seemed to jump, like he was startled or something.'

Ross resisted the impulse to glance at Kennedy, both thinking the same thing: that Trent had jumped because Scolar had given him the prearranged signal. And now, suddenly, he was on full alert, crouching, his gun held, swinging slightly to the left and aiming through the structure.

'Is there something going on?' said Juliet to Jeffrey Coombs.

'I have no idea, ma'am.'

She was watching Abbott, who also seemed to have reacted to something.

And indeed, Abbott had heard it. A ricochet, surely. A round coming off the metal of something very nearby. A shot, surely, and yet there was no corresponding report, which meant . . .

Sniper.

But a sniper doing what? Working on behalf of one of the players?

Warning them?

Which was exactly the conclusion that Heidi had reached. Except that she'd reached it more quickly than Abbott, having already spotted Trent. A third party in an elevated position was tipping him off.

She stopped in her tracks, twisting to level the Sig through the empty windows of the Acid Bath waiting area. Where was he? Where was he?

'Psst.'

It came from behind her, and she wheeled to see Trent grinning in triumph, his finger on the trigger, and threw herself to the side.

Trent fired. A round grazed her side, but she answered at the same time as she called out in pain, a return shot that sent him diving for cover, cursing his hesitancy. It was the rah-rah skirt, he thought. *The fucking rah-rah skirt.*

CHAPTER 55

'Christ, he had the drop on her,' yelled Ross in the conference room. 'Why the hell didn't he just shoot her in the back of the head?'

He and Clifford were both standing, like football fans engrossed in a penalty shootout, watching as their two champions exchanged shots by the Acid Bath.

At the same time, Abbott took off towards the sound of gunshots, staying in the shadow of whatever attraction or structure was nearby, painfully aware that any sniper could at this very moment be drawing a bead on him.

And Scolar? Scolar, a mile away in his water tower, remained calm and steady, shifting the scope, trying to find the woman, needing to protect Yellow. Gunfire in the park was constant now, both firing from behind cover, each trying to keep the other pinned down, which meant that Scolar had a free hand to open fire himself.

His finger curled through the trigger guard.

His breathing was steady.

Below was Abbott, running towards the gunfire. He saw the woman and recognised her as Heidi Kavanagh. Their paths had crossed briefly in Iraq. And didn't she once have a thing with Monroe?

He emerged close to the Acid Bath. At the same time, Heidi saw the movement and swung her sidearm towards him, loosing off two rounds quickly, sending Abbott ducking into cover behind a row of ersatz gravestones.

He peeped out, saw Heidi, wounded. She'd realised that she was outnumbered and decided to make a move to regroup at a better defensive position.

'Heidi,' he called over to her, hoping that she'd hear him over the bark of Yellow's Sig. 'I'm not here to win,' he tried, knowing it was a useless gambit. Even if he wasn't here to win, then she was. And right now, she thought that the best way to do that was to get her ass to a better position.

She rose, coming out of cover and laying down a suppressing fire. Her mistake was to fire in the wrong direction, towards Abbott. But the threat wasn't from Abbott, it was from Yellow.

'No,' called Abbott, rising from behind the gravestones, loosing off two rounds towards Yellow's position. He saw Yellow. Christ, he recognised the guy as well. Name was Trent something. He fired back at Abbott's position and Abbott ducked down as rounds smashed into the gravestone – but not before seeing the back of Heidi's head blown out.

Her body fell, her rah-rah skirt fanned out around her. In the conference room, Clifford buried his head in his hands and sank back down to his seat. Beside him Monroe looked ashen.

As though playing some new version of musical chairs, Lady Norton had stood, as had Ross and Kennedy. Both were watching events on the ground, Abbott and Trent now exchanging gunfire.

Upon his perch, Scolar found himself the judge in a firefight. He had to make sure there was only one winner, though, and he took aim at Green, who was at that moment using the Acid Bath structure as cover to take shots at Trent. He found him. 'Au revoir,' he said, and squeezed the trigger.

Scolar's head jerked up from the scope. Abbott had moved. The bullet meant for his heart had instead grazed his arm.

And down below, Abbott, who knew that he was fighting not one but two gunmen, that absence of gunfire meaning that it was a sniper based – Christ – it could be over a mile away. Whatever he did, he had to take this inside. He needed to find better cover. Cover with a roof, presumably.

He turned and limped away, ripping at the boiler suit to see the wound beneath. Just a graze, thank God. The pain might slow him down, but he wouldn't have to worry about blood loss, at least. He turned, needing to find a better vantage point. He felt the warm blood consuming his arm and a slow tingling and numbness starting to take effect, looking down, realising that he was leaving a blood trail for Trent to follow, and then had an idea. He made his way to the darkened entrance of an attraction called Scales of Justice so that the blobs of blood suggested he had entered it. Next, he stripped off his overalls, bunching them hard up against his wound to soak up the blood, and then moved off to cover behind a booth opposite the Scales of Justice. There the position allowed him a view of the entrance, and that was all he needed.

In the conference room, Lady Norton turned to Kilgore. 'Kilgore, I think they're cheating. The bullet that hit our man, was that fired by Yellow? I don't think so.'

'Of course it was, Grandmama, don't be a sore loser,' roared

Ross, who could barely remember a time when he had enjoyed himself more. If only he had drugs, he thought. If he had drugs, the situation would be perfect.

'No, no,' Lady Norton shook her head. 'Something's not right here. There's another gunman.'

'Somebody on the grassy knoll,' snickered Ross.

'If you like,' she growled, returning her attention to her right-hand man. 'Kilgore?'

'I agree, ma'am,' said Kilgore, looking to Kennedy.

'Well, *you* would,' sneered Kennedy as Kilgore switched his attention to Jeffrey Coombs in search of an executive decision. At the same time, Kennedy turned blazing eyes on Ross. 'Settle down,' he hissed quietly, but not quietly enough.

'I heard that,' roared Lady Norton. 'Why would he need to "settle down"? That's it. That simply proves to me that there is something going on. Coombs? Coombs?'

Coombs was staring at the screens, pale beneath his crinkly tan, mouth working up and down. 'I've no idea, Lady Norton. It's impossible to tell. I've no experience in these matters.'

But now they watched as Abbott stripped off his overalls.

'Oh, he's at it now,' said Ross. 'What's he doing that for?'

'I think I know,' said Kilgore, and Kennedy shot him a hateful look.

Up above, Scolar saw him do it. He saw how Abbott had taken note of his blood trail and then taken off his boiler suit before taking refuge behind a booth nearby. He saw what was in his thinking, and he adjusted his aim accordingly.

In the conference room, Wilson touched a finger to his ear. 'Roger that,' he replied, and then to the room said, 'There's been a breach. Armed unfriendlies inside the park.'

'Well, can your men stop them?' demanded Kilgore.

'Of course.'

'See if you can take one of them alive, so we can find out who's paying them,' said Kilgore, still looking at Kennedy.

'Grandmama, call off your dog. I don't think I care for his insinuations,' said Ross, waving an arm, the voluminous sleeve of his white shirt flapping. 'I can tell you that we have absolutely nothing to do with this. In fact . . .' he turned, saying quietly to Kennedy, 'should we be going? Should I be worried about this?'

Lady Norton echoed his thoughts. 'Well?' she said to Kilgore. 'Should we? Should we be worried?'

Kilgore, who fielded the question to Wilson.

Who shook his head.

'Report is of just three men,' he said. 'We have over a dozen on site. You have nothing to worry about.'

And then the gunfire began.

CHAPTER 56

Abbott heard it. The rattling of semiautomatic gunfire. Nothing to do with him and, as far as he knew, nothing to do with the game. Which meant . . .

What?

That things had gone FUBAR. The game was off?

Should he come out of hiding and go for Tess? He decided to hold his position a moment longer, just until he was more certain of the status outside. Whether he thought the game was over or not was immaterial. The salient detail was whether Trent thought it was over. Whether the people in control of them thought the game was over.

And something else he thought about. That ricochet. It had clearly been intended to warn Trent about Heidi's proximity. The sniper and Trent had no doubt worked out some kind of system. A good sniper, though, a good operator with superb cranial cartography. There was no way they couldn't make the system more sophisticated. Maybe evolve it to go beyond 'the enemy is nearby' and to 'the enemy is in this exact position'.

And that made his mind up for him. He couldn't just stay put. He had to move. And as he raised himself, intending to make a run – oh, OK then, a limp-dash for it – Abbott heard something. A noise from behind him.

'He's behind you!' roared Lady Norton in the conference room. She stood with her palms planted on the conference table, watching the action unfold. Wilson had left the room to coordinate his security force against the three invaders. List remained, M-16 at the ready, although like everybody else in the room he was transfixed by events on the screen and had watched as Abbott hid and waited for Trent. But instead of falling into his trap by following the bloodstained path to the door of the Scales of Justice attraction, Trent had instead taken the long way round to work his way behind Abbott, pausing to cock his head as the sounds of the battle started up from over the other side of the park but otherwise refusing to be diverted from his task.

Coming up behind Abbott, oblivious Abbott, his gun held as Abbott, clearly having made a decision of some kind, rose from his hiding place and then, having heard Trent, wheeled around suddenly.

Oh God, he thought. *You idiot.*

Trent, standing there, gun trained on Abbott, squeezing the trigger.

Then Trent. His head exploding.

'My God.' A collective shout went up in the conference room. Trent's head had literally disintegrated into a mist of blood and bone and brain, as though a bomb had been planted in his skull.

Scolar in his perch knew at once. He knew, and he scuttled into a seated position, snatched up the spotting scope, sweeping it around the park, trying to find him.

A rival sniper.

Down below, Abbott heard a voice that he recognised. 'Abbott,' a voice that he knew at once was Ward. His feelings cycled through plain relief that Ward was here, which meant that Miller was here, which meant that the shooter who had just saved his life was Tom Brace, who was also here, to fear that Ward had put himself in the firing line, and then back to relief.

Ward appeared. He shouldered his AR-15, squeezed off three quick shots and sent a member of the Norton's security team scurrying for cover.

'Miller has an AR-15 for you,' Ward said to Abbott, reaching him and crouching. 'As soon as he gets here we can make a move.'

'No,' said Abbott. 'There's something I need to do first.' He indicated in the direction of the quadrangle.

Ward shook his head with irritation but understood. 'OK,' he said. 'We'll draw them in this direction. You make your way over there.'

'OK, and look, if I don't see you . . .'

'We have plans.' Ward tossed him a phone. 'Use this when you're done and we'll reorg prior to extraction home.'

'Home?'

'Yeah,' said Ward, 'home.'

Abbott was about to move off, then stopped. 'Ward?' he said. 'How did you know to get here?'

'Your mate told us where to come. McGregor.'

'*McGregor?*'

'Yeah, now go. *Go.*'

And with his head spinning, Abbott set off for the quadrangle.

Up in his perch, Scolar found him. The other sniper. He'd made his nest in a huge noose that acted as a tunnel for the rollercoaster. Scolar saw that the other man was using a Barrett and at the same time realised with horror that the guy was aiming directly at him.

'*Mon dieu.*' He scuttled and heard the whistle of the bullet as it smacked into the brickwork.

And now Scolar dived down to his own rifle. He would be forcing the other sniper to adjust his aim, could maybe get a shot off in time.

'Damn,' cursed Brace from his own vantage point. The second sniper had adjusted his height, gone flat, had his own weapon as cover. A round banged into the housing of the rollercoaster nearby. Both men firing a little too hurriedly now, trying to find their aim through a process of trial and error.

'Tom Brace,' came the call from below. It was Miller. 'We're pulling out.'

'I'll be there in a moment,' called back Brace, pulling a face, slightly irritated at having his concentration broken. His opposite number squeezed off another, and he could tell from the proximity of the strike that his aim was improving. This, he knew, was where the Barrett suffered, certainly in comparison to the weapon the other guy was using. Brace was under fire now, finding difficulty in maintaining the composure needed to draw a fine bead on a target so far away. The other guy had the same problem, but by the same token, the other guy had more suitable equipment.

Then again . . .

Up on the water tower, Scolar watched the other sniper doing something. Reloading.

Yes, that was it. Reloading. He put his eye back to the scope, wanting to use the pause in combat to his own advantage. He squeezed off a quick shot, hoping to keep his opponent off balance, prevent him being able to regroup and refine his aim. He flinched slightly as over on the noose, the other sniper fired in reply, a round that smacked harmlessly into the cladding of the water tower below, almost comically wide of the mark.

And then something belatedly occurred to Scolar.

How the Barrett was designed not as an antipersonnel rifle, but to penetrate military vehicles and even buildings.

How the Barrett could be loaded with high-explosive incendiary rounds.

Below him the water tower exploded, and Scolar was swallowed, screaming, in a mass of water and rubble, while over a mile away nestled in the noose at Murder World, Tom Brace paid homage to a worthy opponent, gave his rifle a kiss to thank it, and then began the climb down from the rollercoaster.

CHAPTER 57

The shooting continued behind him as Abbott made his way back to the quad. There would be more guards here, he knew. Men whose only job would be to keep the Nortons safe and who would, no doubt, be stationed on the balcony, able to pick him off from an elevated position, should he get too careless.

'Abbott,' came the call, an accent he recognised. It was McGregor, who clearly had been waiting for him. Were it not for what Ward had told him, then Abbott would have put him down there and then. Instead, he swung his Sig towards him as he came out of cover.

'Talk,' demanded Abbott. 'Tell me everything and tell it now, or I swear to God I'm going to put a bullet in you right here, right now.'

'Come on now, Abbott,' said McGregor, his arms up, not quite in surrender, just in supplication, 'who did you think it was that brought Ward and Tom Brace and the muscleman here?'

'I know that. It's the only reason you're not laid out on the concrete now. You need to tell me right now who you're working for.'

'Me?' said McGregor. For the first time, Abbott noticed a wildness in his eyes. Excitement or anticipation or something else. 'I'm working for *me*. And together, you and me are going to bring these people down.' He shifted slightly, twisting a little so that Abbott could see the gun in the waistband of his jeans. 'Let me pull my weapon, Abbott. We've got to go to work. They have to die. Every one of them. The whole fucking lot of them, Abbott. Come on. Together. You and me.'

Abbott shook his head. And instead of letting McGregor draw the weapon, he stepped forward and snatched it, tucking it into the back of his jeans, much to McGregor's exasperation.

'What do you mean?' demanded Abbott. 'What the fuck are you trying to say?'

'I'll tell you what I mean,' said McGregor. 'Those videos. The ones on the CD. Guess who has a starring role as "little boy on bed"?'

Abbott's face fell. 'No.'

'Oh, aye, that's right. Yours truly. You might say that I hold a grudge, Abbott. You might also say that I'm a man who's happy to bide his time, especially when it comes to plotting my revenge – and you of all people can understand the need for revenge, eh, Abbott? You of all people. I didn't have the special forces training, but I had patience. I had cunning. I had resolve. And then – oh, God must have been smiling on me – I got you. I wasn't able to make Charles Norton pay for what he did to me, but I sure as hell made Doyle pay, eh? And now it's Juliet Norton's turn – she and the rest of her corrupt and poxy brood.'

'So that's it,' said Abbott, who despite the situation, the

need to reach Tess, the battle raging at his back, still felt a numbness creep over him, a sense of shock. 'I thought I was a proxy for Lady Norton, but this whole time, pretty much since I arrived in Derby, I've been yours?'

'You went to Derby to seek justice for your brother,' insisted McGregor, 'I'm helping you deliver it. We're on the same side, you and I.'

Abbott shook his head. 'Fuck this. I haven't got time for this. I've got to get to Tess.'

'There are guards up there. They'll pick you off. I know a back way,' said McGregor. 'Let me take you there.'

He had that same wildness in the eyes that Abbott now knew as a sense of the prize being so close. 'We have them where we want them,' said McGregor breathlessly. 'We'll never have this chance again. We'll never get them together again. We can finish the job.'

The irony of his own intentions repeated back to him was not lost on Abbott, but he followed McGregor anyway as he led them along the side of the building to a wooden fence, ducking through the slats and then around the back to where a fire-escape door had been propped open.

He put a finger to his lips. Abbott acknowledged him and took point, climbing steps to the floor above, where there was another fire exit leading out onto the balcony.

Abbott peered out, saw Wilson with his M-16, the barrel trained on the entrance to the court. Across the way, on the other side of the square, was List, similarly preoccupied, neither of them expecting the direction of attack to change.

Abbott motioned McGregor to stay behind and then stepped smartly out onto the balcony. He took out List with one shot, being forced to use only his good arm as the functionality of the other started to subside. Not ideal but it worked. Just. He swung the Sig and took Wilson.

His second shot had wounded Wilson and Abbott took a quick step forward, looking down at him as he lay in agony on the balcony. 'You bastard,' he said to Abbott, through bared and bloodstained teeth.

'I'm going to have to take a raincheck on that talk me and you planned to have,' he said, and finished the job.

Then he was dashing along the balcony with McGregor at his heel until they reached the 'Guest Suite' where Tess was being held.

At the door they paused, Abbott telling McGregor to take up position on the other side. Inside the room, he knew, was Tess, plus – if the live feed he'd seen earlier was still current – another member of the security team. The last thing this guy would be expecting was Abbott. He'd be anticipating gunfire from the balcony outside, something to herald Abbott's arrival. Or, at least, that was what Abbott was depending on.

He kicked in the door. The guy on the other side was reasonably alert, but not alert enough, and he was still bringing the M-16 up to bear when Abbott double-tapped him.

What Abbott hadn't anticipated, though, was the presence of Morris and Kilgore. Morris was cowering by the door, his arms raised over his head. But Lady Norton's personal assistant stood with Tess held close to him, a gun to her head.

'Hold it there, Abbott,' said Kilgore.

Abbott squinted at him along the sights of his Sig, blood now a constant stream from his left arm, useless and unworkable.

'Put the gun down, you're injured,' insisted Kilgore, trying to sound commanding although his voice betrayed the nerves of the situation. 'Put it down now.'

Tess said nothing. Her head was tilted, pushed that way by the pressure of Kilgore's gun barrel. His finger was through the trigger guard and Abbott could see that the safety was off. If Kilgore, already nervous, was startled or twitched then he'd put a bullet in Tess, whether he meant to or not.

'It's over, Kilgore. The best you can hope for is prison time,' Abbott told him.

'Over?' scoffed Kilgore, a little too loudly and a little too suddenly for Abbott's liking. 'It's not over.'

'It is,' said Abbott, as calmly as he could manage.

'Put down the gun, and I'll explain to you how and why it's not "over",' said Kilgore.

'I'm not putting down the gun,' Abbott assured him. He looked into Tess's eyes. Eyes that told him to maintain his course. He knew enough of her to know that they would be of one mind.

Oh, but please don't let it go bad. Visions of Nathan were swimming in his head. Needing not to have another death in his debit column. *Not Tess. Please not Tess.*

'You couldn't take the shot anyway,' said Kilgore. 'You don't have it anymore, Abbott. Too many years being a pisshead.'

'We'll see, won't we?' replied Abbott evenly. The barrel of his weapon never wavered. His aim remained steady. Tess's eyes stayed on him, trusting him.

'I can take the shot,' said Abbott, and he was speaking to her but also to Kilgore, unnerving him, forcing his hand.

'Then take the shot,' she said, either understanding or perhaps just putting her faith in him.

Abbott was aware of everything – of the sounds of battle in the distance, of McGregor breathing hard with excitement just behind him, but mostly of Tess and Kilgore – and also aware of nothing but himself, his weapon, his aim.

'Wait,' said Kilgore quickly. 'We have men at her house. If you kill her, her family dies.'

Abbott paused, his gaze went to Tess, whose eyes widened, nostrils flaring with fear, and it was all the hesitation that Kilgore needed. His gun whipped forward as he tried desperately to take advantage of the moment, squeezing off a round that would have been a perfect shot if he'd been aiming for Morris. The round killed him outright.

Kilgore just had time to register his terrible effort – an effort that left him even more exposed than he had been before.

And Abbott took the shot.

CHAPTER 58

Kilgore's body fell backwards away from Tess, who launched herself forward into Abbott's grasp. For a second, he felt as though there was nowhere in the world he'd rather be, feeling almost desolate as she then hauled herself away with a look of panic and alarm, maybe even the fringes of hysteria. 'The children,' she said. 'The children? Phil?'

'He was bluffing, Tess,' Abbott told her. 'He was trying it on to get the drop on me, and it nearly worked.'

'How can you be sure?'

The answer was that of course he couldn't be sure, but McGregor came forward with a phone. 'Can you try them?' he was saying to her. At the same time he gave Abbott a look as though trying to exhort him to finish his business here. Abbott ignored it, staying with Tess as she dialled, trying not to interrogate his own feelings too hard, afraid of what they might reveal about him.

'Oh, thank God,' she was saying. Next, she was clearly responding to the worry at the other end of the line, trying to put her husband's mind at rest, telling him she was fine, that she was with Alex. And then taking a deep breath and blurting it out. 'Phil, I think you should get out. I think you should leave the house. Just to be on the safe side.' God knows what he was saying at the other end of the line. 'Just, please, please do as I ask. Just as a precaution. Yes, call the police . . .'

Abbott reached out to her. 'No,' he hissed, 'whatever he does, don't call the police. This lot,' he gestured outside the open door of the room, across the quad to the conference room door, 'they've got the police in their pockets. They've got the whole establishment sewn up. Just tell him to get out of there, go to a hotel. Is there a place that you both know where you can meet without saying so on an open line?'

'Did you get that?' she said into the phone.

Even at one remove, Abbott could hear the bewilderment in Phil's voice.

'I'm sorry,' she tried to placate him. 'I'm so, so sorry.'

'We have to go,' Abbott told her softly, quietly, aware that McGregor was hopping about, wanting Tess to wind-up and trying to arrest Abbott's full attention.

'Abbott, we've got to go. We've got to get them,' said McGregor. He was pointing now – pointing across the quad to the conference-room door.

'Wait,' Abbott told him furiously. 'Wait – we're not doing anything. Nothing until I say so, OK?'

But that wasn't good enough, not for McGregor. Before Abbott could stop him, he'd grabbed his weapon from the waistband of Abbott's jeans and was darting out of the guest suite. He was halfway around the balcony before Abbott could even react.

And something occurred to Abbott. He wondered why they had neither seen nor heard anything of the Nortons.

He wondered why there had been no guard stationed at the door of the conference room.

As he made it to the door of the guest suite, he shouted a warning across to McGregor. If there were no guards outside then they were inside, and if they were inside then McGregor was a sitting duck.

Except it wasn't that, was it? Because as McGregor reached the door and recklessly threw it open to storm inside, Abbott from his vantage point could see directly through the anteroom and into the conference room.

Which was empty.

And too late, he saw the trip wire.

EPILOGUE

The gravedigger sat on a bench beneath a tree watching the funeral that was taking place a hundred yards or so away. Apparently, the deceased who had died of a heroin overdose went by the name Simon Norton. The gravedigger had never heard of him, but since he was the son of Sir Charles Norton, the famous billionaire, also recently deceased, he got a proper send-off and a place in the family plot.

Expensive cars had decanted immaculately dressed mourners who were all now clustered around the grave edge as the priest went through the service. Not a huge attendance by any means. Looking at them, the gravedigger thought that they were probably all immediate family. There was a much older woman, for example, who was probably the widow of Sir Charles. Now, what was her name? There was a glamorous woman the gravedigger took to be the mother of the deceased. Another man. The father? A slightly scruffily dressed young man. A brother, perhaps? It was difficult to tell.

Standing slightly to one side was a cluster of men in dark suits that he took to be assistants and/or security men.

What escaped the notice of the gravedigger – and indeed of

the security men who should have known better – was a figure who, under the gaze of the disinterested chauffeurs who stood smoking by their cars, moved from the perimeter road, past the cars and towards the funeral. To the extent that any of the drivers thought about this man at all, they thought, *This should be interesting. Should be a bit of a show when security get their hands on this turkey.*

The man wore a long mac, suitable attire for the weather. As he narrowed the distance between himself and the funeral, he opened the mac. Slightly awkwardly, thanks to his still-wounded arm, he took from it a Heckler & Koch MP7 that had once belonged to a man named Owen Flyte.

He raised the MP7 to his shoulder and began firing.

The security men died first. Kennedy, being part of that group, also fell, followed shortly by the lawyer, Jeffrey Coombs, who had been reluctant to attend the funeral but thought he should pay his respects. Next to die were Ross, Montana and Cliff.

The last to fall was Juliet Norton, who lay beside her son's open grave with a bullet in her chest, not far from where the vicar cowered, traumatised but otherwise unharmed.

She looked up at the man who had come to kill her.

'You,' she said.

'Yeah,' said Abbott dispassionately, 'me.'

He put a bullet in her head, and then turned and ran to the perimeter road and into the passenger seat of an Audi waiting there.

In the driving seat, Tess.

He looked at her. 'They'll be coming for us,' he told her. 'Everybody will be coming for us. Everybody.'

ALL OR NOTHING – THE TRUTH BEHIND THE FICTION

It's a painful fact that the action of *All or Nothing* was both informed and inspired by real-life events.

At the tail end of the noughties, my career in the special forces was very much in the rear-view mirror, and I felt rudderless and unfulfilled. My life lacked direction and purpose. What's more, I had a drink problem that I lugged around like a sack full of rocks on my back (just like a certain Alex Abbott). I was living in Brisbane at the time, and it was there that I met a bloke at the most unlikely event you can imagine: a fancy-dress party. His name was Simon, and it was just a chance meeting, but it ended up changing my life.

In actual fact, I vaguely knew Simon from back in SF. Catching up on old times, he told me about a charity called The Grey Man, an outfit aimed at preventing child trafficking and slavery, mainly in south-east Asia. The idea was that they would send undercover guys into brothels, identify kids at risk and either alert the cops or send people in to get the kids out.

Would I be interested in getting involved? asked Simon. I looked at the drink in my hand. The ever-present drink. Yeah, I would.

I began in a training capacity but soon moved into a more operations-led role that, in 2011, took me to Thailand. What Las Vegas is to gambling, Thailand is to child trafficking. It was there that we at The Grey Man identified kids at risk and looked to the local authorities for assistance but soon found ourselves up against a wall of ignorance, indifference and outright corruption. A trait I share with my protagonist Alex Abbott is a sense of outrage when I come up against injustice and tyranny. A series of busts going wrong did nothing to cool my temper in that regard. We had heard sickening rumours of children being sold to fishermen and raped for days on boats, then killed, their bodies thrown overboard. Whatever the truth, it was clear that child trafficking was a way of life in Thailand.

I couldn't accept that. Couldn't just shrug it off. It was one thing knowing about it from afar. Quite another matter seeing it for yourself. Meeting an inspirational guy called Mickey, who ran a shelter providing sanctuary to vulnerable girls, was the final spur I needed and, like Abbott in *All or Nothing*, I put a team together: me, plus two . . . let's just say 'similarly skilled' blokes, and Mickey. We had identified villages along the Thai-Burmese border where kids were kept prior to being taken by the cartel and 'distributed' like merchandise. We decided to get them out.

We set off into the foothills, beginning a dangerous mission that I cover in much more detail in my memoir *Break Point*. To cut a long story short, we were able to locate and rescue twenty-two kids in all. We encountered the enemy; guns and knives were drawn at various points along the way of an operation that took place over several days, but no blood was shed, and our daring rescue made worldwide headlines.

In due course my Thailand experience would give rise to the

fictional events in *All or Nothing*. I moved the operation from south-east Asia to the Midlands in the UK in order to show that child trafficking can – and does – happen in all parts of the world, possibly right under your very nose. Plus, of course, I added a few more explosions and gunfights.

The emotion, though? No dramatic embellishment needed, for the fact is that way before I ever envisaged the life of Alex Abbott, I had discovered a sense of direction in myself. For the first time in as long as I could remember I had a feeling of fulfilment. Rescuing those kids had given me a reason to get up in the morning and actually *do* something with my life – something other than pour drink down my throat. I've love to say that it was the reason I kicked the booze right away, but the truth is that I didn't quit the booze right away. When I eventually did, however, it was by summoning that feeling that I helped underpin my recovery.

For reasons too labyrinthine to go into here, The Grey Man charity is no more. As for me, I had to finally accept that the culture of child trafficking is ingrained in society, and there's very little that one man – me, or even Alex Abbott – can do about it.

Or is there? By writing about my experiences both in a fiction and non-fiction capacity and by being active in the media, I hope to draw attention to the issues. It also struck me that true, profound change must come from within – from within society, and thus from within its inhabitants – and it was for that reason that I set up my company, Break-Point, which is all about encouraging change and personal development. Our remit is wide, but the ideology is the same. *All or Nothing* goes the title, and it's certainly a credo by which Alex Abbott lives his life. But I'm not him. Not anymore. I've found a middle path.